I0601008

Winter Falls

By Eddie Skelson

          PANDEMIC PRESS

During the winter of 1927-28 officials of the Federal government made a strange and secret investigation of certain conditions in the ancient Massachusetts seaport of Innsmouth. The public first learned of it in February, when a vast series of raids and arrests occurred, followed by the deliberate burning and dynamiting--under suitable precautions--of an enormous number of crumbling, worm-eaten, and supposedly empty houses along the abandoned waterfront.

H.P Lovecraft – The Shadow Over Innsmouth

Prologue

The seasons change quickly here. The most noticeable being the sudden almost shocking shift from autumn to winter. Mountains and hills hold back the most severe rains unless they blow in from the coast, although there are always one or two of these sea-borne squalls that break through. When these breach the hills and move inland they do so with sufficient rainfall to bloat the lochs beyond their tolerance. In turn, once they have reached their fill, the excess is spewed back towards the waiting sea. Dry beds refill, sedentary brooks become temporary rivers and the homes of unfortunate animals are picked up and carried along with the surge.

Occasionally, when the torrent is strong enough a tributary will form and cut through fields and dense forests. Following an old path it rushes towards the northeast, away from the coast. It brings with it the detritus of the countryside, rotten plants and fallen trees, victims of the nature of the forest, dead things until finally the rushing torrent encounters a ridge that drops suddenly onto the low-lying basalt plain.

Here water smashes against rocks that line the edge and begins to pool behind them, allowing only a steady flow to cascade over as its volume and speed overcomes the barrier. Flotsam and jetsam, ripped and torn from the forest is pushed and pulled in the current and ultimately, they too are cast over the edge.

And suddenly, as though the mountains have agreed to allow the blistering cold air that drives at them to pass their bulk, winter arrives with a singular intensity. It is a blast of such low temperature that it freezes the water as it falls, capturing its essence in a crystalline prison.

'We should have come in the fucking car.' Jonas was repeating what he had said ten minutes earlier but this time a little more emphatically. He was joking, as usual, but he hadn't slept well at the pub and this long walk was working at his patience regardless of the natural beauty the scenery presented.

'Jonas, nok. Du gir meg en hodepinedette,' Trond replied, his tone gruff, but that wasn't unusual as his mood leaned towards sombre more often than not.

'I thought we were speaking in English for this trip.' Jonas continued, gently pushing at his friend.

'You can be real pain in the ass, you know.' Trond replied

'Ha! Jonas laughed. 'That's better though. You need the practice, your accent is awful.'

'Dick head.' Trond replied 'How's that?' He would be the first to admit that his English, although grammatically good, was heavily laden with his Norwegian dialect. Jonas however, having spent twelve years of his thirty-two in the UK had only a slight lilt, his accent had been stretched and diluted through his travels around the island.

They carried on walking. Jonas relinquished his ribbing and the two fell silent for a while. He had hoped that by poking fun at Trond he might lift his friend's mood and that he would become a little more talkative, but since they had left the last village behind Trond had withdrawn into his own thoughts.

Jonas figured that they had walked about five miles with Trond's contemplative silence before they had halted at a point close to an escarpment. It was a steep drop to the lower area of land and Jonas understood why no-one in their right mind tried to cross the highlands at night or in poor weather.

'I need to check our location.' Trond said.

From his thick Berghaus jacket he withdrew an ordnance survey map sheathed in clear plastic. Jonas watched as Trond opened it up and folded it back on its self to make it a manageable size.

They were on the edge of a considerable stretch of land broken up only by dry stone walls. He hadn't seen a single field of crops or livestock of any sort since they had travelled about a mile from the village. It wasn't unusual, not in these circumstances.

He had experienced it before, a corruption that radiated through the air and the soil, a *wrongness* was how he described it to Trond. They had to be close, the signs were there. The weather was turning too. Jonas had an intuition where the weather was concerned and the proximity of the *wrongness* of this place and the violence he perceived in the atmosphere was what had disturbed his sleep.

'Nearly there.' Trond said as if in response to Jonas's thoughts.

'Good, my fucking feet are killing me.' Jonas turned to see Trond looking at him with a concerned expression.

'Ok, yes I know. I *am* taking it seriously Trond. I'm just trying to work though this man, y'know, I didn't sleep well.'

Trond nodded. Understanding. Jonas was sensitive to these places and it upset his well-being.

'According to the map we are close to the boundary.'

'If it's right.' Jonas said.

'Yes, if it's right.' Trond returned the map to the inside of his coat. 'And if the key fits.'

'Ja.' Jonas nodded and frowned realising that he had dropped into his mother-tongue as he occasionally did with short statements.

'You gave one to the villager?' Jonas added. Mild accusation in the question.

'Ja, I did.' Trond replied.

'How come?'

Trond turned his attention from Jonas and looked ahead. 'In case we don't come back.' He fixed his gaze upon a dark line that met the sky on the horizon.

'You told him?' Jonas asked genuinely surprised.

'Nei…no, not really. Perhaps I expanded on what he already knew a little.'

'You think he would come?'

'No, not really.' Trond said and started to walk. He estimated that the dark line of trees lay about two miles or so from where they stood. Their destination would be beyond them.

'Is that the forest in the distance, is that the one?'

'Ja, that's the one.'

'We should have come in the fucking car Trond.' Jonas said.

At this, and despite himself, Trond laughed a little.

Chapter One

Joe Clarke's mood had been black for the whole of the trip from London Euston to Glasgow Central. Frustration, boredom and a touch of anxiety had rested on his mind as he had tried to relax in a standard class carriage where relaxation was effectively neutered by overcrowding. To compound matters an unscheduled change, revealed via a barely audible announcement had advised him there would be a delay. To make sure that he was fully in the picture of a situation he couldn't do a thing about, he was told that this was due to a mechanical fault.

The delay extended his journey time from a barely tolerable five hours to a soul destroying eight and Joe's mood didn't improve when he finally stepped onto the platform at this part of his journeys end. Rain had begun to lightly fall as he had passed through Manchester. By the time he reached Carlisle, the point at which the unwelcome announcement had been made, it had become a heavy sleet, spitting at the window and reducing visibility to almost zero. Upon arrival at Glasgow Station a full-scale blizzard was hammering at the city.

On the platform, an ice-cold wind upon which the winter storm rode cut through the station and easily overcame Joe's inappropriate clothing. His choice of a shirt and tie, trousers, a fashionable but flimsy Nickelson wool jacket and a scarf no thicker than his socks had been just one in a series of bad calls.

To begin with he had chosen not to hire a car and drive to Glasgow. His reasoning had been that he would have to pay for it himself and then claim the cash back as expenses and this was a major hassle. Then there was the prospect of an eight journey each way, along unfamiliar roads that Joe thought were going to be mostly chock full of traffic. By taking an early train he had hoped to be in and out of Glasgow within the day. There was no chance of this now. It was already four o' clock and he still had to navigate to the hospital, speak to Christ knows who about getting the information he required and then physically check and copy the records. Granted he would only photograph the documents with his iPad but he was looking at an overnight stay, which in turn meant more expense claims.

Joe disliked Scotland and things Scottish on general principle, although he had never visited the place before now. He carried with him a weak subconscious suspicion of the country and its people that was based on cultural stereotypes, imagining that every Scottish male was either a psychotic Begby from Trainspotting or a drunken Rab C Nesbitt waster. He also entertained a more general rejection of any society that wasn't based within a London postcode and had summed up his feelings on his upcoming excursion 'north of the border' to a colleague with the sentiment, 'as the Romans had decided that Scotland wasn't worth the effort I'm happy to trust in their opinion on the matter.'

But in truth he what he really disliked anywhere that wasn't a balmy Mediterranean beach, or South West London, his home patch. As far as he was concerned he was being punished with this trip simply for being good at his job and so there was no reason that the whole of Scotland shouldn't take the blame.

He tightened the pitiful scarf and cursed the fact that he hadn't brought a hat, or gloves and that he wasn't wearing anything close to appropriate footwear. He carried a canvas North Ridge backpack slung across his shoulder and pulled his travelling case behind him as if it were an awkward dog.

'*Exiled to the British third world*,' he thought as he passed through the main doors of the station.

Stepping out into the storm caused him to stop and gasp as he took in a lungful of freezing cold air. Snow whirled about him frantically, and the severe wind whipped it into a state of frenzy, buffeting and bashing at him. He quickly retreated into the station.

'Christ all fucking mighty,' he panted.

Recovered from the shock, Joe stepped up to the windows at the side of the door, making sure to avoid triggering their sensors so the blizzard wouldn't get to him. He peered outside. It was hard to make out from behind the protection of the glass but he could see there were no vehicles lined up at the taxi rank This indicated by a feebly lit, barely visible sign. Considering the violence of the storm the bluish glow of floodlights illuminated the parking area well, but all they revealed was it was empty.

Joe wasn't alone at the station, others stood near the doors with him. Couples deliberating venturing out or booking into the station hotel for the night, old people on telephones to loved ones arranging lifts or telling them not to worry. A brave or foolhardy few walked out into the storm as though it were no more than a light shower.

'*Natives*,' Joe thought, and sighed.

He needed to get to the Glasgow Royal infirmary, which Google Maps stated was less than a mile from where he stood. He pulled out his phone. The signal was strong, and he considered his options as they now stood. First off he could sit here in the station, which was only just above freezing, hoping for a break in the weather or for an insane taxi driver to turn up, which was not outside of probability as this was after all Glasgow. However, there were plenty of people who had also chosen not to brave the weather and most likely had the same idea. He didn't fancy tangling with them in the snow while trying to be the first into a cab, should one actually arrive.

His other option was to defy the weather and use his iPhone to guide him to the Hospital. '*The Twenty First Century Solution*,' Joe thought. As he mulled over what to do he sought out a Tie Rack store that he had seen when crossing the station. There he purchased a pair of leather gloves that claimed to have a 'super-warm thermal inner' and a woollen hat.

He tried to find a plain one but the best he could do was a beanie that had a colourful pattern of zigzags ringing it.

'Another twenty quid written off for this trip.' Joe's mental bank statement clocked it up as he handed over his credit card.

Back at the exit to the station he pulled on the gloves and tugged the hat down over his head, another stalwart traveller opened a door and stepped out beside him, Joe bowed his head so that his chin touched his chest and once again walked into the blizzard.

It took forty-five minutes to complete a journey that would have normally taken ten at most and it was hellish. The Tie Rack gloves proved both useless for cold prevention and impractical for operating his Google Maps application. As he clutched his phone, while following the street map, his hands shook and his fingers began to lose sensation.

Joe was staggered that despite the god-awful weather people were still out on the streets and could also be seen in cafes and stores as he roamed across the city. He also became conscious of how ridiculous he must look to the natives. A poorly attired, hapless tourist wandering the streets, clutching a phone which he began to think was worth him getting mugged for.

He decided to try and memorise the route so that he could put the phone away and bury his hands into his pockets, but this proved disastrous. By the time he took the phone out again to check his bearings he had managed to walk a mile out of his way.

Respite came in the form of well-lit signs indicating the direction to the Royal Infirmary by car. Rather than trying to negotiate the confusing snow covered streets Joe followed and walked on the main roads. There were very few vehicles and those that were using them crawled along offering little threat of knocking him over.

Cold, sodden and numb he finally reached his destination. He was surprised how busy the Infirmary was. The waiting area, presumably for triage, was full, every chair taken and a few people standing idly against the walls. Porters and the occasional nurse crossed in front of the reception area. Joe walked to it conscious that his travelling case was dropping chunks of snow as it rolled along.

Despite the busy waiting area the reception desk was clear of visitors. Two nurses, one a dark skinned and amply framed woman, her cornrow hair neatly held in a bunch and the other a slim young man with close cropped blond hair and the makings of an ill-advised moustache sat, being busy.

'Hello, I'm Joe Clarke from Dynamic Systems.' He stated as a trickle of water ran from his beanie and down the side of his nose. 'Could I speak to Mary Burgess please?'

He reached into his jacket for his wallet but fumbled due to the gloves. Offering an apologetic smile, he removed them and tried again. From the wallet, he retrieved his company ID and held it steady for the two nurses to see.

'Just one second my love.' Said the female nurse whose name badge identified her as Dolores. There was no trace of a Scottish accent, instead only a strong but attractive Jamaican lilt to her voice. The male nurse, his badge indicated that he was *Simon*, continued to work, tapping at the monitor in front of him. Dolores squared a pile of official looking paperwork and placed it into a brown envelope. She then added this to a tray that was already piled with paper and envelopes of various colours.

'Now my love Mary Burgess you say?'

'Yes please.' Joe replied.

Dolores pushed aside yet more paperwork revealing a telephone and lifted the receiver. She jabbed at the keypad and offered a Joe a friendly smile, the warmest thing he had encountered in Glasgow so far.

'Hi Chris, is Mary Burgess there?' Dolores asked. 'Thanks Babe,' she said a moment later.

As Joe waited a man wearing a green hospital uniform appeared with a cleaning cart. He dropped down a 'Danger Wet Floor' sign and began to busy himself with a mop around the reception.

'*Good luck with that,*' thought Joe.

'Joe, I'm afraid that Mary is busy at the moment and she's asked if you would take a seat in reception. She will come to you as soon as she can.

Despite his frustration, Joe found it impossible to be sharp with Dolores. Her tone and manner disarmed and relaxed him. Joe didn't wonder she was here on the front line although he suspected that were she to get angry Dolores would also be quite formidable. It crossed Joe's mind that in movies big black women were often tough and intimidating. He then wondered if he was being racist.

'Ah, Ok thanks.' He said. 'I'll wait over there.' He pointed to a row of vacant seats further into the hospital and near to a vending machine.

'Ok Honey, but don't waste your money on the cat pee in that machine. I'll have one of the porters bring you a hot coffee from the canteen.'

Joe was a little smitten with Dolores for a moment and gave her a genuine smile of thanks. He nodded, replied 'that's great, thank you,' and made his way to the seats.

The easy-going warmth of Dolores began to lose the comfort it had given Joe after the first half hour had passed. Once an hour had gone by he caught himself muttering under his breath with boredom. A few people had entered the hospital in varied states of distress and in moments of mild excitement an ambulance would pull up outside with its lights flashing, still bright and shocking even as the snow tried to smother them.

This steady flow had kept his attention on and off but his interest was truly peaked when several hospital staff moved quickly to the door and took control of a gurney as paramedics came hurrying through. On it lay a man, an old man, he wore a tatty, black knee length jacket. He was strapped down securely.

Joe caught no more of this as within seconds the gurney, the old man and the staff had vanished through a security door. Not long after the incident he asked Simon, who was walking past him 'what was with the old guy on the stretcher,' but when Simon stated flatly 'Pissed.' Joe felt a little disappointed.

Up until that point he had been preparing himself to go to the reception and insist that Mary Burgess come and see him immediately, instead he admonished himself. He had resisted reaching a critical point of impatience mostly because he didn't want to cause a fuss for Dolores, who had been so pleasant and the sudden arrival of the emergency patient had also forced him to reconsider his situation. Even though the old chap had just been probably downed by one, or maybe a dozen too many it was down to the hospital staff to sort him out.

'There are people here a lot worse off than you Joey boy.' He muttered. This was a big city hospital in the middle of a blizzard. They were probably a tad too busy to attend to the demands of a data analyst looking for paperwork from sixty years ago.

Resigned to a long wait Joe retrieved a plastic file protecting a wad of paperwork inside it from his canvas bag. He pulled out the paperwork and lay it onto the plastic to protect it from his damp trousers and began to go over the information again.

The job was ostensibly a straight forward one. Collate the data for births and deaths in Scotland since 1900 and identify regions where births and deaths were highest and where the patients were treated, be it on entering the world or leaving it. It was a simple enough task but a heavy workload with twenty people working on it back in London. This data would in turn be processed and used to produce a scaled implementation of the allocation of NHS budget across the regions of Scotland.

For his employer, Dynamic Systems, it was a very big deal. This was the first top line government contract they had managed to acquire but more importantly for Joe it was the pathway to promotion and a pay rise. But there was a problem.

As he had begun to render the supplied data into his program, which showed the rise and fall, year by year, city by city of the births and deaths in Scotland, a Black Hole had appeared. Black Holes were bad. Black Holes indicated a total absence of data in a single defined area or year even worse, both. The problem region lay to the extreme North West of the country.

There were other places that had anomalous data or offered only inconsistent results but they were nothing outside of the expected margin for error. The Black Hole meant that the results were large and consistent, this being that there were no results at all.

As far as he could determine, the hole lay on top of a town called Winter Falls. There didn't appear anything else like a town near to it and according to what he could find on Google it was home to around three hundred inhabitants, but that was taken from the last census information available.

The natural harbour that it sat next to provided its economic base through fishing and there was a small agricultural presence. There was no mention of tourism or of any other industry. The data was old and that didn't help and there wasn't even a reference to which census had been used to obtain the information.

He had first tried to get the records over the phone but had been brushed off by some unhelpful jobs-worth in the hospitals administration department. Records that old were kept in the archives, still in paper format and no personnel could be spared to 'dig through that lot,' Joe had been brusquely informed. Reporting the issue to his boss had resulted in this little trip and Joe was beginning to wonder if a company car and five percent raise were worth the effort.

The shadow of a figure appeared before him. Joe looked up from his graphs and saw, thanks to the photo ID resting upon her cashmere sweater that Mary Burgess had finally arrived.

'Joe Clarke?' She asked

'Hi, yes.' Joe stood and attempted to shake hands before realising that he was clutching the pile of paperwork. He placed it on the next chair and then offered his hand. Mary flashed an impossibly bright smile, made more so by the cascade of thick black hair that bobbed around her shoulders. She was about his age, probably a little younger, he guessed at thirty-two. Her skin, her teeth, her lustrous eyes screamed 'not Scottish' to him. Joe's unrealistic bias stated that Scot's women should be short and round and blotchy, they would have bad teeth and severe hair.

Taking his hand Mary apologised. 'I'm really sorry to have kept you waiting Joe, its hectic here and I don't mean just now, right now it's madness.' Again the perfect smile. For the second time today Joe felt himself utterly disarmed by a woman and once again there was no Scottish accent. Mary spoke with a luxurious American drawl, slightly worn with an English lilt. His bias towards identifying Scottish women gave itself a small tick.

'You're American?' He asked.

'California born and bred but I've been in Great Britain for five years now, two here in Scotland.'

'Wow, that's great!' Joe replied and promptly realised that he was being decidedly uncool and possibly a dick.

'Well it's certainly different.' Mary replied which Joe felt was by way of letting him off the hook. 'So Joe, I'm told you want to see the archives from way back, that right?'

'Yeah, basically 1900 to 1960'

'*All* of them?' asked Mary incredulously.

'Oh, Christ no.' Joe reassured her. 'I just need the records of births and deaths and only those from a particular region.'

'Ok well. I can get you access to them but I gotta tell ya it's not a pretty sight down there.' Mary indicated that they should make for the security door. Joe quickly picked up the paperwork and shoved it into his bag.

'Could I put this somewhere safe?' He indicated his coat and travel case.

'Sure.' Mary walked to the reception desk and leaned over the desk to talk to Delores. Joe watched her every step of the way. Only the white Lab coat, that was unfastened, and her ID badge indicated that she was a hospital employee. She wore grey trousers that fitted snug around slim thighs, the cashmere sweater was light pink and her hair was loose unlike that of every other female staff member that he had seen here. As she leaned on the desk Joe observed how the lab coat curved around her backside.

'Jesus Joe.' he said quietly to himself and stopped staring. As Mary returned Delores came around from behind the counter.

'Causing trouble already Mr Joe?' She said in her voluptuous accent.

'Ah I'm so sorry Dolores, it's just a bit awkward having to drag this thing around.'

'Don't you fret Joe. I'll put this under the reception counter for now, there's plenty of space, but I'll have to get security to lock it away if it's going to be left for a while.'

'That's fine.' Joe replied. 'Everything I need for the archive work is in here.' He patted the bag.

'Ok,' said Mary. 'We are all set then, follow me into the depths Joe, if you dare.' Joe thought he might possibly follow Mary into a pit of snakes if she asked him too.

Just as the awful day had started to look up Joe was led into the archives room and his spirit was instantly broken. The large room, easily the size of a garage forecourt was home to row after row of metal shelving. Crammed onto each shelf were boxes, binders, loose sheets of paper and here and there thick rolls of paper bound with string. On the floor were similar items, some boxes had broken corners and papers bulged out of them.

'Fuck me.' Said Joe.

Mary nodded in commiseration. 'Yup, I'm afraid this is not going to be easy for you Joe.' She walked towards the far end of the room and drew her finger across the shelving there and let Joe see the coating of dust she had collected with that single swipe.

'All of the records from the 1970's onwards have been digitised but there's no funding available to get the rest done.'

She then attempted to pull out a box from the shelf that she had just swiped. 'Could you give me a hand please Joe.'

Joe quickly moved to her and took most of the weight of the box. They placed it on the floor together and Joe could smell a faint trace of attractive cologne on her neck as they bowed to put the heavy box down.

'It's not all bad though,' Mary said as she straightened and wiped her hands together. 'All of the births and deaths should be in boxes like these,' She raised her eyebrows at the box and then pointed at the shelf. 'Each rack should contain about two to three years' worth of records and if you are very, very lucky they will be in order.'

'I only really need the births.' Joe said 'Does that help?'

'Afraid not, births and deaths go into the same box,'

'Ok.' He replied, resigned to the task. He had no choice but to accept the situation. Returning to London today had been a hope but now it was rapidly retreating memory. 'I suppose I should get started'.

Mary offered him a conciliatory smile. 'Ok, good luck soldier,' she said, and left him to it.

At ten o' clock, almost to the minute, a security guard appeared in the archives room. Joe looked up and nodded to him. The guard had been showing his face since six. Joe assumed that his shift had started then. No words were exchanged, the guard glanced around the room, acknowledged Joe, turned and left.

It was approaching five hours of searching through the files and boxes and not one birth certificate had appeared for the region and period Joe required. He had sorted three boxes with various records of birth and death for years leading up to and after the dates but not even one during.

As he sifted through he noticed that many family names were repeated over and over. Not that this was not unusual to him, especially in areas of limited mobility. Macgregor's, Callans, Cambells, Dunbars and Kames were well represented in the region. These families had children before and after the Black hole years but none during, if the archives were to be believed.

He checked the time and decided to call his boss. There was no signal available in the archive room, *'lots of concrete around me'* Joe supposed and made his way back up to the administration offices. The guard who had visited him every hour was sat in there with a multiplex monitor showing at least nine camera views around the hospital, opposite him a colleague was similarly engaged.

'I just have to make a call.' Joe explained.

'Nay worry mate,' the guard responded. Joe realised that this was the first clear Scottish accent he had heard. He stepped outside of the security office and hit Mike Stone's number on his speed dial and waited.

'Hi Joe.'

'Hey, Mike. Sorry to call you at home so late.' Joe took another look at his watch.

'It's not a problem Joe, how's it going up there. The news says there's a fucking blizzard.' Mike sounded genuinely concerned and Joe liked the Boss because of this. He had a close relationship with his staff. He also raced on Superbikes at the weekend which Joe thought made him a pretty cool character by default.

'Yeah, it's pretty bad, took eight hours to get here so I guess I'm stuck for the night.' Joe said without masking his disappointment.

'What about the data, did you get the records?'

'No, and that's another nightmare. I think there are files down here from when the Romans came.'

Joe heard Mike laugh a little.

'In truth, I don't think that I'm going to find any. Unless those particular years just happen to have been misfiled they aren't here.' Joe said.

'Ok Joe. Look, don't waste any more time there. I'm going to book you a room at a hotel near to the hospital. I'll make it a decent one and I'll cover it with the company card so you aren't out of pocket.' Joe rolled his eyes with relief at this news. 'But we need that data Joe; we need it pretty fast to get this contract in on schedule.' Joe knew what was coming next.

'So you are going to have to go to this place, what's it called again, Winterfell?

'Winter Falls Mike.' Joe corrected him. 'Winterfell is from the TV show Game of Thrones.'

'Ha, oh yeah. Alright well, you gotta go there mate. Get copies of the originals and then get back home. All good?'

'All good boss.'

'Great. I'll hire you a car for the week in case the weather keeps you up there for a few days,' Mike added.

'Christ I hope not Mike!'

Mike laughed again. 'Ok Joe, I'll text the details of the hotel shortly and speak to you tomorrow. See ya.'

'Thanks Mike, see ya.' Joe replied and waited for Mike to end the call.

'I'm going to be leaving shortly.' Joe said, to the guard.

'Aye, nay bother,' the guard replied without looking away from the monitor.

Joe returned to the archive room and collected his belongings. He wondered if it was still snowing outside.

Chapter Two

His alarm woke him at eight o' clock. After a hot shower and a late meal he had slept well, but he was a little disappointed he hadn't had time to make use of the hotels amenities. The gym looked amazing. Mike had picked a really nice place and Joe felt a little cheated as he would be unable to get its full value from it.

He switched on the TV and waited for the weather report. When it came on it outlined that today was looking good, tomorrow also. Cold but with clear skies. It started to look shaky towards the end of the week however, more wind, more snow.

'Nay bother,' he thought, he would be long gone by then.

Joe took breakfast in the dining room and then checked out at reception. Once again he was surprised to encounter accents from Sweden to Australia, and it began to dawn on him that perhaps London was not the only truly International' city in the United kingdom. The Swedish girl on the reception desk handed him a plastic zip lock bag with a set of car keys and paperwork inside. He thanked her and made his way out to the parking lot.

The hire car was a Nissan four-wheel drive. Joe opened the driver's door and checked for Sat Nav. No joy.

'Can't have everything,' he said quietly to himself and climbed in.

Escaping Glasgow proved to be another test of patience and willpower. Despite the city councils practiced application of snow removal the city was clogged with traffic. Abandoned cars, minor accidents due to ice and just general bad driving created motorised hell for anyone entering or leaving. After sitting on one stretch of road for over thirty minutes Joe decided to pull over into a MacDonald's and sit out the rush hour.

Here everyone spoke with a distinctive Scottish dialect and for a while Joe was happily lost in the gabble around him. As he sat sipping on a bitter tasting Cappuccino his phone began to vibrate in his pocket. He retrieved it and saw it was the Mike.

'Hi Mike.' he said, trying to sound upbeat.

'Hey Joe, everything Ok with the hotel? You got the car?'

'Yeah it was great, thanks Mike. Car is cool too, four-wheel drive, good call'

'I thought it might be a bit more practical than a Lexus,' Mike replied.

'Sadly, I think you're right.' Joe laughed, but thought he would have risked a Lexus.

'Listen Joe I've tried to get in contact with someone in the town that will have access to the records but its proving difficult.'

'Oh?' Joe replied.

'Yeah, it's fucking crazy but I can't get the number of a police station, a doctor's surgery or even a corner shop.'

'Did you try the Infirmary in Glasgow? They must have a contact for the records.'

'I did, and apparently they don't. The records are delivered each year by hand. No emails either by the way. It's like Middle Earth up there Joe, what the fuck?' Now Mike laughed but Joe could sense a hint of frustration in his voice.

'Don't worry Mike I'm on my way. The weather report is pretty good so there's no reason I can't be in and out today. If the records are in a mess for some reason then I should still be done by tomorrow at the latest.'

'Ok, good stuff Joe, good stuff. Well, have fun in Winterfell.'

'Winter Falls Mike.'

What? Oh, yeah whatever, have fun and get home with the treasure.'

'Will do boss.' Joe replied, and the call ended.

Looking out of the window he could see little change in the traffic situation but he decided to give it another go. He bought a coffee for the road and headed back out.

Once the Nissan escaped the sprawl of Glasgow and its satellite towns the condition of the roads worsened with snow and ice as less traffic had travelled along them, but the 4 x 4 handled it well. Confident, and a little more relaxed, Joe managed to take in the scenery as it was revealed with each rise in the road or corner of a hill he rounded. He had estimated that the journey to his destination would be three hours, so long as there were no surprises on the way.

Google Maps had drawn a blank on Winter Falls and he had trawled the Internet for anything that featured the town, finally coming across a PDF of an Ordinance Survey map from 1948. It showed that the port lay about twenty miles northeast of a place called Lochnivar. It was nestled against the ragged north-eastern coast and surrounded by a vast wall of dense forest. Lochnivar looked promising as there were entries for it all over the net. Tripadvisor alone listed over two dozen vacation spots in an around the town.

Several villages were scattered further inland, and although they lay on a more direct route than Lochnivar Joe decided to take the extra miles to ensure he would have a garage available.

The journey allowed his mind to wander, much more than while travelling up from London, and as the Nissan cruised alongside Loch Lomond thoughts of Mary Burgess floated into Joe's mind. He wished he had taken a break to go and talk to her, but searching through the archives had consumed his attention. That was how it had been of late.

He had spent most of his free time working on the NHS software recently. A lukewarm romance. with a girl he met at his gym. had cooled to tepid quite quickly because of this. His friends had given up asking him to join them at social events, even trips to the cinema, which Joe loved. He had always been a movie buff, especially for sci-fi and horror flicks, and until his job with Dynamic Systems he enjoyed going to triple bill and late night showings of genre classics. He knew he had allowed work to become life, but it was something he could fix once he had this project wrapped up.

Perhaps it was the stunning natural beauty of the Loch and its surroundings that gave him space to think of an existence outside of, or at least after, the NHS contract. Maybe just being away from Glasgow, which he had found uncomfortably similar to London, allowed him to begin actually enjoying being away from it all. He couldn't say for sure, but by the time he reached Lochnivar Joe found his outlook was positive and he felt his mood warm for the first time since departing at Euston.

The holiday town seemed deserted, and as he pulled on to the forecourt he worried the garage might be closed due to the weather. Despite the ESSO sign being illuminated he wasn't even certain that the pumps would be live.

'*The winds might have knocked out the power to them,*' he thought anxiously.

He pulled up to a pump, saw the readout was illuminated and relaxed a little. Once he spied a cashier in the garage store his mild anxiety completely faded. He climbed out and attended to re-fuelling the Nissan.

Once the tank was full, '*sixty quid's worth of expenses full,*' he went inside to pay. He hadn't eaten since breakfast which made the colourful array of sweets and drinks tempting. He plucked two bags of chicken flavour crisps from a box, a bottle of cherry coke from the refrigerator and a Galaxy bar from a display that lay by the cash register, deliberately enticing to snackers like himself.

The cashier was a short, thin man with salmon pink skin. He tapped on an electronic register a couple of times as Joe approached, each hit producing a beep.

'Just arrived or about to leave.' The cashier asked in a friendly manner and with a well-spoken but distinctly Scot's accent.

'Just got here.' Joe replied

'Where'd ya travel from, Inverness?'

'Glasgow.'

'Glasgow! Sweet Jesus, how are the roads?' His expression was one of genuine surprise.

'Actually it's been Ok,' Joe said. 'The snow is deep but there's not much drifting.'

'Just as well then.' The cashier began to scan each of the items 'Some of the roads around here can disappear even when the weather is fine.'

Joe laughed a little but then realised that the cashier wasn't joking.

'That's sixty pounds for the fuel sir and two pounds fifty-eight for this lot, sixty two fifty if you please.'

Joe pulled out his wallet and produced his credit card. Inwardly he winced at the fuel cost.

'Are ye staying at the Lochnivar hotel?' He handed over the card machine into which Joe slipped his overburdened Visa and entered his pin.

'No, no I'm moving on, further North. I'm headed to Winter Falls.'

'Oh aye,' said the cashier as he waited for the debit to be accepted, 'what's that then?'

'It's not a what, it's a where.' said Joe 'A fishing port about twenty or so miles from Rhicarn.'

The card machine beeped and threw out a printed receipt which the cashier tore away. He pressed another button on the register and the cash draw popped out. As he placed the receipt inside a copy was printed which the cashier took and offered to Joe.

'That's your VAT receipt sir.' Joe took the copy and secured inside his wallet. 'Winter Falls ye say. Canna say I know it. Caravan Park?'

'No it's the name of the town, or the port I suppose. '

'A town near Rhicarn?' The cashier said as he leaned on the counter. Joe had begun to pick up his snacks and deposit them in his pockets. 'Are you sure you have the right place?'

'Yes, quite sure.' Joe smiled. 'Right on the coast, well obviously on the coast, it's a port. There's a pretty big forest around it and I think the next nearest village is Roscregan.'

'Aye well, I know of Roscregan and the forest you must be talking about is Ardach Coille, which is Gaelic for 'big forest' by the way, I guess back then flowery names weren't really required.'

Joe half smiled because he wasn't sure if the man was trying to be amusing, informative or sarcastic.

'But canna say I've heard of a place called Winter Falls though.'

'Oh.' Joe replied uncertainly. He wasn't really interested in this man's knowledge of Scottish geography but he did feel that the 'big forest' thing was a bit of a dig. Had the cashier not pressed him he would have left it at that.

'Are you *absolutely* sure you have the name right? I only ask because the area from Roscregan to Ardach Coille is pretty tough going. Very few signs to guide you and there are no villages nearby should you have a problem.'

A small flicker of doubt did cross Joe's mind. The town *had* been difficult to locate and the map he had used was something like sixty years old.

'Ok look would you mind looking at my directions? I have them written down in the car.'

'No problem laddie, I don't think I'm gonnae have much more to do this afternoon.'

'Thanks, I'll just be a second.'

Joe left and moments later returned with his notepad. He flipped the pages until he came to a sheet headed 'Winter Falls.' Underneath the title was a neat list of road designations, the names of towns and villages these ended with the initials 'WF'.

The cashier looked at the list carefully. Joe could see him making the journey in his mind as his eyes scanned the directions in sequence.

'Does it look Ok?' Asked Joe when he thought that the cashier had taken it all in.

'Aye well, it looks Ok as it goes.' He returned his gaze to Joe. 'But I tell ya I've no heard of a town called Winters Fall anywhere around here. I've lived in Lochnivar all my life and while I may not look much of an adventurer now I've travelled across the hills and peaks of this place a good deal in my youth.'

Joe frowned. If his directions were wrong this would make him look pretty stupid back at the office. Days wasted, money down the toilet and no advance on getting the contract completed.

Seeing Joe's obvious concern the cashier decided to offer some support. 'Look, head to Roscregan and stop there. According to your directions it's the last village before this town you are trying to find. If it's near and you just have the name down wrong or its perhaps further North or even, he wagged his finger 'one of the smaller Isles perhaps, rich people occasionally buy those godforsaken rocks and rename them, then it's likely that the folks there will know and can save you making a moose of yourself.'

It was solid advice and Joe nodded in thanks. He definitely didn't want to make a moose of himself.

'Thanks. I'll do that.' The cashier handed the notebook back to him.

'You just have to hope that the weather doesn't turn as well. You'll not want to be driving across Rhicarn with a storm blowing, trust me.'

'It looks to be Ok, have you heard anything different on the news?'

'No.' replied the cashier. 'But this is Scotland laddie, the weather here doesn't really care what the news says.' He offered a smile but Joe understood that it was actually a friendly warning.

'Well thanks for your time.' said Joe

'Nae bother, and good luck,' the cashier replied.

Joe's upbeat mood was truly drained by the time he climbed back into the Nissan. With the state of the roads it was still a good two hours before he would reach Roscregan, which in turn virtually guaranteed another day in Scotland. He had no idea if there was a bed and breakfast in the village so if the directions to Winter Falls were wrong he could be sleeping in the car. What had been a gradual softening of attitude towards the realm of the Scots in the face of its beauty and friendly natives was once again hardening fast.

'Unbefuckinglievable.' He said, as he looked into the rear-view mirror.

He pulled off the forecourt and slowly drove out from Lochnivar. Not bothering to soak up the beauty of the town that wore a clean smooth blanket of snow or its picturesque harbour. He glanced up at the sky, it was clear of clouds and the sun was bright despite its reduced heat. Joe wished he had brought his Ray-Bans.

As he carefully negotiated the main road through the town could see that Lochnivar was, as the tourist information on Google had suggested, clearly a popular tourist destination. Signs announcing 'Bed and Breakfast' and 'Holiday Break Special Offer' could be seen standing in almost all of the gardens and nailed to fences, but as he journeyed further north the houses began to thin out and the signs disappeared altogether.

The journey took him through a few patches of light forest and upon exiting one of these there was a noticeable change in the quality of the road surface even with the buffering of the snow. After an hour there was no doubt in Joe's mind that he was now travelling upon a dirt track. The road had narrowed so much that had he opened the doors on each side they would have scraped the drystone walls that enclosed it.

There were passing places where the wall was set a little further away from the road but these were badly spaced with up to a mile between them. The Nissan coped well with the occasional dips and rises and what caused real problems was that the snow was deeper here than on the main roads and Joe was forced to drop his speed to almost a crawl. He had hoped to reach Winter Falls by mid-afternoon but he was satisfied just to see a few farm buildings ahead indicating that he was approaching what he hoped was Roscregan, the last stop before his destination.

As he entered the village Joe could see about two dozen houses clustered around a grass square. In a few houses lights were visible, shining through nets or curtains. A butchers and general store stood next to each other and appeared to be the only shops, at least with visible signs, but at the end of the street on which they lay was a larger building with a traditional hanging board usually found on a pub.

He pulled into a car park to the side of the building. It had room for another seven vehicles but no other space was taken. Stepping out of the Nissan and into the snow his shoes disappeared into about four inches of it. He stomped around to the pub entrance. The sign that swung a little in the mild breeze read 'The Silent Piper' and a bas-relief carved in the wood depicted what Joe presumed was a pipe player in full swing, clearly unaware that he was silent.

It had not yet started to grow dark but a small light that was fixed into the top of the wooden porch which protected the doorway was lit. Joe walked into the porch and pulled the heavy wooden door open. A wall of heat, rich with a strangely alluring pine scent engulfed him and he stepped inside.

Immediately to his left was the bar, very well stocked with various spirits and sporting a half dozen hand pumps. Ahead were tables with round or square tops, almost all of them occupied and predominantly by men. On his right a large open fire blazed away as it ate into a pile of logs that it had been fed. At the very far end he could see bare wooden stairs leading to the first floor.

The movie An American Werewolf in London, sprang to Joe's mind as every head turned to face him and the conversation dropped to leave an expectant silence. Eyes looked him up and down, absorbed the suit, the shoes, the ridiculous hat and jacket combination and then turned back to whatever had previously being occupying them. He recalled that one of his favourite comedians, Rik Mayall had been in that scene. It was one of his bits of movie Trivia he liked to test people with.

He figured that the best course of action here was to buy a drink before he asked any questions, a 'when in Rome' sort of thing. A single step placed him in front of the bar but there was no one attending that he could see. He stood for a few seconds trying to look confident and at the same time relaxed, but the effort made him look strained.

A man stood up from a table that was near to the fire. Joe casually turned to see where he was going and to his surprise the man walked over to the bar and lifted a portion of it to allow him behind.

He was shorter than Joe who was what he thought of as a respectable five foot eleven, *'my family couldn't afford the extra inch,'* he joked to girls if asked his height. The barman was around five nine Joe guessed but he was stocky and looked powerfully built. His face, broad and dangerous looking, sported a pair of metal framed spectacles, his hair was thick and black with a few lines of grey weaved into it and he had a light beard flecked with the same sign of age. Joe thought that he was probably in his late forties.

'Ken ah get fer ye?' He asked in the broadest Scots accent Joe had heard yet.

'I'll take a half pint of beer please,' Joe said half expecting the barman to sneer at him.

'Nae bother, any particular?' He indicated the pumps lining the bar. Each had a fancy or outlandish name on a plaque in front of them. Steam Beer, Orchard Pig, Monks Folly, and one that really caught his eye 'Stone Oaked Arrogant Bastard Ale.'

'I'll try a pint of Bastard please.' Joe risked a smile.

The barman reached under the bar, pulled out a traditional pint pot and began draw dark liquid into it from Joe's chosen pump. He wore a light blue polo shirt of no recognisable brand and this showed off arms that were thick and muscular; each was decorated with tattoos a few of which Joe thought had military significance.

'Passin through?' The barman asked as he handed the pot over.

'Sort of.' Joe said. 'But I may need to stay over, could you tell me where the nearest B&B or hotel is.'

'We've rooms here if you need to stay a night. Nearest hotels would be in Lochnivar but that's aways from here.'

'Yeah I actually just came from there.'

'The roads no bad then?' Asked the barman

'Not bad no, well the snow is pretty thick but no drifts and of course it's a clear day so I got lucky I think.' Joe sipped at the beer which was thick, like oil and at first taste very bitter.

'Aye I guess yer did.' He watched Joe as he struggled with the beverage. 'That's a braw one no?

'Yes it is a bit... er, braw.' Joe hoped that the stocky barman would not take offence at his mimicry. He was rewarded with a kindly flash of white teeth.

The barman turned to a small cash register and rang in an unseen amount. 'Takes some getting used to that one, I would try the Steam Beer if you'll be having another.'

'I will, thanks.' Joe pulled out a five pound note which he thought should cover the cost.

'That's a pound fifty please.' It came over as 'poond' but the pronunciation wasn't what shocked Joe

'One pound fifty! Seriously?' Joe said as he handed over the fiver.

'This is no London my friend,' replied the barman taking the note and handing back change.

The barman then leaned on a pump causally. 'So if ye have come *from* Lochnivar where are ye headed to? If I may say yer don't look like yer might be mountain climbing.'

'Ah, well I hope I'm on the right track here. I'm looking for a town called Winter Falls.' Joe said.

The smile on the barman's face evaporated and the conversation throughout the bar once again became muted. Joe glanced around and saw that as before all eyes were on him.

'Ah see.' Said the barman. 'And why would ye want to find Winter Falls?'

'I just need to get some information from there.' There was silence. 'For my work,' Joe added.

The barman's expression was flat and undecipherable. Joe decided to expand on his reason

'I'm an analyst.'

'An analyst?' asked the barman.

'Yes.'

'And you need information on Winter Falls?'

'Yes.' Joe repeated.

'Could ya no call? It's a long way to come, from London, no?'

'Well, no I have to get copies of some records. And yes, I'm from London." Joe thought for a second then continued 'it's a government contract so everything has to be bob on, you know.'

'The government eh?'

'Yes,' said Joe, conscious that his conversation was now the focal point of the entire bar. 'Plus we tried to get through to the town, well my boss did, and we couldn't obtain any numbers.'

Joe felt a sliver of nervousness creeping into his voice. He couldn't explain why. The barman had not been aggressive or rude in his questions, far from it. But he felt his questioning to be more than mere curiosity. *'Still'*, Joe considered, *'why wouldn't the locals be interested in the Londoner, in a beanie hat, wandering around the highlands like a twat?'* He took a proper gulp of the oily beer.

The barman reached under the bar and produced two small glasses. 'Ah'm Kevin,' he said, 'will you no join me in a shot to help wash that doon?'

Joe wasn't overly fond of spirits but he figured that the Whiskey couldn't be any worse than his 'Arrogant Bastard,' plus this was a friendly gesture and he didn't want to appear rude.

'Sure, thanks.' He replied.

'Nae bother.' said Kevin.

'I'm Joe, Joe Clarke.'

Kevin poured an equal but generous measure of Whiskey into each glass. Joe could smell the rich and potent aroma of it as it splashed into them.

'Nice to meet you Joe.' Kevin said and raised his glass 'Cheers, as you folks say.' He took the contents of the glass down in one swift and practiced move. Joe instinctively copied him and regretted it immediately. The Whiskey was like a fire in his throat and whilst he managed to avoid coughing his eyes watered up as he tried to hold back his reaction.

'Jesus.' He finally spluttered

Kevin smiled. 'Very brave lad. Keeping in step with a Scotsman.'

Joe became aware that the patrons of the pub had resumed their conversations. He couldn't decide whether it was mentioning Winter Falls or the fact that he was sort of working for the government that had caused the disruption but he was glad to longer be a focus of attention.

'When will ye be headed off to the Falls then? Kevin asked.

'Well first off I'm glad to hear it exists, I was beginning to have my doubts'

'Oh. How's that?'

'I spoke to a guy in Lochnivar and he said he had never heard of it. He knew about this place but said that there was no such town as Winter Falls.'

'It's no surprising to be honest Joe, It's not really a tourist area and if you can't sell a stick of rock with the name on it Lochnivar people tend to lose interest.'

Joe detected the teeth in Kevin's statement but decided not to press the matter.

'Still good to know it's really there. Are there any easy routes I should know about?'

'No. There are no short cuts.' Kevin replied bluntly.

'Oh. Ok fair enough. How long will it take me to get here, if the roads are good all the way?'

'You won't find it.' Kevin said flatly.

Joe paused for a moment, unsure what Kevin meant. 'Won't find the road?' He asked.

'No Joe, you won't find the town.' Kevin looked serious. His words were not menacing or threatening, simply matter of fact.

'Surely it can't be that difficult Kevin. I appreciate that the snow is a bit of a blanket but the road seems easy enough to follow.

'There are more roads than you might think around here.' Kevin said.

'Ok well I'll bear that in mind. I'll make sure to keep to the coastal road that should get me there right?' Joe asked hoping that Kevin would agree.

'I guess we'll see.' Said Kevin, not giving the answer Joe had wanted. 'But look, if you have no joy just head back here. I'll have a room ready for yer and a meal if yer need it.'

'Right, that's er good of you, thanks for that.' Joe decided that now was a good time to get out and start his journey. 'I'll be on my way Kevin and thanks for the Whiskey, phew! Good stuff mate.'

'Nae bother.' Kevin replied.

Joe repeated his 'thank you,' smiled and turned to leave.

'See you later.' He heard Kevin call as the pub door slowly shut behind him.

Chapter Four

Joe left the Silent Piper at four and the sky had been clear of clouds. When he arrived back at the pub it was almost two am, above the heavens were brilliant with stars. He parked in the same spot as he done earlier, there were still no other cars, and wearily trudged back to the front door. To his surprise the Piper was fully lit and the door clearly unlocked as it opened as he pulled on the handle.

Inside a few villagers still occupied tables and the fire still burned, although not as fiercely as it had earlier. The first of the occupants of the bar to turn his head was Kevin who was sat alone reading a newspaper. He offered a consoling look when he saw that it was Joe who had entered.

'Welcome back Joe, no luck then?'

Joe said nothing. He walked over to Kevin and pulled out an empty chair. 'Do you mind?' Joe asked indicating the seat.

'Not at all.' Kevin replied.

Joe sat heavily and yawned. 'I think I've been around that fucking coast a dozen times.' Joe said with obvious resentment. 'I couldn't even find a road to the forest. Every time I took a turn towards it I ended up five fucking miles further away.' He let out a terrific sigh. 'Jesus Christ. What a nightmare.'

Kevin stood 'I'll get ye a drink son, what'll ya have?'

'Oh great, anything...just...anything.' Joe replied

Kevin went behind the bar 'A pint o' Arrogant Bastard maybe?'

Joe managed to laugh a little, 'No perhaps not that'.

Kevin returned with a mug of Steam Beer and a shot of Whiskey for each of them.

'How come you are open so late?' asked Joe as he sipped at his drink. The Steam Beer was much milder than the Arrogant Bastard and had a sweet, nutty aftertaste that Joe found appealing.

'When the snow is bad everything stops around here. My place is where most of the village spends winter so I stay open as late as I can for them.' Kevin said. 'Besides I knew you would be coming back.'

'Why were you so certain?' Joe asked.

'Ach, you know. The roads around here are awful, no sign posts, no landmarks and what with the snow and all, well I was pretty confident.

Joe thought about this. While at first it sounded vaguely reasonable it was also pretty weak given the steps he had taken to try and locate the town. He had driven carefully. Maintaining as best he could a view of the coast on any road he took. Eventually he had found himself driving on roads with tyre tracks in the snow that only his vehicle could have made. He was going in circles.

Kevin was wrong about the landmarks though. There was one, a Cenotaph. A tall, grey structure that stood on a stone base with two steps leading up to it. He had passed that landmark at least three times.

'So what's your plan Joe? You heading back to London tomorrow?'

'Back to London, God no. I've got to find this place, my job depends on it.' Joe drank more of the beer. 'I couldn't even phone my boss. No signal.' At this he pulled out his phone and saw the same lack of bars which he then showed to Kevin. 'It's like being on the moon around here.'

'Dunnae worry about that. You can use our landline to make your call.'

'I would appreciate that, thanks. I'll call in the morning I don't think my boss will be happy with me waking him at this hour.'

Kevin nodded. 'So you are going to look again tomorrow?'

'Yeah, first thing I'll head out. Clear head, positive attitude, you know.'

'Aye, I suppose.' Kevin replied. 'Well your room is at the top of the stairs on the left, the key is in the door. Twenty-five poonds fer the night and ye will have a breakfast waiting for ye if are up no later than eight.' Kevin stood and Joe followed suit. 'Pay in the morning son. Go and get your heed doon.'

Joe picked up the Whiskey and knocked it back. This time the fire was welcome and he let the sensation linger.

'Thanks Kevin. I'll see you in the morning.'

Joe made his way up the stairs and found his room, the key in the lock. It was compact but looked comfortable. He undressed and wanted to wash himself down but tiredness won him over and with barely a thought he crawled into the bed. He was asleep in seconds.

Chapter Three

Joe awoke two minutes before his alarm was due to go off. The digital display on the small travel clock read 7:58. He had always been quite a morning person. He had been jogging since his late teens and only missed a run if work or perhaps an excessively heavy night out forced him to grab as much pillow time as possible.

He felt pretty good. The frustration of yesterday was a distant memory and he was ready to get the job done. As he dressed the smell of bacon frying began to permeate the room. He recalled that Kevin had offered breakfast. He dressed, happy that he had packed jeans, a sweatshirt and trainers in his travel case.

Downstairs he found Kevin sat at a table facing the stairs. He was busy eating from a plate filled with everything an unhealthy breakfast should consist of. Across from him was another plate comprised of the same ingredients.

'Mornin.' Kevin said.

'Good morning!' Joe replied, brightly.

'Breakfast.' Kevin said pointing to the plate opposite his with his fork.

'Great!' Said Joe. 'Good job I'm hungry that looks like a lot of food.'

'Start your day with a good breakfast and it won't matter if you miss your dinner.' Kevin replied.

'I suppose that's so.' Joe said as he sat and commenced an attack on the bacon.

They ate in silence for a few minutes until Joe felt compelled to offer some conversation. He asked Kevin about the village, the bar and as many questions about the area that he hoped would not seem naive or stupid. Kevin happily answered and in turn questioned Joe about his work and life in London. Whenever Joe brought up the subject of Winter Falls though Kevin deftly ignored the question or quickly moved on to something else.

Something had begun to niggle Joe about the cryptic way that Kevin spoke, or rather didn't speak about the town. Despite him at least acknowledging its existence he had offered no actual directions and there had been no discussion of if he had ever been there. Kevin had also been so certain that he wouldn't find the place. He rationalised this as best he could, yes there was snow on the ground, certainly no signs that indicated where it might lie and yes as he had said the roads were very confusing. But still, the man was so certain that he had prepared his room and hadn't been at all surprised to see him return.

Joe was surprised at how quickly he finished his meal. In London breakfast was a fruit juice and a croissant. By the time he had finished his run there was little time for sitting down and eating so he would grab what he could en route to the office.

Kevin had finished before him and left the table, returning a few minutes later with two mugs of steaming coffee.

'What's your plan then Joe?' he asked

'I want to get out there as soon as possible Kev. Find this place, get my work done and be home to be perfectly honest. I'm against the clock and I can't really afford more fuel and stop overs.'

Kevin took a few sips from his tea. He appeared to be thinking, ruminating on something. He placed the mug down and closed his hands around it as though soaking up the heat from it.

'What will you do if you can't find the place today?' He asked.

Joe blinked. He hadn't even considered this. 'I can't imagine that'll be the case to be honest Kevin.'

'You could'nae find it yesterday.' Said Kevin.

'Well yes, but I had been travelling all day, there wasn't much daylight left when I set out and let's face it, as you said, the roads around here are confusing to say the least.' Joe countered.

'Aye, there's that.' Kevin said. 'But see. What if ye still cannae find it. Will ya be away to home, to London?'

Joe thought about this for a moment. 'I guess...yes I would. I'm not entirely sure what my boss would think about that but yes I would.'

'Aye.' Said Kevin. 'Well I need to get started here. Roscregan folks are farmers so they are up and aboot already and they have very little tae do come the afternoon.'

Kevin nodded. 'Yeah I need to get moving too. Thanks again for the breakfast Kev, really good.'

'Nae bother.' Kevin replied. 'And listen if this is stretchin yer finances a bit just send up the payment for the room when ye get home, okay?'

Joe was almost speechless, he stammered out an attempt at a polite refusal. 'Kevin...that's good of you to offer but...'

Kevin waved Joe's attempt at rejecting the offer away, 'It's nae bother, just send a cheque or something. There's none of us going hungry up here and I don't want you running out of fuel and getting stuck in the middle of nowhere.'

Joe felt incredibly humbled and began to redden a little. He did have limited cash in his wallet and if there was no cash machine in Winter Falls it would mean surviving on a few pounds until he got back to Lochnivar at the earliest.

'That's very kind of you Kevin, thanks.' He said.

'Nae bother.' Kevin replied. He gave Joe a smile and turned to leave but then remarked. 'Oh, one other thing, on your way back just head to Inverness. It will cut your journey time loads and you can get a train home or down to Glasgow if you need to.'

'Cheers, good idea, thanks again.' Joe replied. He had expected another 'Nae bother' from Kevin but instead the nicest Scotsman he had met smiled and walked towards his bar.

Joe was out on the road within fifteen minutes of finishing his breakfast chat with Kevin. It was only when he had made decent headway into the trip that he realised that he hadn't called his boss.

'Fuck,' he cursed out loud as he pulled out his phone and saw that there was not a single bar showing.

Against the evidence he tried calling but was met with the 'Beep Beep Beep' that indicated no signal. He placed the phone on the dashboard and made a mental note to check it every time he came to a passing place. He forgot for most of them.

A light dusting of snow had fallen through the night but not enough to cover the tracks he had made yesterday. Joe was pretty certain from the look of the road that his had been the only vehicle to have travelled upon them since the blizzard. He glanced up at the sky. It was no longer clear, patches of cloud moved at a slow pace and each had a dull grey base.

It wasn't long before the coast came into view on his left. The road was for the most part at least the length of a football pitch away from what he presumed was a steep drop, but every now and then he came close enough to witness the sheer fall from the edge down to dangerous looking rocks being bashed by the sea. His grip on the steering wheel increased.

As before he tried to maintain a route that kept the coast in view. His logic was that as Winter Falls was a port it had to be by the sea. Stick with the sea, find the port. Unfortunately, the road occasionally turned away from the coast and headed inland. Usually because a sizeable hill or fast moving stream or a river blocked the way but sometimes, Joe was convinced, for the sheer hell of it.

After such a diversion he would try to find his way back to the coast and would eventually do so, but only after a great deal of driving around empty expanses of snow covered fields or between large and ominous looking hills. He also looked for virgin snow, free of his tracks from the previous day to see if there may have been a route he had not previously taken. He had no luck in such a find.

Every road he took featured furrows he had made earlier. Occasionally he came across roads in which he saw wider track marks but figured that this would be where he had started to go in circles.

Once again he began to lose his patience with the situation. No signs, seemingly random roads and a landscape that was at once different yet almost impossible to tell apart one mile to the next. It began to grate at his nerves. He checked his phone. No signal. He pulled over on to a passing place.

'This is insane.' He said out loud.

He sat, tapping his fingers on the steering wheel. He could just turn around and go home, just drive on to Inverness as Kevin had suggested and be back in London by tonight. He had no idea what the fallout would be but surely there was some way around the problem that could be managed from home.

He sighed and started off again, looking for a road to bring him back to the coast.

A short while after this a familiar object came into view. The large Cenotaph stood proudly against the snow. Joe could see the vast forest beyond it, which had been his first proper glimpse of Ardach Coille, the *'big forest'* he thought wryly. He pulled up alongside it and decided to look, deep down hoping that it might offer some clue as to where he should be going.

He had not noticed from his car that the obelisk had names and dates cut into it. At the bottom on the side facing the road was a plaque but this was obscured by snow. Joe crouched down and wiped it away so that the whole of the text was visible.

1914-1918   1939-1945   ·
In Remembrance of the brave souls of Winter Falls
Who gave of themselves that we may live
In peace and freedom.

There was another line at the bottom that Joe couldn't make out. The metal looked to have been hammered and scratched, mutilating the text. He studied the names that filled the rest of the monument and realised that he had seen many of these in the records he had gone through in Glasgow. What he joked was his 'super power' a superb memory flicked through them and highlighted those that were the same. There were Macgregor's, Callans, Cambells and more made up long generations of Winter Falls families.

He knew that in the First World War almost the entire population of men eligible for service had been wiped out in some villages. For some reason he hadn't associated that with places in Scotland and now realised his ignorance as to how far the sacrifice for the wars had been felt.

He placed his hands on his hips and looked around. He could hear the sea crashing against cliffs somewhere beyond the forest ahead. He contemplated walking through it to find the town. It was a passing fancy. Water was already seeping into his training shoes and a short bluster of wind reminded him of the fact that he was wearing a jacket that wouldn't keep him warm and certainly not dry.

He got back into the car and considered his options. If he returned to Inverness now there would be time to try to sort out a solution. If he spent the rest of the day looking for the town and didn't find it he wouldn't be able to get home until tomorrow. The weather was due to turn again. God knows what he would do then.

He could always return to Roscregan and from there call home and get Mike to look into getting some decent directions. And there was Kevin, perhaps he could introduce him to a villager who would be prepared to escort him there. Joe felt that this idea had merit. Maybe he could even drag Kevin away for an hour or so. He settled on this. He had no intention of wasting any more time.

He jumped back into the Nissan and started back towards Roscregan, following his own freshly made tracks in the snow.

When he returned to the Silent Piper this time the bar was busy. It was early afternoon and the fire was back to its fearsome heat. Kevin was serving a big man with a large and expansive beard. The patrons looked up from their drinks and conversations once again but quickly lost interest in Joe's reappearance.

Kevin saw him and Joe thought his gracious host looked a little confused. He finished serving an old gent who wore a drab brown coat. Once a pint had been pulled for him the old fellow walked to a table where he and Kevin had eaten earlier. Kevin left the bar and came to Joe.

'I did'nae expect tae see you.' Kevin said.

'What can I say, you were right, the place is fucking impossible to find,' Joe shook his head, 'however I had an idea'.

'Oh?' Kevin said cautiously.

'Yeah, I figured that there *has* to be someone here who can give me some decent directions or even better perhaps someone could accompany me, or at least escort me there. I'm absolutely positive that my boss would pay them for their time.' Joe beamed at Kevin and hoped that he would offer to go along.

Kevin didn't return the positive smile. Blank faced he replied 'No, I don't think you will find anyone Joe.'

Joes face fell 'Really? I mean it couldn't take long with someone who knows the way, surely?'

Kevin turned his head to look at the customers; they were all doing their utmost to appear to be occupied. He put his hand on Joes shoulder and Joe could feel the strength in it as Kevin gently guided him toward an empty table close to the entrance.

'Come here a second Joe, take a seat.' Kevin said quietly and the two sat facing each other. Kevin leaned in a little towards Joe and Joe mimicked the move. 'Listen mate, I'll not mess you around. You seem like a nice fella and yer also seem smart so I want yer tae listen tae me carefully okay?'

Joe wasn't sure how to deal with the situation. Kevin had not threatened him but he felt as though a tension had suddenly insinuated itself into the atmosphere.

'Absolutely Kev.' he said.

'This is the Gods honest truth Joe.' Kevin said and paused.

Joe nodded to indicate that he understood that Kevin was about to speak as a 'man of his word'. He had no reason to doubt him.

'If you were to ask every single person in this village, or at Kilicolm just to the east or away to Inchroch in the north how to get to Winter Falls they couldn't tell you.'

Joe eyed Kevin carefully, searching for any hint of humour or general piss-take. 'Do you mean couldn't or wouldn't.'

'Joe, this isn't a Scotsman versus Englishman thing. To be honest your average Scot does'nae really give a fuck where people are from so long as they don't try to screw him over.' Kevin pushed his spectacles up, twitching his nose as he did so. 'I have never spoken to a single person who has been to that place and come back. Now don't get me wrong, *their* people come to us on occasion. They buy supplies from us here in town, they buy in bulk and pay in cash. A *lot* of cash. Much more perhaps than you would think was fair, but I have never spoken to anyone who has simply visited that place...do ya ken?'

Joe understood from this only that the people of Winter Falls were charged considerably over the odds for their goods.

Kevin continued. 'My father never spoke about the Falls other than to warn me about it. See that Cenotaph you mentioned? He told me that the memorial was the closest I should ever go to Ardach Coille, the forest beyond it. He said that it was an evil place Joe and he *meant* it, believe me. My father was afraid of nothing, *nothing* Joe,' he emphasised. 'But any mention of Ardach Coille or Winter Falls and he would go as pale as a ghost.'

'I'm not really sure what you are suggesting here Kev.' Joe said 'Are you saying the forest is...what? Haunted?'

'I don't know!' Kevin said. 'I don't know if it's haunted, plagued by locusts or full of Nazi's, what I'm telling you is that the scariest, bravest man I have ever known, a man who I loved and who would *never* lie to me was terrified that I might try to find that place.'

Joe thought about this and then asked, 'So what about the people from the town, you say they come and buy all this stuff what are they like?'

Kevin mulled over this question for a moment and then clasped his hands together, crossing his fingers. His thumbs rubbed against each other.

'They are...different. I mean physically. How they look and move.' Kevin appeared to be struggling to find the words to express himself. 'When they come they are always dressed in large black coats, dirty things that stink to high heaven of fucking fish and Christ knows what else. They wear those hats, from the 1920's, like Gangsters wore.'

'Fedoras?' Joe offered.

'Aye, that's them.' Kevin agreed. 'I mean they're fucked too, dirty, battered. But with those hats, and the big collars lifted up on the coats it's difficult to really see them. You can just about make out their eyes, sometimes a nose, sometimes and a mouth.' Kevin brought his hands up to his face, one just above his eyes and one below his mouth indicating the visible area. 'That's all ye see.'

'And?' Joe asked, confused.

'They're not right.'

'Not right how? Joe asked.

Kevin puffed. 'I don't know, it's hard to say ya know?' He looked around, searching for the words to express himself or perhaps to see who might be listening. He leaned in again.

'You know those poor people who get that look about them when they have a problem, a disease from birth...makes them look, different?'

Joe grasped at terms that came to mind 'Uhm, like Dwarfism, Thalidomide, Downs Synd...'

'Down Syndrome, that's it.' Kevin interrupted.

'You think they have Down's syndrome? Joe asked

'No, no I mean like, they have that *look* you know. The wee kids you see with it they all have that same look and *you know* that something isn't right.'

Kevin forked two fingers on his right hand at Joe's face. 'These guys, their eyes are wider apart than you would expect, their noses are...more flat, not always but you know, a lot of the time. Their mouths are wide and thin lipped. This *look*...they all have it in some way or another.'

Joe could tell that Kevin was being utterly honest but couldn't see where he was going with it. Was he saying that the town was inbred? Some highland twenty first century version of a back-woods Deliverance type town? And even so, what of it?

'Kev I'm not really sure what that means, you know. Ok if this place is a bit backwards it still...'

Kevin cut him off. 'It's not backwards Joe, its fucking *evil*.' Kevin said it sharply and with conviction.

Joe noticed a few heads stir from their drinks. Kevin realised that he was becoming too agitated and held silent until he felt that attentions had drifted again.

'Look, the simple matter is that Winter Falls has a history and the truth is I don't know what it's all about. My father did and he wouldn't share it, no one's parents here would, but we all got the same warning, to stay away. Most of the old folk from Roscregan have moved away now, ironically it's the money from the Winter Falls people that keeps this place alive, if that's what you can call it. The old folks used the cash to leave ans we use it to send our kids to University, as far away from here as possible. One day I hope I have enough to go too.'

Kevin clasped his hands together on the table. 'All *you* have to do Joe is drive to Inverness.' He said.

Joe couldn't understand what Kevin was driving at other than that he had some deep-seated fear of the town, or at least its people. But he knew it was a genuine concern that the Scotsman was expressing and that sharing his concern was somehow a risk for him.

The two looked at each other in silence. Joe struggled to make Kevin's strange revelation meet with anything approaching reason. If it was true, was Winter Falls some kind of drug running zone, a town taken over by a cartel or mafia, a secret government installation for biological research or perhaps it was a massive Paedophile haven and the men were products of in-breeding.

They were all farfetched ideas but then so was the concept of generations of villagers being too afraid to go near a place.

'I'll go home tomorrow.' Joe said. A look of relief passed across Kevin's face. 'To be honest I'm sick to the back teeth of driving around like a twat. We can sort this out from London.'

Kevin nodded. 'Aye, good, good. Take the same room and I'll get the train times for ye.' Kevin stood. 'The phone is behind the bar if you want to call your boss.'

'No.' Said Joe. 'I'll leave it until I get to London and tell him face to face. I'll need to time to come up with something that doesn't make me we look like a total failure.'

'Aye well, I think it will turn out for the best Joe.' Kevin said by way of comfort.

'I fucking hope so Kevin, I really fucking hope so.' Joe left the table and made his way back to his room.

Joe spent the rest of the evening completing crosswords he found in newspapers that were piled next to the fire. None of the locals that came to the bar attempted conversation with him but occasionally one would nod in greeting or say 'Evenin' as they passed by him.

Kevin had been busy. A delivery truck had arrived and cases of spirits were hauled in. Joe helped with this along with another villager named Tim. Kevin and Tim appeared to be good friends and the tall thin man, who Joe discovered was a mechanic was friendly and exhibited a dry wit.

While he and Tim had worked together Joe had interrogated him lightly about Kevin and the village. He wasn't surprised that Tim was guarded and evasive, it seemed to be the norm here but he did reveal that Kevin had a military background and that he was considered a 'hero in the village' but he wouldn't expand on this.

'You'll no find a better bloke than Kev when ya need a fella wi some steel at your side.' Tim said by way of closing the discussion.

While Joe and Tim had worked on emptying the truck of supplies Kevin had noticed Joe struggling with the metal kegs made cold by their journey. He dug out a pair of strong gloves and very a thick woollen hat with ear flaps which was a hundred times warmer than his Joe's Tie Rack beanie.

Later when Joe tried to return them Kevin told him to keep them as they were 'proper' and 'not like the shite' he had bought from city.

The beer truck driver mentioned that the weather was beginning to turn and Joe made a mental note to check with Kevin the forecast for the rest of the week.

The outside air was still very cold and the previously clear sky had been replaced with a dull flat canopy of grey that met the hills on every side.

After the delivery had been brought in Joe had considered exploring the immediate area but as his trainers were already damp he decided that with his current luck they would most likely fall apart if he tried to be adventurous. By nine o' clock the monotony had finally gotten to him and he told Kevin that he was going to go to bed early, ready for the journey home.

Kevin gave him a mock salute and smiled, his mood clearly elevated by his decision to leave. Joe took the time to wash himself down before relaxing on the bed. He tried to push the spectre of the conversation to be had with Mike away and instead allowed thoughts of the appealing curves and fetching smile of Mary Burgess to entertain him. As he started to drift away he pulled the covers over him and sank into sleep.

Chapter Four

Joe woke feeling fresh and fairly alert at seven am. He washed and brushed his teeth, dressed and began to pack his travel case. He had left his trainers on the radiator and the heat had dried them out completely. They were pleasantly warm when he pushed his feet into them. Once satisfied that what few items he had bought along were in the case he headed for the bar.

As he came down the stairs there was no smell of breakfast although Kevin was sat at the same table and watched him as he descended the steps. In front of him was a small brown envelope.

'Good morning Kev.' Joe said.

'Mornin.' Kevin replied

Joe was disappointed that there wasn't a plate full of eggs, beans, bacon and sausage waiting for him. He had forgotten what a guilty pleasure eating 'bad' food with such abandon had been. Kevin didn't look happy. As Joe approached the table the Scot pushed the envelope toward him.

'This was delivered for you last night.' Kev said.

'Oh? What time?'

'About eleven.'

Joe picked up the envelope. In neat script written in biro across the front was his name. No stamps or postmark were visible and the envelope flap was reinforced with sticky tape.

'Who delivered it?' Joe asked 'Not the postman surely?' Although Joe then considered that out here perhaps it worked like that.

'No, not the postman.' Kevin replied flatly.

Joe picked at the tape and then drew it off in a strip, lifting the flap. He pulled the envelope open and retrieved a folded letter. Opening it up and resting it on the envelope he read it to himself.

Dear Mr Clarke,

My name is Dr. Alan Peake and I have been informed that you wish to come and collect copies our of local health records but have had difficulty in finding us. Do not worry, you are only one on a very long list of people who have got lost in the labyrinth of roads and woodland around our town. One day I'm sure we will manage to make signposts that don't blow away every time the wind changes direction.

I have included with this letter exact directions to the town including landmarks to help guide you on your way. Please make sure to bring this letter with you and use it by way of introduction to Officer Alex Macgregor at the Police Station. He will be happy to guide you to my office and I can furnish you with any information you require.

I look forward to seeing you soon.

Dr. A. J Peake

'Fuck me.' Joe said. He looked inside the envelope and withdrew a second slip of paper. A few directions were scribbled onto it. He noticed that one of the landmarks was titled, '*The Cenotaph.*'

'Who bought this in?'

'One o'*them.*' Kevin said.

'Right.' Joe replied. 'One of the downs guys.'

'It's no downs ah said.' Kevin replied sharply.

'Well this is great.' Joe said, ignoring the rebuke. 'I can head over there straight away and get this thing wrapped up once and for all.'

'So you're not headed to Inverness?'

Sure, once I've got this sorted.' Joe couldn't hide his joy. 'Kev, this solves everything. I can be done in Winter Falls by the afternoon at the latest and then I'm off to Inverness for the train home this evening.'

Kevin shook his head. 'I think you should go home Joe. Put that letter on the fire and drive to Inverness right now.'

'I can't do that Kev. Come on mate, this is from the Doctor there.' Joe checked the name again, 'Dr Alex Peake. He's basically said that's he's expecting me ASAP and that the records are waiting.'

'Can ah take a peek at the letter?' Kevin asked.

'Sure.' Joe said, handing him both the letter and slip of paper with the directions.

Kevin studied them both carefully and then pointed to a mark at the bottom of each piece of paper.

'What's that?' He asked.

Joe hadn't paid any attention to the mark on the letter, only the directions. At the bottom right corner of each sheet was a faint reddish brown symbol. It looked like a spiral with a line through the centre. There were two dots at the bottom and at the top what looked like two dashes.

'I don't know.' Joe said. 'Perhaps it's his signature?'

Kevin scoffed at this. He pointed to the pages. 'Ya think he signed the directions? Who would put his signature at the bottom of a scrap o' paper with directions on it?'

Joe thought he had a point but couldn't see what relevance it had. 'Well, maybe it's not. I don't know what difference it makes.'

Kevin became exasperated. 'It's fucking weird Joe. Like that town, like the freak faced guy that brought the letter, like everything about the whole business of Winter Falls.' He handed the papers back. 'Ever since you mentioned that you were looking for the Falls my back has been crooked with worry.'

'Listen Kev I just think that...' Joe was cut off mid-sentence.

'I need to tell you one more thing Joe, before you make up your mind.' Kevin said urgently. This time he looked behind him to check that the door was shut and no one had entered the bar. Joe stood patiently, ready for Kevin to deliver his final argument.

'People used to go missing around here.' Kevin said. He could see that Joe was about to speak and so held up a finger to silence him. 'Not for a long time mind, but in my Dad's day, occasionally, when I was a nipper folks would disappear.' Kevin lowered his voice. 'Visitors to the hills, the coast and from the other villages just vanished'

'Oh come on Kev, this is a highland region, people are always falling down holes and wandering off cliffs. Christ, I thought I was going to end up in a Loch just driving here!'

'Aye Joe, we do lose the odd clueless rambler who doesna look where he's goin, but I'm talking about kiddies vanishing from their beds at night.'

Joe shifted in his seat. Kevin's voice was now a whisper.

'There used to be another half dozen villages within sixty miles of here. All gone now. Because children and young women were being taken from their homes and snatched off the streets. Families packed up and left, moved as far away from that godforsaken town as they could, and that Joe is what we are all about to do here. In a few years Roscregan will be a memory, a mistake on your road map.'

Joe wasn't prepared to let this new bombshell deter him. Kevin was pushing the very highest level of credulity that he would allow. 'You said *used to* Kev. I take it this is no longer the case.'

Kevin sat back. 'No, it's not. Once the police started to get involved in a serious way it stopped. After FIFTY years it stopped Joe, but then again did it? I mean what if they just started to hit places like Glasgow and Edinburgh eh? How many kiddies and girls vanish from those shite holes and it doesn't get reported or fucking noticed?'

'Wait, Ok so now the townsfolk of Winter Falls are child snatchers and what, serial killers?' Joe folded the letter and returned it to the envelope. 'Listen Kev you have been an absolute gent and I would've been screwed without your help but this is just...it's getting silly mate.' He tucked the envelope inside his jacket. 'I've got to go. I'm going to get this business sorted and get back to London so that I can fire some cash up to you and a very big thank you present, Ok?'

'I don't need a present Joe. I just want you to get home safely.' Kevin said with resignation.

'I will, don't you worry.' Joe said and offered his hand.

Kevin took it and they shook. 'Thanks again.' said Joe

'You're welcome.' said Kevin with regret in his voice. Joe was surprised that he didn't offer his usual 'nae bother.' For a moment, he looked as though he was about to give one more word of caution, but he didn't.

As Joe fired up the engine on the Nissan he saw Kevin come towards him from the back door of the bar. He wondered if he was going to start with more stories as he brought the window down. Kevin carried a bulky winter coat in his arm.

'Take this with ya. That fucking thing you're wearing couldn't keep a dog warm.'

'No really Kev it's Ok...' Joe started but Kevin pushed the bundle through his window.

'There ya go. The next time I see you that's a full set o' winter clothing you owe me.' Kevin forced a smile.

Joe took the coat and placed on to the passenger seat. 'Thanks Kevin, you are...well you know.'

'Aye. Well, go steady. The radio said the weather is going to turn to shite tonight, and that it could get very bad by tomorrow.'

Joe had forgotten to check the radio and was glad for the heads up.

'I'll be finished within a few hours, should be fine.' He gave a final nod of thanks and then pulled off the car park.

The journey out of the village and along the coastal road was starting to become familiar. When he reached the first place that the road split he pulled over and checked the scrap of paper with the directions listed on it. The route was straight on from here and this was the route he had taken for the other journeys.

A couple of landmarks were highlighted which he had seen but had not thought of as such, where the road veered around a large hill and forced him away from the coast, a passing place where just beyond it was a broken-down barn with rubble strewn about it like little cake decorations covered with ice. Finally, he came to the Cenotaph with the forest looming to the rear of it. The direction said to carry straight on from here and then to take a road off to the left.

Joe would have bet a month's wages that there had been no left turning on the road for a good five miles after the Cenotaph and yet, after driving no more than a thousand yards a break in the drystone wall that divided the road from snow covered fields, revealed a junction. There were furrows in the snow and Joe couldn't decide if he had travelled along this route and forgotten in the confusion, or if these were perhaps the tracks left by the man who had delivered the Doctors letter.

He paused at the junction for a moment, fingers tapping on the steering wheel. The road was clear as far as he could see but at some point it would have to cut through the forest as the lay of the land suggested that it would end up going over a mountain if not.

He thought about the barn. Kevin's voice drifted into his thoughts *'there used to be a half dozen other villages around here.'*

He indicated left, despite there being no car or person within view for miles, and started down the road towards Winter Falls.

Chapter Five

Joe noticed a steady decline in the road as he approached the forest ahead, the dip made the hills seem larger, and the forest more vast. The trees were incredibly tall and dense throughout. The foliage of the perennials was rich and dark and that darkness was amplified under the canopy it created as the Nissan entered it.

He couldn't say whether it was the weird stories spun by Kevin that produced a chill in him as he followed the road though the trees, or if it was because the air was simply cooler, but he turned up the heat from the air-con to counter it. Despite the gloom and the danger of driving along a road that could have hidden potholes and icy sheets under the snowy cover Joe increased his speed.

After a while he had begun to wonder just how far the forest would stretch, it seemed that he had been driving for far more than the ten minutes the clock displayed. He pulled his phone from the canvas bag. He had bundled the coat on top of it which made it a struggle. As his attention was diverted from the road for just a second, to loosen the zip on the bag, something dashed past the front of the car.

Instinct forced Joe's foot to hammer the brake pedal to the floor and the Nissan lurched for a brief moment and then began a graceful slide which in a heartbeat started to become a skid. Joe was struck with a mild panic and overcompensated on the steering wheel, exacerbating the angle at which the Nissan turned. As a drystone wall came into view through the windscreen he managed to push away the panic and started to tap the brake pedal and carefully and eased the wheels against skid.

The Nissan did its job and regained traction bringing it to a halt almost sideways on the road and close to the wall. Joe let his head fall back against the padded seat and let out a long breath.

'Jesus Christ.' Sweat began to pour from his scalp. He looked out of the side and then the rear window but couldn't see anything. The heat of the air-con seemed hellish and he felt a little nauseous. He opened his door and climbed out. Cold air raced around his body and quickly extinguished the sweat but Joe decided to stay outside until he was sure he wasn't going to throw up.

He leaned on the bonnet and rested his forehead onto his forearms, breathing heavily.

'This is too much.' He said between short pants of breath. 'This is getting way too fucking much.' A series of loud cracks made him quickly lift his head and he spun to face the forest. He scanned the gloom, looking deep into the trees but couldn't see anything, until suddenly '*crack...crack...crack*' noises came from just beyond where dark began.

He stood and walked towards the wall. From the corner of his eye he detected movement, a flash of colour, brown, white. Joe felt the hairs stand up on the back of his neck and just as he started to back up towards the car a stag bounded into view. It leapt in and out of the trees weaving through them with graceful ease. Joe gasped.

He had never seen a live stag before. The creature was magnificent, as big as a horse and sporting a set of antlers towering above its head. It continued its wild and erratic prancing through the trees and then abruptly turned back into the forest. Further cracking of dead branches could be heard as it galloped away,

Joe continued to gaze in the direction that the stag had run until he realised that his teeth were chattering. He gathered his wits and got back into the car. The warm interior was intoxicating and Joe took another moment before he manoeuvred it back into position.

He couldn't decide whether he was more excited about seeing the stag, which he supposed had almost caused him to crash, or whether he was concerned at just how scared he had been that something 'weird' had been in the forest.

Before he started off again he finished what he had been doing. He unzipped the pocket of the bag and checked his phone. No signal.

'Brilliant.' he said. 'Fucking brilliant.' He put the Nissan in gear and moved on through the forest.

The first sign of civilisation was a bicycle propped up next to a stile. Joe slowed the car and brought the passenger window down. On closer inspection he could see the bicycle was practically ancient. It looked like the type of bike he had seen in old movies the kind the police or postmen rode. The tyres were reduced to ragged strips of desiccating rubber and the paintwork had been replaced by a rough coat of rust.

The edge of the forest was the closest to the road he had seen so far and he half expected to the Stag to appear, leaping in and out of the trees. Ardach Coille didn't not appear to thin out at all, it was just a solid mass of trees, gorse and bramble right up to its edge.

He closed the window and carried on along the road. Eventually houses began to appear, cottages with long gardens that led down to the road. Joe couldn't help but notice that even with a blanket of snow covering the rooves and creeping up the corners, the cottages looked to be in a poor state. There wasn't a double-glazed window to be seen and the wooden frames looked rotten.

As he progressed, still moving downhill, the cottages became semi-detached and terraced homes. The gardens became shorter and street lights appeared. What didn't change was impression of dilapidation and age. The same rotten frames and soiled windows marked each house. Joe wondered how bad this place would look without the snow masking it.

The road curved and as the Nissan came around a bend the whole of the port was visible below. A cluster of houses interspersed with large buildings that Joe assumed were warehouses huddled up to the water's edge. Two jetties ran straight out into the harbour and a number of boats, fastened to posts that stuck up like twisted fingers from the jetties, bobbed gently on the water.

The road split here, he could carry on down and into the port proper or go straight across to where a row of large houses stood. Joe thought that they had an official look to them and decided to head there. As he pulled up outside a house that had a large wooden notice board outside it Joe realised that he hadn't seen a soul on his way in. Nor could he see anybody now.

He looked at the notice board. Faded letters at the top revealed that this was the 'Winter Falls Police House.' Underneath the notice board was free of any messages. No parish notes or lost dog posters, just worn wood and blistered paintwork.

'Bingo.' Joe said.

He decided to wear the coat. It had been insanely cold when he had got out of the car after the stag incident and it was not looking to get any warmer. He picked it up and also grabbed the canvas bag. The coat was too bulky to slip on inside the car so he got out and put the bag between his feet and he wrestled it on. It was a big coat, clearly made for Kevin's stocky physique but it was well padded and lined. It felt good.

Joe zipped it up and reached for his bag. As he did so he felt something jab at his hip. He stopped and put his hands into the pockets. In the right pocket he felt something cold and hard. He gripped it and withdrew a revolver.

'Fuck!' He gasped.

His surprise was so great that he almost dropped the gun into the snow. He turned to face the car in case anybody was looking out of the nearby windows at him.

'Jesus fucking Christ Kevin.' He said. Carefully he broke the chamber open to see if it was loaded. The bases of six bullets started at him back at him. He snapped it shut and returned it to his pocket. He felt a little more carefully in the other. His fingers came into contact with the cold cylindrical cases of more bullets.

'It's not a big deal.' Joe said to himself. 'Kevin is just a little paranoid.' He picked up his bag and turned back to the Police Station. 'Now, I'm just going to stroll into this cop shop with a loaded gun and everything will be fine.' He said under his breath.

He walked up the steps that led to the front door. He wondered whether he was supposed to knock. This wasn't like police stations he was used too. '*Police station, police house,*' he thought, was there a difference? He decided to knock. Just a few seconds after delivering a short but audible rap he heard another door open inside the building and footsteps approaching.

Joe wasn't sure what to expect. He recalled Kevin's description of the men that came to buy goods in Roscregan. Strange people that hid their faces, revealing only widely spaced eyes, flat noses and thin mouths. Is that what would be on the other side of the door?

When the door opened Joe was not sure if he was not actually disappointed as the man before him exhibited none of these characteristics. He wore a police uniform although it looked a little worn and possibly not the cleanest Joe had seen. He was also an incredibly large man, easily six and a half feet tall and well built, although his gut revealed that he was not big through exercise, at least not these days. Joe thought him to be in his fifties but the thick black beard he sported disguised his age a little. His hair was thick and somewhat long and unkempt for a policeman.

A large hand with hairy fingers was offered and Joe accepted the handshake. He had half expected the big man to crush his fingers as some sign of dominance however the shake was firm but not painful.

'Ye must be Mr Clarke' He said. His voice was surprisingly gentle and the accent mild. Much easier on the ear than those of the Roscregan villagers, Joe thought.

'Yes, that's right, but please do call me Joe'

'As you wish Joe, my name is Alex Macgregor but just Macgregor is fine. I don't think I've been called Alex since I was a bairn. Come in. I've a tea brewing'

Macgregor stepped back from the door and gestured for Joe to enter.

It was just a few steps from the front door to a small room with a counter that ran the length of it. There were two doors in the room both behind the counter, on one it read CELL and the other read PRIVATE.

Macgregor moved ahead of Joe and lifted a portion of the counter up just like Kevin did to access his bar. This was clearly the business end of the station. A few official looking notices were tacked to the walls and a faded poster on the front of the counter announced that there was to be a SUMMER FAYRE.

'Come through.' Macgregor said.

Joe followed him through the door marked PRIVATE. To his surprise it was actually a living room on the other side. There were two large chairs and a matching sofa, a dinner table with four chairs set around it at the far side and an assortment of cupboards. A small fireplace burned gently producing enough heat to chase away the cold. On the right wall was another door and Macgregor made his way to it.

'Take a seat and I'll get ya brew. Do ya take sugar and milk?

'Just milk please.' Joe replied.

'It's only powdered milk.'

'That's fine, really, thanks.' Joe said.

He settled into one of the sofa chairs. As he got comfortable he felt the hard shape of the gun barrel on his hip once again and stopped fidgeting. Macgregor entered with a large mug in each hand. 'There ya go,' he said handing the leftmost mug to Joe and sat on the sofa.

'I was told to give you this note.' Joe said. He placed his mug onto a small table he spied to the side. He was going to ask about a coaster but saw that the table was covered with rings from numerous hot cups and the varnish was worn away so took a chance. He reached into his jacket, withdrew the envelope and offered it to Macgregor who took it and placed it onto the arm of the sofa.

'Thanks.' He said, and then took a sip of his tea.

Joe was a little surprised that the policeman didn't take out the letter to read it. He had been expecting him anyway he supposed but was assaulted by the nagging question, *'then why have me bring it to you, you twat.'*

'Will the Doctor be coming over?' Joe asked.

'Aye,' said Macgregor. 'He has a few things to attend to in the town and then he is coming to meet you.'

'Good.' Joe said. 'I'm hoping to get away before this evening, the weather is supposed to be turning tonight and I don't want to be caught in it.'

'Don't you worry son,' Macgregor said, 'we want to get you finished up and on your way too.' The policeman seemed to think about this for a minute and then added, 'I mean, you know...the Doctor is a busy man, yer ken?' Macgregor looked at Joe intently as if worried that he might react badly.

'Hey, I understand. I'm sorry that I've had to take up any of his time at all.' Joe replied apologetically. He sensed that this was all hard work for the big policeman, he was trying hard to appear congenial but really had no interest in Joe or his mission.

Joe studied him. Even though the mug Macgregor held was a good size it seemed comically small compared to his huge fist, he was a mountain of a man. The uniform didn't just show signs of age it strained at the seams. Macgregor's broad back and meaty arms threatened to rip them open at any moment.

'Have you got your tickets? The gun show is in town.'

He examined the contents of the room. No photographs, paintings or decoration of any sort adorned the walls, other than wallpaper that wouldn't have looked out of place in an episode of Downtown Abbey. No television or radios were visible, no books resting on the cupboards. Joe wondered what the huge man did to pass the time. He couldn't imagine that there was a great deal of crime to deal with out here.

Macgregor said nothing. Small talk was obviously not his thing. As Joe pondered what a man with nothing to occupy him might do on a day to day basis. A gym around here probably consisted of lifting boulders and chasing bears. The police officer sipped at his tea and stared malevolently at the fireplace.

Joe was startled as a clear *'Ding'* rang out in the room. Macgregor rose from his chair and headed for the door leading to the reception room. Joe surmised that a bell, hidden somewhere, must be activated when the front door opened. A new voice could be heard as the door closed.

'I see our guest has arrived Macgregor.'

'Aye, he's sat in ma livin room.' Macgregor replied to the visitor. Shortly afterwards a slim man wearing a parka entered.

In contrast to Macgregor this man was short, no more than five foot five and had a thin, weasel face and equally thin hair receding from the temples. Joe stood to greet him. The man immediately offered his outstretched hand which Joe took.

'Alan Peake.' He said in a friendly and confident manner.

'Joe Clarke.' It's good to meet you Doctor Peake. I was beginning to think I would never get here.'

The Doctor gave a good natured laugh. 'Ha ha well, when I was advised that there was a young man driving up and down the length of Rhicarn in the snow I thought I had better act!'

Joe felt a little sheepish and started to redden in his cheeks. 'How did you know I was looking for Winter Falls?'

'Ach, one of the lads from the town was in the Piper and overheard that you were looking for the Falls. Of course, I didn't get to hear about it until late yesterday but as soon as I did I got him to travel back with the letter and directions.'

'That was good of you, thanks very much.' Joe said.

'No, no, it was not a bother at all. We can't keep the government waiting can we? I have the records waiting for you at my office. Why don't we head over there now and get them sorted?' Peake said, clearly keen to get on.

'That would be great Doctor, thanks.' He handed Macgregor his mug. 'Thank you for the brew Mr Macgregor.'

'Welcome.' Macgregor grunted.

The Doctor left the room and Joe followed behind. When he exited the police house the first thing he noticed were snowflakes falling lazily around him.

'Jesus, it's snowing already.' Joe said.

'What? Oh yes, not to worry it's not heavy.' The Doctor didn't stop to look around, instead he continued to the path moving briskly along. 'My surgery isn't too far,' he called back as Joe picked up pace to keep up with him.

'We could take my car?' Joe suggested

'Nonsense, by the time we have got into it we will be there.' Peake said and gave a dismissive wave of his hand.

They soon reached a line of buildings and stopped about midway along the street beside another worn sign. This one advised that it was the **Surgery of Dr. A. Peake** and that the visiting hours **were 9.00-3.00 Closed on Weekends**. Underneath was a handwritten note protected with polythene that stated that if there was an emergency to try at the Doctors home, No. 18 Ramsey Close.

'Here we are then,' said Peake. He flashed Joe a toothy smile and nimbly skipped up the steps to the large grey door at the top. Joe followed and upon entering the building as Peake held open the door from him he found himself in another small reception area. Like the police station there were no posters, informative or otherwise. The walls were an off-white colour but it looked as though this shade was through age and not a decorative choice.

Peake moved in front of Joe again and led him to the door across the room. At about eye level was a name plate.

'My office.' Peake said and entered. Joe noticed that the plaque read Dr. Charles Roberts.

'Is Doctor Roberts in today?' Joe asked.

Peake stopped mid stride in the doorway and turned to face Joe. 'Excuse me?'

Joe indicated the plaque. 'I assume you share an office.'

Peake looked at the plaque and looked a little startled. Joe thought he looked like a man caught in a lie.

'Oh! Doctor Roberts.' He said and gave a nervous laugh. 'My word no. Doctor Roberts has been gone for some fifteen years now.'

'Gone?' Joe asked.

'Deceased! Dr Roberts was the physician for Winter Falls before me, he put in fifty years of service to the town before he finally went to his rest.' He tapped a knuckle on the plaque. 'I never got around to taking this down. Everybody here knows everyone else so it seems a little pointless to have my name up there, and I don't know, perhaps I am a little sentimental. Dr Roberts was *my* GP when I was a child of course.'

'Right.' said Joe. The story, made up on the spot he was sure seemed ridiculous to the point that he half expected Peake to follow it up with 'I'm pulling your leg.' He didn't. Instead he eyed Joe for a moment, almost certainly gauging whether he had bought the story and then carried on into the office.

This room was larger than the reception. A tiled floor and white walls that didn't appear as clean as they should be for a place of medical care, and it looked eerie in the overly bright light from the two large bulbs.

'*Not strip lights.*' Joe thought.

A desk, large and impressive lay almost to the back wall and at the side of it was a folding screen where patients could undress. The usual examination bed was a next to this and other than that the room was home only to a few cupboards and a set of scales. There was a large window that would look out over the front of the building but the glass was frosted, obscuring the view.

On the desk were four boxes, open at the top, and Joe could see that each was full with paperwork. Peake walked over to them and placed his hands on either side of one.

'Here we are, the records for the dates that you were enquiring about and you should find them not only in order of year but also alphabetical.' Again, Peake presented Joe with his toothy rat-like smile. 'That should save you a great deal of time.' He added.

Joe's mind was beginning to fill with questions but he wasn't sure whether he should ask any of them. He had already been made uneasy by the strange story of the name plate and now he was in what could only be described as a filthy surgery and with a man who had somehow known that Joe was looking for paperwork from a certain set of years. He hadn't told anyone at Roscregan about the data he required. There was a chance that the hospital had called ahead and advised him but this hadn't been mentioned if so.

He knew he should be over the moon that his work here might be finished soon, possibly within a couple of hours. He didn't, he felt a little nervous and he began to wonder why the good Doctor and Officer Macgregor seemed so damn keen to have him gone as soon as possible.

'Well, I'll let you get on shall I?' Said Peake.

'Won't you need your office? Joe asked.

'Oh no, no... I just have a few house calls around the town and folks can call me up at my house if they need me urgently.' Peake replied.

'No receptionist?'

'No.' Said Peake. Joe detected a hint of annoyance creeping into the Doctors voice. 'She's off today, got a cold.'

'What if someone comes to the surgery while you are out?'

'No one will come.' Peake replied impatiently. 'This isn't some big town practice with a constant stream of drug addicts and hypochondriac old ladies. It's quiet here and people know when to come and when not too.'

'Ohh kay.' Said Joe. 'I'll *get on.*' He placed his bag on the desk and started to haul wads of documents from one of the boxes.

Peake licked his lips and made for the door. When he reached it he turned his head back to Joe, 'I'll be gone for about two hours. I imagine you will be done by then. Feel free to just scoot off if you like.' He said and added, 'When you are done.'

'Thanks.' Joe replied. Peake turned and left the room. A second later the front door opened and shut.

'Jesus fucking Christ.' Joe said out loud. He took a deep breath and then exhaled slowly. 'Well Kev had the fucking creepy factor nailed.'

He picked up one of the files. It was the record of birth of Mary Macalister, born in 1912 and without complications. There was some scribble on the page, probably by the Doctor or midwife, but it was illegible to Joe. Everything seemed in order. The sheet was well preserved considering its age, this however was not the period he was after. It was two years too early, he dug down a little and lifted an inch or so of the sheets out and checked the next one visible.

'Adam Campbell, born 1914. Bingo.'

Joe set the sheet aside and checked the pages from the bottom of the pile he held. He pulled free a further six pages that were within his time frame and placed them on top of the 'Campbell' sheet. He then delved deeper into the box, checking the dates until he came to records showing births in 1917. He pulled the documents up to that point out and piled them on top of the others.

He took off the big coat, conscious of the weight of the revolver inside the pocket, and lay it onto the examination bed. Then he moved on to the other boxes and performed the same procedure for births dated between 1939 and 1941, 1966 to 1968 and 1991 to 1993. All the missing years were there, his mood lifted a little. From his bag he pulled out his iPad, removed the protective cover and turned it on.

All he had to do now was take a snapshot of each record and he was done, '*Adios Scotland.*'

He looked at the iPad. It looked back with a black screen. Joe held the power button down for ten seconds, nothing happened.

'Fucks sake.' He said. He reached further into the bag and pulled out the power cable and adapter. There was a power socket immediately behind the desk and he plugged it in. Joe then dragged a chair closer to the socket and rested his iPad onto it.

'Please, please, please let it be because I'm a dick.' His whispered.

He plugged the power cable into the Pad and a few seconds later the low battery icon appeared in the middle of the screen indicating that the device was charging.

'Oh thank fuck.' Joe sat on the edge of the desk. He couldn't believe he hadn't checked the power on the iPad before he left Roscregan and as he remonstrated with himself a knock sounded at the office door.

Joe quickly stood. 'Och, *no one will come!*' He said, quietly mocking the Doctor.

'Hello?' He called out. 'I'm afraid the Doctor isn't here.' The door opened a little and Joe was a taken aback as a girl who looked to be in her early twenties popped her head around the door.

'You're alone then?' She asked quietly. Her eyes darted around every corner of the room. Joe wasn't sure what to say. He found himself taking a quick look around the room himself as though to confirm the fact.

'Uhm, yes I suppose I am.'

The girl cautiously entered the surgery and pushed the door shut behind her. She was average height, had a mess of auburn hair and an appreciably curvy figure. She wore a raincoat, fastened up, and a pair of faded jeans was visible beneath it. She spoke with the same accent as the Doctor and Macgregor, some words, like 'alone' sounding almost musical due to the intonation she applied.

He also couldn't help but notice that she was pretty and not at all weird looking, which was starting to be less surprising than it being the other way around if Kevin was to be believed.

'You need to leave right away.' She said.

'I'm sorry, who are you.' Joe asked.

'My name is Melanie Peake.' She replied.

'Any relation to ...' Joe started but was interrupted.

'I'm his daughter.' Melanie said. 'You need to leave Mr Clarke, right now.'

She walked towards him and looked at the boxes on the desk. 'That's all nonsense.' she said indicating the records Joe had pulled out of them. 'They have spent the last two days getting all of this ready, you have to go right now.'

'Melanie, I'm very sorry but I'm not entirely sure what you mean.' Joe decided to stay behind the desk so that there was a respectable distance between him and the strange girl. 'I understand that the hospital may have called so that...your Dad could prepare these for me.'

'No hospital has called.' She said flatly. 'No one calls this town. Billy Duggan told my dad what you were after, he heard you talking in the pub.'

Joe began. 'Right...well I...,' but stopped. He was suddenly at a loss for words. His grasp on the situation was beginning to slip. A thought entered his mind that he may be in shock after the incident with the stag. He had almost crashed, and what with the stress and the weather and...

Before he knew it Melanie was standing almost toe to toe with him. He found himself looking down into hazel brown eyes. Her hair, the auburn mess, fell back as she looked up at him. She placed the palms of her hands onto Joe's chest at which Joe almost jumped backwards in surprise.

'Please leave Mr Clarke. Go now, before the blizzard locks you in.' She said softly.

Joe snapped to his senses. 'Blizzard! What are you talking about?' Joe looked up at the frosted window. Outside of the rippled glass he could make out the rapidly moving, twisting shadow of a wall of falling snow.

He stepped around Melanie and dashed to the front door of the surgery. As he swung the door open a blast of freezing cold air packed with snow launched into him. The cascade seemed to be falling as far as he could see, which wasn't very far. The wind was strong enough to sweep the moving curtain in different directions and whether through primordial senses or just plain pessimism Joe knew that the wind was going to get stronger and the snowfall heavier.

He slammed the door shut and quickly strode back to the office. Melanie had moved back to the front of the desk and stood with an expectant look on her face. 'Do you see now, you have to leave.'

Joe began to pace the room. He wiped at his forehead as thick flakes had melted in his hair and began to trickle down.

'I cannot believe my fucking luck.' He stopped and looked at the frosted window again 'JESUS!' he shouted in pure frustration. He closed his eyes and once again took a deep breath, to calm himself and to take stock of the situation. He could stay, get the job done and then attempt to drive out. He was in a 4x4, the odds were good so long as no more wildlife decided to play chicken.

At worst, at the very fucking worst he might have to stay in the town and leave tomorrow, (deep down a small voice reminded him that blizzards can last for days) *or* he could leave now. Just go home and sort out this cluster fuck from London.

It wasn't even an option.

He turned to Melanie. 'Listen, thanks very much for letting me know about the blizzard. If I was a superstitious person I would think it was following me.' He smiled to try and lift the tension he felt he had created with his outburst.

'You'll be leaving then?' Melanie asked.

'Yeah, definitely. I'll give it a go anyway. I've just got to get this job finished, *well* started, and then I can get out of here.'

'NO!' Melanie shouted. You have to go *NOW*.'

Joe moved back a step. The girl looked panic stricken, her eyes were wide and her hair waved around her face. The image of an insane gypsy women flashed thorough Joes mind as his ability to create stereotypes conjured from movies switched into gear. He felt he should say something but couldn't. The situation was back to being almost surreal and possibly dangerous and he couldn't get a grip on any part of it.

Melanie stepped toward him but this time Joe didn't step back, worried that such an obvious movement would exacerbate whatever was going on with the girl.

You don't know these storms like I do Mr Clarke. 'This,' she pointed at the frosted window and its shadow play behind it 'hit from the sea within thirty minutes of there not being a single flake of snow in the air, and it's going to get a lot worse and very quickly.' She stepped closer. 'You won't be able to *try the road* because there won't be one.'

To Joes surprise she brushed past him, making for the front door. 'Leave while you have the chance Mr Clarke, get your key from my Dad somehow. If I could get out of here trust me I would.' As she opened the door and the blizzard made its way inside she pulled up her hood and turned to Joe once more.

'Don't believe a word he says, he's insane.' She bowed her head and walked out of the door, leaving it open. Joe Walked over and shut it quickly then returned to the desk, lifted the charging iPad and then sat, placing it on his lap. He had to do something normal to give him time to settle.

'*I think the weirdometer just went off the scale.*' He thought. '*Get the key!*' Was he supposed to lock the Surgery?

He once more considered just packing his stuff and leaving. It was going to take him at least an hour to copy every document, probably more. The girl was right of course, if the storm got worse visibility would be zero and drifting could hide the drystone walls. With no point of reference he would be in a ditch before he had travelled a mile.

He sat for a few minutes turning the options over in his head. He had to get this done. The job was sat right in front of him. Once it was copied all he had to do was get home, whether it was today, tomorrow or the day after was secondary to this. He stood and moved the iPad to the floor, taking care not to dislodge the cable.

He then took a page from the top of the first pile and placed it onto the chair. It was an awkward position to work from but he had to keep the pad charging. One by one he placed the records onto the chair and took a photo of each with the pad.

Chapter Six

Doctor Peake appeared back at the surgery sooner than the two hours he had said he would be. He was still wearing his parker, which was soaking wet, the shoulders still had snow clinging to them. He didn't see Joe, who was on his knees behind the desk, using the chair to hold the documents as he snapped them with the iPad.

'Are you done?' Peake asked once before he realised where Joe was. He didn't seem concerned that he was using a chair to work on rather than the desk.

'Not even close.' Joe replied.

'Well you need to leave. There's a blizzard.' Peake gestured towards the surgery door.

Joe was about to say 'Yes, your daughter told me.' but decided against it '*don't believe a word my dad says, he's insane.*' Her words pricked at him. 'Yes, I saw earlier, it looks pretty bad.'

'Pretty bad?' Peake looked aghast, 'It's bad and it's going to be a nightmare, you need to be on your way son, right now.'

'I'm afraid I can't Doctor Peake, I need to get this finished.' Joe didn't stop his steady routine of moving a record to the chair and then taking a shot as he talked. Peake looked flustered.

'Well how long will you be?'

'I'm not sure but I think another hour, maybe slightly longer" Joe replied.

Peake shook his head and puffed a little. 'I don't know, I don't know.' He said and paced a little.

Joe finally stopped. 'Look, no offence Doctor but I need to get this done and talking to you about the state of the weather really isn't going to move things on.'

Peake stopped his pacing and looked at Joe as he stood with the iPad in his hand. 'What will you do if the roads are blocked?'

'I guess I'll have to stay the night and see what it's like in the morning.' Joe said. 'You have a hotel or B&B here I guess.'

Peake stared at him as though he were talking a foreign language.

'Somewhere to stay.' Joe said 'this is a port, you must have somewhere for people to stop over'.

'Well...I suppose there is the hotel.' Peake said with a transparent degree of uncertainty.

'Great. Well, if needed I'll book in there.' Joe said.

'But...it might be full'

'Are you fucking kidding me?' Joe said, annoyed. 'We are two hundred miles from anywhere and in the middle of winter and you think your hotel might be full?'

Peake tightened his lips and his eyes darkened. Joe raised his eyebrows in a 'well?' gesture.

'I'd better go and check. See what I can do.' Peake turned and marched out of the surgery. As he opened the door the wind pushed at it and swung it wide, it howled through the surgery. Joe watched with grim resignation. He was here for the night; he hadn't been so sure of anything for the whole journey. He went back to the records and recommenced his photography.

Joe's estimate had been good. The last record was copied within an hour of the Doctors visit. He had tried to keep his mind free of worry as he worked through the documents but the girl Melanie hung around his thoughts.

He had decided that she was attractive, not in the way that Mary Burgess had been, polished and professional, slim and having that perfectly spoken American accent. Melanie was pretty in a less obvious way. Her clothing was from the seventies, her hair was amazingly wild and on anyone else he thought it might just appear untidy but on her it was sensual and provocative. She clearly had a curvy figure but he didn't think was carrying any weight that detracted from what he considered a sexy physique.

'*I have hidden shallows.*' Joe mocked himself.

She was a little scary though. When she had pressed her hands against him he had almost toppled over. Melanie was strange and possibly a little dangerous he thought.

By the time he copied the last record Joe realised that he had developed quite an interest in meeting her again. He wondered what it was about the women in Scotland that had this effect on him.

Once he was finished he returned the documents to their respective boxes and packed away the iPad. It was now fully charged. He pulled on Kevin's big coat and felt the weight of the pistol and bullets in each pocket. He hadn't decided whether to just bury them in a field on his way home or return via Roscregan and hand them back to Kevin. Either way he wanted the thing out of his possession as soon as possible.

He decided to take a look outside and made his way to the front door, opening it carefully in case the wind blew it wide again. It was a wise move, the wind had picked up to true gale proportions and the snow was dancing insanely outside. Visibility was to all intents and purposes zero. He pushed the door shut and returned to the desk. He was now certain of being here for the night, which was shit. But it also entertained the possibility of meeting with Melanie again, which had something going for it.

He wondered what her problem was with her father. Weren't girls supposed to be Daddy's favourite? Maybe she wanted to escape the small town life and head to the bright lights. He could imagine Doctor Peake being a bit of a killjoy. There certainly no immediate family resemblance, '*thank god*' he thought.

As he mused over what the evening might bring the front door finally swung open again and Peake walked in, closely followed by the towering Macgregor. Both were wrapped up with thick hats and scarves and they were covered from head to foot in snow.

The Doctor entered the surgery while Macgregor waited in the reception. 'Well there is already a foot of snow on the ground and no sign of it letting up, so it looks like you are here for the night.' Peake said with obvious displeasure. 'There is a room for you at the Tall Pines Hotel. Macgregor will walk you to it. I need to attend to some personal matters but I'll see you off in the morning.' He said.

'Ok thanks.' Joe replied. He picked up his bag and slung it over his shoulder. 'I've returned all of the records to the correct boxes and they are in the proper date order.'

Peake looked at him blankly. 'What?' He asked.

Joe gestured to the boxes. 'I've put the records back, tidy, in order.'

'Oh right.' Peake replied. Joe could see that the man had absolutely no interest in the records.

'*I probably could have just burned them as far as he is concerned.*' He thought.

Joe started for the door where Macgregor stood, watching him. 'Well I'll see you tomorrow.' he said. 'And thanks for sorting out a room for the night.'

'You're welcome.' Peake said dismissively.

Joe carried on towards the entrance. Macgregor pulled open the door and stepped out ahead of him.

Once he was outside properly Joe could feel the strength of the wind. It buffeted him from different angles, it was like being in an icy pillow fight.

'Come on.' Macgregor said impatiently and started to march away.

Joe had to take longer strides than he felt were safe in the thick snow to keep up but he didn't want to ask Macgregor to slow down. He suspected that the big man thought very little of him as it was.

He quickly realised that they were walking along the road that curved down to the harbour. At one point he almost walked into a lamppost as the snow became so thick that even their glowing tops were hidden. A couple of times he fancied he saw the shadowed outlines through the snow, other people braving the storm, but no one came close enough to be seen properly.

The road began to level and straighten after a few minutes and Joe reasoned that they must now be in the harbour area. Some of the buildings here were quite tall and helped to block a little of the winds ferocity and in turn lifted visibility a little. He could make out warehouses and other large structures. A few of them had ageing signs. Macready Fresh Fish, Denton's Motor and Engineering and one in the shape of a swordfish that said, 'Supplies – All waters.'

MacGregor came to a halt outside a set of double doors. He pushed at one and entered the building. Joe followed and found himself inside a hotel lobby.

'Another fucking reception.' He thought. He looked around the place. It looked practically derelict.

'Jesus.' He said under his breath. A single unshaded light bulb dangled from the ceiling and was all that lit the area. Against two of the walls were plush but dusty looking chairs, one had a table in front of it with an ash tray sat in the middle. Joe couldn't recall the last time he had seen an ashtray in a public building. The carpet he stood on showed signs of wear and near the door where he had entered there was no protective mat. Strands of bare carpet cord were visible.

On the far right was a set of stairs that led up to the first floor. The reception counter took up almost the entire wall in front of him and was made of dark wooden panels. Behind it a man stood looking at him, a pen in his right hand that he tapped repeatedly onto a large open book.

Joe finally saw the look that Kevin had been talking about. He thought the man to be around thirty or so but it was difficult to be sure. His hair was sparsely allocated to his head revealing a pallid and blotchy skull. He had the wide spaced eyes that Kevin had described and a similarly wide mouth with razor thing lips. His nose was not particularly flat but it seemed almost out of place on that broad, chinless head.

'He looks like a fucking frog,' Joe thought, *'or a Guppy.'* He tried not to stare. Macgregor went over to the counter.

'This is the lad. Sort him out for the night, he's leaving tomorrow.' Macgregor said in his no nonsense manner.

The receptionist, 'the guppy man' nodded and reached down under the counter, his hand returned with a key attached to an oval wooden fob. 'Room eight.' he said in a voice that was deep and guttural. Joe thought he spoke as though he had a chest problem, as though his throat was blocked with phlegm.

Macgregor took the key and tossed it to Joe and he snatched it from the air, 'Cheers.'

'Aye.' Said Macgregor who then turned back to the guppy man. 'Send him up some supper.' He looked at Joe, 'You eat bacon, potatoes beans, that sort of thing?' he asked.

'Sure.' Joe replied.

Turning back to guppy man Macgregor grunted. 'You got that?' Guppy man nodded and uttered 'Yes.' with a gargled voice.

Macgregor turned back to Joe and fixed his gaze on him. 'Don't leave the hotel.' He said. Joe thought it sounded as close to a threat that Macgregor could give without him actually producing handcuffs. 'The storm is heavy and you don't know your way around, you could end up in the sea.' He added by way of explanation.

'Right, yeah of course.' Joe replied. 'To be honest I just want to get some sleep and see the back of today.'

'Good then.' Macgregor murmured. He strode past Joe and exited the hotel.

Joe looked at the receptionist and pointed to the stairwell. 'Upstairs?'

Guppy man nodded.

'Cheers.' said Joe and headed to the first floor.

At the top of the stairs he was met with a long corridor with pale wooden doors on either side. The first door on his left had a little white disk screwed in at the top that indicated that it was 'Room 5'. He walked a few yards until he saw 'Room 8' on the right. He inserted the key into the lock and it turned easily, the mechanism made a 'Clunk' noise as the lock slid back.

Joe entered the room and took it in. It was smaller than he had anticipated. There was a single bed, a chest of drawers with a mirror on top of them. A tall but slim wardrobe stood near to the room's only window. There was also a table near to the bed with a single chair under it.

There was no TV. There didn't appear to be a bathroom but there *was* a dank and musty smell. Joe fingered the sheet and blankets on the bed, they at least appeared to be dry and clean. He supposed that the dampness lay in the walls and the carpet.

He stepped back outside and walked down the corridor until he came to a door with a small sign that read 'W.C.' He tried the handle and the door pushed open. Inside was a grim, ceramic toilet with a pull-chain flush and a sink. Joe couldn't see any soap or towels.

He left the toilet and went back to his room. Sitting on the small bed he looked at the window. The snow danced and whirled outside.

'What a shit hole.' He said.

He opened his bag and withdrew the iPad. As he powered it on realised he had left his travel case back in the car.

'Fucks sake.' He mumbled.

There was no chance on earth that he was going to walk all the way back up the road to the street he was parked on. As abrupt as Macgregor had been he was right, stumbling about in this weather, right next to the sea, was not a good idea. He took off the big coat and hung it in the wardrobe.

He considered taking the pistol out and putting it into his bag but decided to leave it where it was for the time being. Having taken off his coat he felt the cold in the room envelope him. A small radiator hung by the side of the sink. Joe went over to it and laid his hand onto the surface. Cold. He shook his head.

A quiet knock sounded at the door. Joe stepped away from the sink. 'Hello.' Joe said.

A whispered but familiar voice asked, 'Mr Clarke?'

'Yes.' Joe answered. 'Melanie?'

The handle moved down and the door slowly opened. Melanie's face appeared and upon confirming that it was Joe she stepped in to the room, easing the door shut behind her as she had done in the surgery.

She was wearing a large waterproof jacket this time, the same denims he thought but now they were tucked into a substantial pair of wellington boots. Joe thought that this girl would look good in anything she decided to wear no matter how unfashionable it might be. What a shame she was probably crazy.

'Why did you stay Mr Clarke?' She asked.

'Look first thing.' Joe raised his hands, fingers spread wide in a 'stop' position. 'Please call me Joe, my dad is Mr Clarke.'

Joe dropped his hands down and Melanie stood silently, her mouth pouted slightly as though she was about to say something but had decided against it. 'And second, what the fuck is up with this place? It's like the town that time forgot.'

Melanie took a step forward 'Please, keep your voice down.' She said calmly. 'We can't let anyone know I'm here.'

Joe made to speak but stopped. He paused while he thought out what to say next. Melanie waited.

'Ok, look I don't know why you are so keen for me to leave but I can promise you that I'm not here for anything other than to collect some data for my job.' Joe indicated the iPad on the bed, 'Which is done by the way, I've finished. And come tomorrow I'll be on my way home...Ok?'

'I know why you are here Joe.' She said.

Joe liked it when he heard her say his name. He stuck mental pins into his hands to help him keep some focus.

'I told you, I heard my father discussing it with Billy Duggan.' She took another step closer. 'I want you to leave because the longer you are here the more dangerous it is going to be for you.'

'Dangerous?' Joe gave a short nervous laugh. 'What do you mean *dangerous*?'

'Winter Falls isn't like any other town Joe. There is something horrible here. The whole place is...' Melanie paused, she looked down as she struggled to find the right words then returned her gaze back to Joe. 'The town is rotten. It's a cursed place and its people are evil.'

Joe had no response. He raised his eyebrows and stood with his mouth open. His mind raced with possibilities. The girl was having a laugh at his expense. She was disturbed, a mental case of some sort or maybe seeking attention having fallen out with her father. Should he just ask her to leave? He didn't want to do that. She was the only thing about the place that was attractive, but he couldn't envision this conversation going anywhere comfortable. Melanie broke the silence.

'The only reason they let you into the town is because you work for the government.' She said

'Let me in?' Joe said, puzzled and added. 'And look, I don't work for the government directly I'm just doing some contract work that they need.'

Melanie bought a hand to her mouth. 'Oh my God! Do they know that? She said, and quickly followed up. 'No, they can't know that, they wouldn't be this cautious if that was so.'

'Cautious? What are you talking about? Why? Is this a problem?

'Yes. Look, that's complicated Joe...it's all complicated. The important thing is that you have to convince them that you do have important government connections, can you do that?' She said with an expectant tone.

'Why?' Joe said. 'Why, would I want to do that? My request is completely legitimate I'm not breaking the data protection act or anything.'

Joe could tell that Melanie had no idea what he was referring to. He wondered if her reaction to what the iPad could do would be like showing an Amish farmer holographic movies.

'Because then they won't kill you Joe.' Melanie said flatly.

Joe's wry thoughts about the situation came to a halt. They turned to instead to something numb and grey. She had said the words with a deadly earnest and her eyes, the big hazel orbs that Joe had almost sunk into were nothing other than honest.

'Why would anyone want to kill me Melanie?' He asked nervously.

Melanie pulled her sleeve back a little and revealed a watch, an old tarnished thing with a worn brown leather strap. She looked at the time.

'I can't go through all of it with you now Joe, my Dad won't be at church yet. I think he's gone to see Billy Duggan. I need to get back before he does.' At that she made for the door.

'What the fuck!' Joe exclaimed. Melanie turned. 'You can't just hit me with all that shit and then leave.'

'I'll come to you in the morning, early, they won't rise until at least eleven and the snow should keep the others at home.' She turned back to the door and opened it.

'Look just wait...' Joe said

'I'll be early.' Melanie said quietly. 'Wrap up, we will need to leave the hotel.' She gently closed the door as she left.

Joe's head spun. He sat down on the bed and ran the last hour through his mind. Not much of it seemed real. The incredible storm, the hotel that looked creepier than the one in The Shining, the fit doctor's daughter who had a screw loose, the hotel receptionist that would be at home in Deliverance. None of it seemed to stick. Every time he tried to form an opinion on the matters they drifted away into a fog.

He wasn't sure how long he had sat on the bed before there was a knock on the door. This was solid and deliberately loud. He doubted that it would be Melanie. Joe stood and approached the door. 'Hello.' He said through the wood.

He could barely make out the words but it sounded like 'Mr Clarke I have food'. He surmised that 'Guppy Man' had brought up the meal that Macgregor had ordered. Joe opened the door. It was Guppy Man. It took Joe all of his reserve not to pull his nose at the somewhat rank odour that appeared to emanate from the receptionist.

The man stood with a tray bearing a bowl of soup and a plate that had a pile of potato and beans, topped with rashers of well cooked bacon.

'Thanks.' Joe said taking the tray. Guppy Man said nothing. He turned and made his way, with a peculiar waddle, down the corridor to the stairs. Joe watched him go and then shut the door with his foot. He placed the tray onto the table and pulled out the chair. He hadn't realised just how hungry he was. He hadn't eaten since the previous evening and as he sat at the table his stomach growled.

Before he ate though he had to put the gun away, he shuddered a little when he thought about it. *'Fucking thing,'* he thought. He took it out of the coat pocket and examined it. It looked like a pistol from a police film, the kind the tough old cop would use rather than some 'fancy gun the kids used,' where was that from he thought, Lethal Weapon?

He shook his head. *'Kevin, you mad fucker.'*

The food actually smelled reasonable once the receptionist's unique odour had left his nostrils. He tried a spoonful of the soup. It was tomato, thick and sweet and almost certainly out of a tin but it tasted good. He tried the potatoes, they were made from powder and were bland but the bacon and beans were Ok if a little salty.

He sat down to eat properly. As he tucked into the soup he reached over to the iPad and set it up on the table via a small stand affixed to the back. Once it was powered up he tapped at the screen between spoonful's of his supper.

He chose the 'slideshow' option from the menu and the images he had taken of the birth records began to roll by every three seconds. After the tenth image Joe hit 'pause.' On screen was the record of birth of Samuel Kames. Samuel had been born in January 1914, the son of Elizabeth and Kenneth Kames. Joe had seen that name before; the date was poignant for some reason.

He rolled back the images to the start and went through them again. He extended the time between sliding to eight seconds and studied each one a little more carefully.

He paused again just a few slides in. James Brownsword's details appeared. Born January 1914, the daughter of Sarah and Michael Brownsword. Something was sparking in the deeper parts of his mind. Joe pushed the names around looking for patterns. It was how he worked with data. His memory for information was good, possibly genius he had been told, he could recall dates, figures, names and almost any sequence of them by the patterns they made.

He let the slideshow continue and stopped just two more images later. This record was for Peter Bannen. Born in February 1914 to Alice and Charles Bannen. Bannen, Kames, Brownsword the surnames began to appear in his mind's eye as a strong text with deep grooves scoring them, chiselled into stone. He let the first names join them and a grey background appeared. The names began to wrap around a tall object, angled, forcing the text to turn at a right angle.

Joe saw the Cenotaph clearly now. For its entire height, from top to bottom, there were names cut into the stone and the names in front of him were upon it. He flicked through the images quickly, swiping his finger across the screen to speed up the slideshow. Henry Carpenter, James MacDougal and Frank Whittaker whizzed by and Joe immediately recalled their position on the obelisk. Jack Draper, Finn McCarthy, and Harold Broad. All male he noted.

It could mean nothing of course. This was a small town with close knit families. He thought of 'Guppy Man' and thought just how close some of the families might be. But so many names the same as those that had died during the war? It struck Joe as odd. There was also an absence of any kind of Doctors notes. Most of the others had at the very least an indecipherable scribble casually jotted down in the father's details or in a corner.

Joe had to draw his face away from the screen for a moment. A sudden ache caused him to rub at his eyes and a deep tiredness started to sweep over him. He blinked and yawned. Looking at the screen once more the names were too difficult to make out, they were blurred. Joe closed his eyes again, he shook his head to try and push away the tiredness but it had no effect.

He could hear his breathing becoming heavy and slow and he began to rock in his chair. He hadn't realised how tired he was, it was still early evening wasn't it? His thoughts were becoming muddled. Was it dark outside? Why were people going to church in the evening, perhaps they were Catholics. Did Melanie fancy him, she looked good even in that huge coat. Joe folded his arms and rested his head on them. *'I'll take a nap,'* he thought.

Chapter Seven

Joe woke to a firm hand pushing his shoulder. Lifting his head from the pillow he had made from his arms a pale face and familiar hair came into focus. He took a deep breath and as he did so he brought up a hand to his mouth to stifle a yawn and realised that he had drool on his lips and chin.

'Ugh, Jesus.' he said, wiping himself free of it with the cuff of his shirt. Melanie had now become clear and palpable in his vision. 'God, I'm sorry about that.' He felt deeply embarrassed and suddenly realised what was wrong with this scene. 'Hey, how did you get in to my room?'

'You didn't lock the door.' Melanie replied.

'Wow.' Joe took a look around the room. Everything seemed as it had before he had dozed off. 'I must have zoned out for a while, what time is it?'

'It's seven.'

'Ah right.' Joe said. He yawned again and as he placed his fist against his mouth he asked. 'Why are you back? I thought you were coming tomorrow.'

'It is tomorrow Joe, it's seven in the morning.' Melanie replied.

'What? I slept through the whole evening?'

'You were drugged.' Melanie said in the same tone as she might say that it was raining outside.

'Drugged?' Joe's eyes bugged. 'What the fuck?'

'The meal you ate.' Melanie picked up a fork and poked at the remnants of potato Joe had left on the plate. 'Probably the soup but I imagine there was some in the Smash as well, just to be sure.'

'Just to be sure of what?' Joe wasn't sure whether to believe Melanie or not but he felt he had the right to be annoyed.

'They didn't want you getting bored and deciding to take a walk around the town Joe.' Melanie offered him a consoling expression but nothing more. 'Grab your coat and put these on.' She said before Joe could ask more questions. He hadn't noticed that she had been carrying a large brown paper carrier bag. From it she withdrew a pair of old but solid looking boots.

'I guessed you would be about size nine to ten in shoes.'

Joe nodded 'Uhm, size ten.'

'Good, these should be dead right then.' She offered them to him, holding them up by long black shoe laces.

'Why would I want to wear someone else's boots?' Joe asked

'We need to go out. There is something you have to see.'

'Go out in the storm?' Joe asked although deeper in his thoughts was a part of him very willing to take a walk out with Melanie regardless of the weather.

'It's stopped, at least it's calmed down for the moment.' Melanie answered and held out the boots closer to him. 'Please hurry, we need to do this quickly.'

Joe decided to roll with it. He still hadn't decided whether Melanie was perhaps a little crazy, the drug thing seemed at once highly unlikely and yet coldly plausible with regards to how he had been affected. He also wanted to take the opportunity to spend a little time with her and had to fight the rational thought that it was a very pointless thing to do for more reasons than he could count. He took the boots and set about getting ready. As he hauled on Kevin's big coat and pushed his feet into them he wondered what would be the next set of hand me downs he would be wearing on this trip.

The boots were a perfect fit although they felt strange having worn flimsy trainers for the last few days.

'All set?' Melanie asked.

'I suppose so.' Joe replied. 'But listen, I don't mean to sound like an arse or something but can you please tell me what the fuck is going on?'

Melanie looked directly at him, her eyes wide and serious. 'I'll tell you as much as I can Joe, but not here, we need to head out into the forest.'

'*Of course we do.*' Thought Joe. '*Why wouldn't we need to walk out into the middle of a forest, knee deep in snow?*'

'Lay on Macduff.' He said.

'What?' Melanie asked.

'Let's go.' said Joe.

Melanie guided Joe through to the rear exit of the hotel, taking back stairs that avoided the reception. The door they went through wasn't locked and in fact didn't appear to have a lock. When Melanie pushed it open Joe could see that there was still a steady stream of flakes coming down. They were far lighter than the previous day and fell lazily as there was no gale tossing them around.

It was extremely cold though. Despite the big coat and his hat Joe felt the chill of ice in the air upon his face. Melanie had tucked her hair into a large, colourfully knitted hat and Joe though that it looked good against the white of the snow. He realised that there was a very real lack of colour about this place, everything was dark and lacked any kind of lustre.

He guessed the snow to be about three feet deep which meant the storm must have absolutely raged while he was asleep.

'*No way could I have slept through something like that normally.*' He thought.

The route they took out the town was clearly one that Melanie knew well. She guided Joe through a couple of alleys, the houses that lay either side of them looked as though they were unoccupied but Joe thought that most of the buildings here had that look about them.

Once past the houses, they came to a small stone bridge that ran over a stream which was currently solid ice. Melanie insisted that they walk over the stream thereby avoiding being seen from the houses that lay just to the right of it. Joe didn't question this. He followed her down the slight embankment and they walked a hundred yards or so along the stream. The ice was so solid that at no point was there any indication it might crack.

Once Melanie was satisfied that they were out of view, thanks to the appearance of large clumps of snow-covered brambles like small hills leading up to the forest, Joe broke the silence he had maintained so far.

Is this really called 'Big Forest' he asked pointing at the looming trees.

'Ardach Coille,' said Melanie, 'yes that's a rough translation. How do you know that?'

Joe shrugged 'Tourist information.' He said as they began to enter the forest proper. There was a very definite line of trees that marked the forests boundary and Joe wondered if this was natural or if the trees might be cut back on purpose.

It had been heavy going through the snow and Joe was thankful for the sturdy and waterproof boosts although his feet were still cold. He only ever paid attention to the colour of his socks, not the thickness. Now he wished he had some of the ridiculously thick army-green walking socks his father had in seemingly endless quantity.

As the trees grew thicker the snow began to become less dense. The evergreen canopy that towered above them had shielded the forest from much of the fall. Occasionally a 'whump' sound would catch Joe's ear as straining branches finally gave way under the weight of a snow deposit and drop to the floor. He wondered when Melanie was going to start talking. At present she seemed to be on a very determined path straight ahead. At least Joe *thought* that was how they had travelled but he wasn't entirely sure that they hadn't made slight deviations here and there. The monotony of the snow and the trees was quite disorientating.

They had been moving steadily downhill. The land to the right of him had begun to rise and by the time Melanie drew to a halt a ridge of at least thirty feet was on his side. To his left the trees continued perhaps another hundred yards or so but it looked as though at that point they formed a new tree-line.

Ahead was a haphazard row of boulders that looked icy and dangerous. Certainly not something that Joe wanted to cross so he was pleased that they had stopped here.

'Down that way is the coast, the Ardach follows that line for about three miles until it meets the cliffs.' She said indicating the tree-line.

'Ok.' Joe said, unsure as to whether the information was pertinent or not.

'We need to go over these rocks. The ridge bends here and we have to be on the other side of it.' Melanie made for the base of the boulders.

'Great.' Joe said glumly.

He watched as Melanie nimbly negotiated the obstacle. She pushed her hands into the snow, despite not wearing gloves and felt for hand holds and eased herself up the to the top. Joe tried to follow and almost immediately slipped. Fortunately, he had barely climbed more than a foot and only dropped back to the floor, bringing a pile of snow with him, some of which managed to find its way down the back of his neck.

'Fucking hell.' He shouted brushing the snow off him.

He thought that Melanie might be laughing at him but when he looked up her saw her looking serious, pensive.

'Try again Joe.' She said.

Joe puffed his cheeks and recommenced his climb. He took a little more time with his footwork and found decent niches on which he could push himself up. Near to the top Melanie took his hand. She felt warm in his grip but he suspected that he was just colder than she was, but her hand felt good and he liked it.

Her grip was strong and Joe was grateful for the help. He clambered on to the top of the large boulder that Melanie knelt upon. When he looked out to what lay on the other side he caught his breath. The ground below dropped about another three feet below the rocks. Across it at a width of about six feet was another body of water, frozen solid as the stream under the bridge had been but this was different. Whereas that had been a flat and dull thing, the natural result of slow moving water gradually freezing to its base as layer upon layer succumbed to the cold this was something else.

This stream had been fast moving, perhaps even violent as evidenced by the frozen sprays that projected at various angles, the torrent having impacted upon boulders and errant logs from dismembered trees. The cold snap must have been literally that, so sudden a drop in temperature that every ripple and wave was caught in a perfect iced version of its former self.

But this was nothing compared to the view presented to Joe on his right, where the land had been gradually rising to become the ridge that stretched as far through the forest as he could see. The source of the frozen stream was a waterfall that cascaded over the top of the ridge. The entire column of water was a thick trunk of ice. At the top frozen spray hung precariously, held in place by fragile threads of frost. As the falls swept down it grew thicker until it reached the base of the ridge and there it exploded into the stream. This too, every aspect except for perhaps the first few drops that had splashed away from the tumult as it crystallised, was captured as a frozen sculpture.

'Good god.' Joe said. 'It's beautiful'

Melanie said nothing. Instead she descended from the rocks to the stream and walked towards the base of the fall. Joe followed, gingerly treading where he thought Melanie had trod. He breathed a sigh of relief when both of his feet contacted the solid water. He walked up to the falls carefully, noting how slippery the ice was with every step.

Melanie was stood amongst the frozen ice at the falls base, apparently not caring whether she destroyed any of the fragile natural art. Joe was more considerate and manoeuvred as close to it as he could without trading on the iced foam and spray.

The ice glistened despite the poor light. Joe marvelled as flakes of snow drifted down and appeared to be pulled onto the ice wall, there to become an additional layer on the natural sculpture.

Joe saw Melanie staring at the fall with deep concentration. *'No, not at it.'* Joe thought. *'Into it.'*

At one side of the ice column he could see a branch that protruded for about six inches. He tried to follow its dark body deeper into the body. Looking closer he could see small objects, probably little pebbles, dark lengths that could be more twigs, sticks or long slender stones, picked up by the current and thrown over the falls only to be suddenly imprisoned by the plummeting temperature.

'What can you see Joe?' Melanie asked, looking at him.

'It's beautiful Melanie, it really is.' said Joe truthfully. He turned to look at her and was surprised to see that her serious expression had not altered at all.

'Come here.' She said.

Joe paused for a moment, looking to see if there was a way to get to her position without disturbing the ice. He stepped over it as best he could, wincing when he scuffed a section and it collapsed into a frosty powder. He looked up apologetically at Melanie, because he felt he should, but she appeared to have no interest in it.

As he drew up close and stood next to her she pointed a finger at the ice directing his attention to something deep within it.

'What can you see?' She said

Joe peered into the column where she indicated. It was a little like trying to view a Magic Eye picture, the longer he stared the more shapes came into focus, a twisted dark finger of wood, little bricks here and there and something deeper that had a familiar shape, dark patches on it, rounded on one side. He moved his head slightly to allow the light to fall at a better angle. The object, though blurred and obscured through the thickness of the ice, came into view. It was a skull. It looked like a human skull.

Joe jerked his head back from the ice as though something was about to come out of it.

'What the fuck is that? He barked.

'You saw it then?' Melanie asked, unnecessarily Joe thought.

'That's a fucking skull.' Joe said with an accusatory tone. 'Is that a human skull?'

Melanie nodded.

'What the fuck is that doing in there?' Joe shouted at Melanie. Fear suddenly gripped him and he felt the cold, *all* of the cold, surround him.

'What is this place?' Joe jerked his head around, searching the ridge as though there might be someone watching.

'*This* is Winter Falls Joe, and *that* is a part of its secret.' Melanie said.

Joe stared at her incredulously. 'I don't understand this.' He began to feel a little sick. The events of the past few days roared into his mind like a fast-moving montage, designed to drive him insane. The storm, the missing records, the deer, the creepy doctor, the monstrous police officer, guppy man, Melanie, the gun. His hands clamped down onto the pockets of the jacket. The gun was in his bag.

'Shit, SHIT!' He shouted, on the verge of panic.

'Joe please don't shout. I can't be sure that no one else is out here.' At this Joe clamped his mouth tightly shut. His chest rose and fell with exaggerated breaths.

'I think we are Ok.' She said to try and reassure him. 'I just don't want to risk it Ok?'

Joe gave a quick nod. 'Ok.' He said in a whisper.

'You have to see everything Joe or you are not going to believe what I'm going to tell you.' Melanie stepped towards him and placed her hands on his chest as she had done at the hotel. Once again Joe almost stepped away.

'You have got to be calm Joe, you have got to know why that...' She flicked her eyes towards the skull, '...is in there.'

Joe started to pull himself together. The shock was subsiding and his adrenalin had warmed him a little.

'I don't give a fuck why *that* is in there.' He said. 'I just want to leave this fucking town right now.'

'You can't leave Joe, not now, it's too late.' Melanie said without malice or threat.

'Fuck the snow.' Joe hissed. 'The Nissan will piss it.'

'It's not the snow.' Melanie pressed herself close to Joe. 'The snow won't keep you here, there is something else. It keeps me here too Joe, I can't leave either.'

'What do you mean?' Joe gripped Melanie's shoulders, her face was so close now. She looked up at him and he could feel her breath, warm against his chilled skin. To his surprise she placed her hands on his cheeks which had the effect of setting his face on fire with a sensual heat, weirdly stoked by his fear.

'Please come with me. You have to see the rest and I'll tell you *everything* that I know.' Joe could hear pleading in her voice, he had begun to think that Melanie was incapable of such a thing.

'Ok.' He said. 'Ok, Ok,' and moved his hands down her arms. Melanie released his face, but slowly as though it pained her to do so. Even in his state of mild panic Joe knew that there was something there, a heat stirred inside his stomach. It was a shit time to fall for someone. He should have had a dinner break and gone to see Mary Burgess. He should have asked her to dinner, spent the night in a bar with her and who knows, maybe he would have woken up at her place. Joe shook his head, now he was in love in crazy land.

Melanie took his hand and led him to the far side of the stream. The climb here was not as tough and Joe managed to ascend almost as quickly as she did. From the top of the rise they followed the base of the ridge for a short distance, perhaps a hundred yards, until a narrow pathway presented itself.

'Convenient.' Joe said, he felt that his resolve was returning.

'It's not natural.' Melanie said. 'It was cut into the ridge ages ago when there were pirates and smugglers. They used it to get to the shore from caves deep in the forest. The whole town was in on it apparently. This place has been bad for a long, long time.' She began to walk up the path.

The path was steep and Joe was relieved that it wasn't just him that slid on the snow. He was thankful when he reached the top having twice thought he was going to tumble back down. They walked back along the ridge to where the stream became the waterfall.

The view of the falls from here was not as spectacular as it was from its base. The stream, although it had frozen just as fast, didn't have the same dynamic appeal. Not that Joe was in any kind of mood to appreciate the artistry of nature.

He had wanted to ask Melanie questions, a lot of questions, but had decided to wait and hear what she had to say, or see what other sight she might have to show him. He was also quieted by the fact that she now held his hand as they walked. It could have been for mutual support, in case one of them slipped and went to tumble over the edge. But it wasn't, they both knew that it wasn't, and for now this would have to do.

At the top of the falls Melanie guided Joe along the edge of the frozen stream and back into the forest. The trees grew thicker as they travelled and brambles and ferns also appeared to take up more space of the space between them. With snow on top of it all Joe thought that the whole forest was beginning to look like a vast white sea that threatened to pour in on them. Abruptly Melanie stopped.

Ahead Joe could make out a clearing, the early light of morning streamed down into it.

Melanie turned to him and took both his hands. 'Joe I can't even begin to tell you what you are going to see.' She looked deep into his eyes as if searching for some indication of what his reaction might be. 'This is one of the places where they worship.' She said.

'Who are *they*?' Joe asked, allowing 'worship' to slide for the moment.

'Most of them,' Melanie said. 'Most of the townsfolk. Not everyone comes from what I have been able to gather, certainly none of the girls, not yet anyway.' Joe felt a shudder run through her. 'They are here from about eleven until dawn. This is why we were safe to leave this morning, they are asleep, the ones that matter.'

'Your father?' Joe asked.

Melanie nodded. 'Oh yes, he would be here.' She looked disgusted.

'So what is this?' Joe asked. 'Some kind of pagan church we are talking about, some kind of Wicker Man thing?'

Melanie looked at him blankly, 'Wicker Man?'

'Doesn't matter.' Said Joe. He rephrased, 'Is it a weird church thing?'

Melanie thought for a moment. 'Sort of yes, I suppose, except that this is...' she looked in thought again and then asked, 'Do you believe in God?'

Joe shrugged a little, turning the ends of his mouth down. 'No, I don't think so. Religions not really my bag.'

'No Gods at all?' She said.

'Well no, if I don't believe in one I'm hardly likely to believe in any am I?' He replied and wondered if he had made an error in being so flippant. Melanie could be a Born Again or Jovo or some other flavour of Christian.

If he had annoyed her it didn't show, instead Melanie looked at him with what could only be considered sympathetic eyes.

'Ok. Well, we will need to talk about that later.' She said. 'But for now I've got to ask you to promise not to make any loud noise, don't shout or scream Joe, please.'

Joe knew that ordinarily he would have laughed at such a request but he had to admit to himself that he had almost screamed at the bottom of the falls. The sheer look of dread that was etched into Melanie's face, as she asked him essentially to 'be a man,' extinguished any sense of bravado he may have had.

'Ok.' He said. 'I promise.'

Melanie turned from him and led him by the hand into the clearing. There wasn't a single tree or clump of ground foliage in a rough circle of about twenty feet. The snow had been thoroughly trodden in two distinct lines leading up to what looked like a large stone table, a dark grey rectangular block. On top of the block sat two pottery bowls at either end of its length. Between these bowls were variously sized objects coated with snow and frost. Melanie let Joe's hand slip from hers as he slowly approached the scene.

As he drew in nearer he could see that the area immediately surrounding the base of the block was stained with a dark substance. It coated the top and sides and was also mixed with the mud and snow at the bottom. He moved around to the side nearest bowl so that it no longer blocked his view.

Joe stood still, as though instantly frozen into place like the falls had been. His mind began to register what he saw piecemeal, to allow it all to be taken in without driving him into madness. The irregularly shaped pieces on the top of the block were a man, had *been* a man.

There was a torso, no arms or legs were attached. The head was near, but not connected to the neck. This had been obscured by the pottery bowl. The head looked down upon the rest of its body with empty sockets where there had once been eyes. The torso had been gutted, a gaping hole just below the breast bone cut down to the navel. It was now a gore lined cavity with a glaze of frost and ice.

Joe knew it had been a man because the genitals had been cut away as one and laid to the side of the chest. There were other objects too. One of which was a heart, raggedly cut at each artery. Next to this were two small rises of snow Joe suspected had eyes underneath.

He wanted to back away but found himself moving closer. There was no sign of the man's legs or arms but each pottery bowl was full. Although snow had settled on them both Joe could make out frozen intestines that took up the bulk of one of them as a pale length of the organ hung over the lip and had stiffened against the side. He couldn't be certain what was in the other but a torrent of options flooded his mind.

He was almost ready to look away, ready to dash from the scene and puke his guts up into the snow. Into *fresh* snow where no one had walked but first he had to see the upper section of the man on the block. The heart had not been cut directly out of the chest. Joe assumed that it must have been severed and pulled out from the open stomach because the whole of the upper chest was intact except for a design that had been carved into the skin.

Satisfied that he had not been mistaken and that the design was what he had thought it was Joe turned away and walked towards the edge of the clearing, away from where Melanie stood. He dropped to his knees and began to retch.

He didn't hear Melanie run over to him but was glad to feel her hands on his back. She pulled off his woollen hat and ran her fingers through his hair as his body lurched.

'It's Ok Joe.' She said. 'It's Ok.'

When the last spasm had faded Joe spat bile, which had collected at the back of his throat, into the steaming mess he had deposited. He wiped his mouth one with one sleeve of his jacket and then wiped away his tears with the other.

Melanie didn't take her hands off him as he stood. Instead she nestled herself under his arm and wrapped hers around his waist.

'Fucking hell...oh fucking hell.' Joe cried. Fresh, warm tears spilled down his cheeks. Melanie lifted his arm and pulled back the sleeve revealing his watch. She looked at it and told Joe that they had to start moving back.

'Fuck that!' Joe snapped. 'I'm fucking out of here.' He started to move off away from the clearing but Melanie held onto his waist and pulled him back as best she could.

'You can't Joe, you'll get lost. You will never find your way out of the forest.' She moved in front of him, almost sending them both tumbling into the snow.

'Listen to me Joe.' Her hands grasped his face and he looked down at her through red rimmed eyes that were still filmed with tears.

'You need to know what is happening here, it's the only way you will understand how to get away.' She stood on her toes and at the same time pulled Joes face closer to hers. Once again her sweet breath intoxicated Joe and he allowed his mind to swim into it as though he were swimming for the safety of the shore.

'We have to get back to the town, we need to get you to your room so that no one knows you have or I have been here.'

Joe's head had begun to spin and Melanie sensed the loosening of his muscles just before he dropped to his knees. She knelt with him and maintained her embrace.

'Joe, you have to keep yourself together. They are scared of you and they think you work for the government.'

Somewhere deep in his miasma of thoughts Joe knew that this was incorrect and shook his head to let Melanie know that she was wrong.

'I know you don't Joe. I understand that, but they don't and it's why you're still alive. You just have to convince them that you work for the government and that your job in Winter Falls is done. That everything is perfect and you see no reason to come back, ever.' She pressed her cheek against his and wrapped her arms around his neck.

She whispered into his ear. 'I need to get out too Joe. I *have* to get out, but we are going to need each other to do it.'

Joe didn't have the strength to argue or rationalise what was happening or what he was hearing. He nodded dumbly into Melanie's shoulder. Melanie pulled her cheek away from his and kissed him gently on the lips. When she broke the contact Joe felt that he would cry again, his heart ached for her touch, but Melanie stood and coaxed him to his feet.

'We need to get back before the town starts to wake.' Joe nodded. 'It will take less time to get back as we don't need to go via the falls.'

Joe had no problem with that, he never wanted to see that waterfall again, not as long as he lived. Melanie took his hand and started off back towards the town at a brisk pace, pulling him along.

During the walk Joe began to regain his wits. He needed to start making sense of things. It was his nature to put pieces together, to read data and assemble it so that the big picture could be seen.

'Do you know who it was on that table?' He asked

'I'm not completely sure.' Melanie said 'But there were two men in the town last week who I've never seen before. They looked like hikers or climbers of some sort. I don't know how they got in but I'm fairly certain they didn't get out.' She squeezed Joe's hand. 'I didn't get a chance to talk to them.'

'If that's one of them where's the other?'

'I don't know.' Melanie replied. 'There are lots of places to hide people in the town Joe, if he's alive anyway.'

'Why did they kill him? Why did they kill him like *that?*' Joe said it through clenched teeth.

'It's a ritual Joe.' She hitched her head backwards 'The stone back there, it's an altar, it's where the people of Winter Falls offer sacrifices to their god.'

'Fucking hell. It's the bloody Wicker Man. I knew it. This place is full of psychopaths.'

'Trust me it's worse than that Joe, much worse.' Melanie said darkly. She pointed ahead. Joe could see that the tree-line near to the town was coming into view. 'Ok listen we have to meet up later but I can't get away until my dad goes to worship.'

'Jesus, are they going to kill someone else, this other guy?' Joe asked his eyes wide with fear.

'No I don't think so.' Melanie said. 'I've never known them to offer someone up again straight after...' She stopped, as Joe looked as though he was on the verge of losing it again.

'Joe!' She snapped at him. It did the job and she could see that he was with her again.'

'They will meet at the Order House tonight which is on the far side of the town, near to the harbour. I can get away from eleven. I'll come to your room as soon as dad leaves the house.'

'What about Kermit?' Joe asked.

'Who?' Melanie asked, confused.

'The frog man on reception.' Joe said.

'Oh Henry.' Said Melanie. 'He won't be there. He will be at the Order house too.'

'Right.' Joe said.

'He will bring your food up. Don't eat it.' Melanie advised.

'Don't you fucking worry, I won't.' Joe replied.

They reached the edge of the forest and scanned the town for signs of activity. It was quiet. The snow had begun to pick up pace and Joe thought that Winter Falls looked a little like a Dickensian snow globe from this vantage point, but this wasn't a positive image. Something about Dickens stories had always scared him as a child. Dickens' London was dark and dangerous and full of people who were cruel to children.

He thought that the snow was there to mask the horror of the place, to veil its filth and vileness. A shit-hole town of murdering, religious nutbags that shunned the outside world and killed people who happened to wander in to it.

Melanie tugged at his hand. 'Come on, let's get going.'

Joe nodded and jogged along with her, helping them to quickly reach the rear of the hotel. Melanie pulled open the door and Joe stepped inside.

'I'll be here shortly after eleven.' She said as Joe stood in the doorway. 'Act normal, try to mention your government work and that you are happy with everything.'

'Yeah, no problem.' Joe said. He wanted to kiss her but wasn't sure if he should try. He had been upset back at the falls and maybe she had just done what was needed to calm him down. He wondered if he should ask her if maybe she liked him a little but decided that it wasn't really appropriate to try courting in the middle of Psychoville. His thoughts were halted as Melanie reached a hand behind his neck and pulled him down to her mouth. She kissed him, deeply this time, he felt her tongue slip against his briefly and his balls stirred with an aching passion.

When he felt her grip loosen on his neck they pulled apart as one. Melanie beamed a smile at him. 'I'll see you later.'

'See you.' Joe said, dazed.

Melanie turned and vanished around the corner of the hotel. Joe stood in the doorway for a moment in case she suddenly reappeared. He hoped she would.

When he was satisfied that she really was gone he closed the door and went up to his room. On arriving he unlocked the door carefully, subconsciously fearful that someone might be waiting inside for him. There was no one.

The room looked its usual drab self and nothing appeared to have been moved around, Joe wished that he had taken more time to position things, allowing him to know for sure anything had been interfered with. He locked the door behind him and sat on the bed.

Now that he was alone and in his room he felt relatively safe. He allowed his body to relax a little. The panic and fear that had wound up his thinking process so tightly now uncoiled and thoughts began to spread out across his mind. He lay back and closed his eyes as he tried to make sense of what he had seen and heard.

Most, if not all of the townsfolk, were involved in some form of pagan worship. They had murdered a man, most likely a traveller, some poor sod out walking the hills with his mate, as part of a ritual or offering. *No,* it must be more than one, other murders, because there was the skull embedded in the frozen waterfall.

Apparently he was safe if they thought he worked for the government, this is what Melanie had said. Joe decided they were probably worried about the heat that would come down if a government official suddenly disappeared. Not so easy to cover up a missing civil servant. Not like it would be to snatch and kill a prostitute or homeless person from the streets of Glasgow. Kevin had mentioned that. He wondered just how much the amiable barman really knew.

He found that lying stretched on the bed made him feel uneasy so he sat up and swung his legs over the side. Despite his tension easing he realized that he was still too tightly wound to totally relax. He untied his bootlaces and eased off the boots as his feet were beginning to throb from the heat. The bottoms of his jeans were soaked through. He took his trousers back out of the travel case and put them on. Checking the radiator he found that it was as cold, if not colder than it had been yesterday.

He returned to his thoughts of the situation. He was simplifying it all, leaving holes in his picture. He knew this. Some things were not answered by the crazy townsfolk or 'Wicker Man' theory as he now labelled thought it.

Why couldn't he find the place initially? That had been odd to say the least. Kevin had insisted that he wouldn't find it, until the day that the person with the letter arrived that is. Melanie had said that he wouldn't have got into the town unless they wanted him too. What did that mean? She had also said he wouldn't be able to leave, not now, and more than once she had stated this. He had assumed she meant because of the storm but now he wasn't so sure that this was the context she had used.

The symbol he had seen, carved into what was left of the man on the block had been the exact same icon on the letter and directions, which of course was the same as the tattoo that Macgregor wore on the inside of his forearm. Was that the symbol of their church or cult?

A knock sounded at the door. Two firm raps. It startled Joe and his heart leapt to his mouth. For a second he thought he may have been talking out loud and that *they* had overheard, but he regained control quickly.

'*You didn't say anything out load dickhead*' He thought.

He closed his eyes as he remonstrated with his paranoia. '*You are fine. It's probably Guppy Man come for his dinner plates. Come to remove the evidence of drugging your guest you fuck.*' Joe thought bitterly. He wanted very much to punch Guppy Man, *Henry,* in his frog face.

He got up and approached the door but stopped and checked the room first. The boots he had been given were by the bed and were wet. He quickly stepped over to them and pushed them underneath so they couldn't be seen. Two more knocks sounded at the door.

'Coming.' Joe said, not having to feign irritability. He decided to hide the big coat under the bed as well. Satisfied that nothing provided any indication that he had been out of the hotel he unlocked the door and opened it.

To his surprise it wasn't Henry on the other side. Nor was it Macgregor or the Doctor. Instead a new face stood before him. Equal in height to Joe but more filled out across the shoulder. A stocky man but not absurdly so like Macgregor. Once again the *Winter Falls look* that Kevin had described in detail wasn't present which made Joe think that Kev had been exaggerating that aspect.

What the man opposite did look like was a criminal of some sort, according to Joe's super power of stereotyping people he didn't know. The man had a mop of black greasy hair held in place by a tatty corduroy flat cap. His dark skin was complimented by a week's growth of stubble. He wore a bulky donkey jacket that looked quite new and his pale blue denims were met below the knee by a pair of black wellington boots. He eyed Joe without saying a word. A smirk played around his lips, partially obscured by the black hair of his fledgling beard.

'Can I help you?' Joe asked.

The man said nothing for a moment, sizing Joe up. An unspoken drawing of lines in the sand was occurring. Joe was sure of it. He couldn't say why exactly, but he found himself instantly disliking the man. It wasn't because of his appearance, although Joe thought he had a touch of a Bill Sykes about him, but because he could see a nasty, brutish nature *in* him. He was certain that this was the kind of person who would set old ladies on fire to get their pension books.

'You must be Mr Clarke.' The man stated rather than asked.

'Yes.' Joe replied.

'Macgregor sent me down. Says I'm to tell you that the road is closed.' The man's voice was deep and rich with the accent of the Falls. His words cascaded into each other almost like a melody.

'He says the weather is going to turn again later today and its best if you don't go wandering off.'

Joe caught a hint of threat in this and surprised himself as he lashed a response back at the messenger. 'I'm not just some bloody tourist. I know better than to go strolling around strange places during storms.'

If it had any effect on the man he didn't show it at all. The laconic smile still lay on his lips. Joe thought that he might be handsome. If a woman liked the rough, Oliver Reed type persona this guy had it in spades.

'Well, he told me to tell ya, so I have.' He touched his cap as a farewell gesture and turned to leave.

Joe stepped into the doorway and asked after him. 'What's your name?' The man didn't pause in his lazy stride away but called back. 'I'm Billy Duggan. I'll be seeing ya.'

Joe watched as Billy disappeared down the stairs. Once he was gone Joe stepped back into his room and locked the door.

'Wanker.' He said under his breath.

He moved to the window to see if Billy appeared in the view but he didn't show in the half a minute or so that he waited.

'So, that was the legendary Billy Duggan.' He said to himself, his breath steaming up the window as he spoke. The snow was light but constant outside. He wiped at the misty patch he had created and looked out across the town. No one moved about, hardly surprising given the weather but it still seemed odd, eerie even. No one was clearing their path, no one walked a dog or chatted to a neighbour over a wall.

It was as he mulled over the emptiness of the town that a memory came back, reminding him of what he had been doing before he had slipped into unconsciousness the previous night. He snatched up his iPad and turned it on. The red 'No Power' icon lit up.

'Fuck!'

He had left it on overnight and with the app running, thanks to Guppy Man and his drugged soup. He had set the damn thing so that it wouldn't turn off when he went to get a cup of coffee at work.

He scowled at the pad and searched for the charger. He couldn't find it. He checked under the bed, in both his bag and the travel case. It wasn't there. The room was tiny and there was only so many places it could be. It wasn't in any of them.

Someone had to have taken it while he was out cold. Except that made no sense, surely they wouldn't want his suspicions raised. Joe paced the room, chewing his lip as he tried to figure out a scenario in which alerting him to the fact that someone had broken into his room, with a spare key he imagined, would be in their best interest.

Joe stopped pacing, his train of thought was going off the rails again. He rewound. Why had he wanted the pad? He looked at the dead, black screen. *'It was the names!'* He pulled out his phone, he hadn't even looked at it since yesterday and was pleased to see that there was still 56% of charge remaining.

Joe swiped his finger across the screen until the 'Notepad App' appeared. He pressed it and once the little digital lined page filled the screen he began to type in the names he could recall from the Cenotaph.

He visualised pulling up to it in the Nissan, he got out and walked towards it. Extending his hand he ran his fingers across the letters sunk into the stone. When he had finished, satisfied that he couldn't haul anymore up from his memory and that what he had written was accurate he performed the same mental trick with his viewing of the pad the night before. It was more difficult than the Cenotaph recall had been. He guessed that the drugs had messed up his usual storage method but he did manage to type out eight names.

They matched perfectly to the names on the memorial list. If the two sources were correct eight men had died in the same year that eight men were born with identical names. It was probably more, he was sure of this, but without the pad he couldn't check. He needed that charger.

Joe stood and took his trainers from under the useless radiator. After putting them on he shrugged on his Nickelson jacket, unlocked the door and marched out of his room. He headed towards the stairs with a determined pace.

Melanie had told him that she thought they were scared of him because they thought he worked for the government. That he had to convince him that this was the case. He decided to do just that.

When he reached the stairs he could see Henry sat behind the reception desk with his huge oddly spaced eyes half closed. Joe approached with a degree of stealth and once he was directly in front of the sleeping receptionist, slammed his hand down on the counter top.

'Excuse me.' He said loudly.

Henry almost fell from his chair and made a strange 'errggle' noise as he grasped the lip of the counter to prevent him actually dropping to the floor.

'Where is my fucking phone charger?' Joe bawled. Henry's strange face seemed to change in pallor by the second.

He blinked like a lizard, huge lids over large pale eyes. 'What?' Henry said in his raspy, phlegm soaked voice.

'I left my fucking charger in my room. I've woken up only to find that it's apparently disappeared.' Joe flicked his hand in the air like a conjuror to emphasise the point. He wondered if he might be overdoing the indignation but was quite enjoying seeing Henry squirm.

'That charger is government property and if it goes missing I'm going to have to report that it was *stolen* from this fucking shit hole of a hotel.' Joe jabbed a finger at the hapless receptionist 'Your fucking hotel,' he added.

'Wha...wait', Henry stammered. He reached under the counter and produced the charger, dangling it between his fingers.

Joe snatched it off him 'and what the hell is it doing under there?' he demanded.

'Handed in.' Henry croaked the words 'handed in by guest...was by your door...was gon tell ya,' he said.

Joe decided to reign in his temper now. He had his charger and Henry looked genuinely terrified. *'Mission accomplished* 'he thought. 'Bloody good job.' Joe warned him. 'I have to submit a pile of paperwork when government property goes missing,' he said.

'That should be enough.' he thought.

'Right, I'm going back to my room, and I would prefer not to be disturbed by Officer Macgregor's lackeys if you don't mind. The sooner I'm home and can forget about this place the better.' Joe sniped.

He walked back to the stairs making sure to give Henry a filthy look as he mounted them. *'Yup, that should do it,'* he reassured himself.

When he got back to his room he immediately plugged the charger into the pad and waited while it stored enough energy to power up. He believed that he knew why they had taken the bold step of stealing his charger. They wanted to gauge his reaction. Perhaps to see if he would just 'let it go' because he was scared of something maybe, or to see if he was some government big mouth or not. He hoped they thought the latter now.

The iPad chimed indicating that there was enough power to turn it on. Joe eagerly picked it up from the bed and swiped to the photo-gallery. He rolled the images along the screen as he had done before but this time checking off each name that married up to the names on his phone. He had recalled eighteen names that he was certain of on the Cenotaph. Before he had worked his way through a third of the images for 1914 he had found them all.

The records had to be faked. They were good though. Whoever had forged them had produced them on original documentation he was certain, the texture and age of the paper could possibly be duplicated but Joe thought this wasn't the case. He was prepared to bet that the pages were the ones that *should* have been filled out during that year. But they had been rushed. The forger had just copied the names from death records of those who had died in the fighting during the War that year. The lack of doctor's scribble lent weight to this.

Joe sat at the table feeling quite pleased. The little task and bawling at Guppy Man had helped to push the sickening thoughts of the morning away. He wasn't sure what it meant and he still couldn't be a hundred per cent certain that he was right but he knew that he had revealed *something* about the town that Melanie hadn't mentioned.

Thinking of Melanie reminded him that he wouldn't see her until this evening, after eleven she had said. He had the whole day to spend sat in his room and he wasn't sure that he could bear that. Feeling emboldened by creating a scene at reception and sowing the seeds, he hoped, of his connection with the government Joe decided that he should venture out, to show he had some spine.

He could use the back door of the hotel as he had done with Melanie but decided against it. It was probably better to be seen to wander around, like the tourist he had denied he was to Billy Duggan. If someone came to his room, thinking he was still in it, suspicions could be aroused.

Decided, he stood, unplugged the charger from the iPad and inserted it into his phone instead. It was better to have the mobile on full power and ready to go if and when he got a signal. He pulled his boots and coat from under the bed. His jeans were still very damp at the bottom but he figured that it was better to wear them while the snow was still falling rather than the thin cotton trousers. As he changed into them he looked out of the window and saw that the steady fall had not altered one way or the other.

Finally, he delved into the bottom of the bag. The pistol and bullets were hidden under the stiff canvas-coated board which stopped the bag from sagging at the bottom. He lifted it and withdrew the items.

He turned the gun over in his hand as he debated whether to take it. Part of him insisted that he would be insane not too. A man had been brutally murdered by these people and he was only alive because of a misapprehension on their part as to who his employer was. However, the thought also repelled him. He had never fired a gun in his life and although he supposed he could be considered fit and thanks to his passion for the gym was fairly strong, he certainly wasn't a fighter. Perhaps having the pistol would make him decide on a course of action that he needn't take.

He pressed his lips together as he considered the options. If they came back to his room while he was out they might find the gun, then he was definitely screwed.

He settled on a compromise. Finding the release lever on the pistol he opened up the chamber and tipped the bullets into his hand. He would keep the gun in one pocket as before and *all* of the bullets in the other. He felt sure that if he pointed an unloaded gun at someone the effect would be pretty much the same as if it was loaded. So long as only he knew that the bullets were where they couldn't cause any harm it should be fine.

Joe picked up the tray with the plate, bowl and cutlery on them and exited the room, he didn't bother locking the door, he couldn't see the point. He made his way to the reception where Henry was once again half way to sleep. Joe let the tray drop onto the desk from about an inch above it and the sound of the crashing ceramic startled the receptionist as before.

Henry looked at the tray and Joe thought he detected a reddening in his strange skin. To prevent Henry from thinking he harboured any suspicions about his meal Joe pointed at the remnants of potato. 'Don't you have fresh potatoes? I hate that powdered stuff.'

Henry stared at him, thin mouth slightly open, but said nothing, he just shook his head a little.

'*He looks like a mental patient.*' Joe thought. 'Well I don't want that tonight thank you, just the soup.' Joe handed his room key over. 'I'm going for a stroll around the town. I'll be back later.' Henry remained silent. Joe frowned at him and then left, this time by the front door.

Chapter Eight

Upon leaving the hotel Joe was struck by the rise in temperature compared with when he had travelled through the forest with Melanie. No doubt the flat grey layer of clouds that floated above had helped. The light was poor though, almost a twilight.

Joe decided to follow the path in front of the hotel down towards the harbour. He could see that there was a glow of soft lighting coming from some of the houses and store fronts. The path down was quite steep and Joe occasionally felt his grip on the snow fall away. He would lurch violently, swinging his arms comically to maintain balance. Each time he looked to around to see if anyone had seen his display but there still appeared to be no one on the streets.

All of the houses on the path right down to where it finally eased its decline, whether they had the lights on or not, had curtains tightly drawn across every window. It was not until he reached the main street that ran the length of the harbour did he see them unguarded. The first lit building was the second along in a row that backed on to the docks. At the rear of it a jetty disappeared out into the sea.

Joe approached and saw a sign, old and weathered like the others he had seen yesterday. It was nailed up, a large three foot square wooden panel that may have once had a painted white background, now there were only grey patches stencilled onto which was text, barely visible.

Pat Lawton

Food and Beverage est: 1900

Joe wondered if the signage might actually be over a hundred years old, it looked it. As he stared at the sign the door to the premises swung open. A man emerged carrying a brown box, gripped by large un-gloved hands. He held it against his chest. Joe could see that the top layer was tins with bland labels. Unbranded canned goods. The man halted when he saw Joe and looked straight at him.

Joe immediately saw the Winter Falls *look* in this man. Much more than was evident in Henry. He was short and stocky, wearing a large black coat similar to Billy Duggan's donkey jacket except this went down to his knees. His head, large and oddly shaped wore a few lonely strands of long black hair that lifted and fell with the breeze. His eyes bulged from his head, not only larger than Henry's but more widely spaced. A flat nose sat below, almost flush with his face and beneath this a razor thin mouth that traced a grim line atop what passed for a jaw line.

The big eyes performed the 'lizard blink' as snow attacked them. Joe thought that he had seen the small dark nostrils flare for a moment just before the man turned away from Joe and continued along the street towards the other side of the harbour.

Joe watched him shuffle off. He walked with the speed and of a man in his nineties but there was strength in his steps.

He decided to take a look inside 'Pat's' store. As he stepped in to the shop, which was large inside, he noted that it was no more sanitary than any of the other Winter Falls places of business. Dust, cobwebs and here and there patches of grease or mud could be found in corners and on the walls. The goods were displayed on ancient metal shelves still in their boxes.

Joe walked down one of the aisles and ran his finger along the plain printed text that informed him of the contents of each box. Tuna, Ham, Dried Onions, Powdered Soup, Boiled Rice, Peas, Carrots, Stewed Steak. There didn't appear to be any kind of order to the type of goods, there were no helpful labels on the boxes with details of the price or weight.

There was a deep freeze unit filled with plastic-sealed bacon and sausages. It looked as though boxes of the product had just been tipped in until it was full.

'*Tesco shares are safe at the moment,*' Joe thought. As he turned the corner he was surprised to see a woman picking a can out of one of the boxes down the next aisle. She looked young, probably Melanie's age give or take a year. She drew a sharp breath when she turned and saw Joe.

'Hi, good morning.' Joe said and smiled. The girl stared back blankly, holding the can in her hand as though it were a mug of coffee. There was none of the *look* about her, in fact Joe thought her a little plain looking, a slight face and a straight cut fringe that underlined the rest of her thick black hair that was held up with an elastic band. She said nothing in reply and continued to stare nervously at Joe.

Whatever confidence had prompted Joe to talk to the girl now left him and he groped around in dark corners of his social repertoire for something to say.

'I don't suppose there's a McDonalds around here?'

The girl quickly replaced the can and walked to the opposite end of the aisle, away from Joe, and hurried out of the store.

Joe stood still, feeling sheepish. '*So much for communicating with the natives.*'

He heard the sound of something heavy being dropped onto the floor further up and across from where he stood, perhaps two aisles over. A second later another *Falls* man appeared at the end of his aisle.

'*Just like shopping box guy!*' Joe immediately saw what he now thought of as the *advanced* Falls look.

Not even an apologetic strand of hair clung to this one's head. It was the same oddly bulging shape and the face was almost identical as far as the eyes, nose and mouth could be considered. If there was a difference it was that this man blinked a little more, even without snow to bother him. He wore a large work coat that was probably once khaki but was now a perfect camouflage against the cardboard boxes being pale and worn.

The man opened his mouth to speak but what came out sounded more like a clogged drain trying to empty.

'Whaaaghyouuuheeeerrreforrr' he said in the gargled manner Joe had heard Henry use.

'Just shopping.' Joe replied.

'Nooothinggheereeeyouhhh.' Shop guy pointed at him. Joe stared at the thick finger that had a nail that looked grey and pointed, almost like a talon. He noticed a fold of skin hung from the base of the finger and melded into his knuckles.

Jesus does that guy have webbed fingers?'

'I think you're right mate.' Joe answered. He nodded a farewell and like the young woman had done before him hurried out of the store.

He decided to carry on his adventure down the street, away from what he thought of as the Satanic Lidl. Between buildings gaps were filled with what he assumed was mostly sea fishing equipment. There was certainly a great deal of nets, piled up into snow covered domes like little Christmassy hobbit houses. He also determined that there were oars, long poles with nasty looking hooks on the end, broken crates with weights spilling out of them and other sea fishing supplies.

He came to a space between two unlit buildings that was occupied by a large tarpaulin, stretched from one side to the other. Snow covered it completely but the shapes of whatever was underneath showed up as ripples across the surface.

Joe decided to investigate this. He took a look around to see if anyone was walking by and seeing no one he pushed some of the snow away to find an edge to the tarp and upon locating one lifted it up. The weight of the compacted snow made it heavy and awkward but with a little pushing and shaking Joe was able to raise a sizeable portion above his head.

What he found under the tarpaulin was row after row of statues, no taller than three feet high and each sculpted in what he could only think of as a tribal style. They looked like the kind of thing Indiana Jones might encounter deep in a South American burial chamber. From what he could see they represented some kind of aquatic creature, or creatures in fact because he observed that whilst some bore a similarity they all appeared to be unique in overall design.

The object nearest him was set upon a ragged stone base. The figure had a vaguely humanoid shape to it but there its humanity ended. Folds of loose skin had been carved into the stone. A distended belly protruded out of them, moving up to a chest that had runes or sigils carved into it. The scene in the forest flashed across his mind although he couldn't see the same design on this creature, and what a creature it was.

The head was large in comparison to the body, perhaps artistic license had been at work here. A gaping maw, filled with two rows of shark-like teeth, top and bottom, was surrounded by a hairstyle that consisted of snakes, or perhaps tentacles that writhed about it. Above the mouth Joe couldn't see anything that might indicate a nose but there were widely spaced eyes, almost to the sides of the face. Those eyes appeared to glisten in the half light.

Joe peered a little closer. There was something decidedly unnerving about the sculptures. They were ugly little things, lined up in rows, disappearing in the darkness beyond the lifted portion of the tarp and it was like looking at an army of dwarven monsters. All of the statues had the same twinkle where the eyes were located. He stretched his free hand out and ran his fingers over them, they felt like metal, extremely cold to the touch but smooth unlike the rock they were set in.

He took his hand away and pushed the tarp further back to allow more of the weak light from across the road to spill onto the front row. He could see that one of them didn't have the shiny eyes, just two dull sockets. Again the forest scene was with him for a moment but he managed to cast it aside.

He wet the corner of his sleeve with a little saliva and then manoeuvred under the tarp so that he could polish one of the eyes of the statue nearest to him. It produced a dull yellow patch. Joe rubbed harder at the metal revealing more of the same from under the tarnish. Where he had cleared most of the dirt and grease, the metal took on a rich shine. Joe was almost certain that what he was looking at was solid gold.

He looked around again, checking for sure that no bulbous eyes were observing him. The tarp was starting to get heavy but he quickly rubbed at the other eye producing the same result, a lusty gold orb set in the grotesque stone.

'Fuck me. There must be a fortune here.'

He stepped away and let the tarpaulin drop sending a small avalanche of snow to the floor. His arm ached a little from holding up the sheet and he swung it around to get the blood flowing. He looked again at the area taken up by the tarpaulin sheet and the numerous little bumps in the snow. He reckoned that there must be thirty or so statues.

'Why the fuck would they just leave them out here? Perhaps it isn't gold.' He thought, but he knew it was. He was no jeweller but he knew gold when he saw it. Perhaps most men did. The statues looked like relics, probably from an ancient civilisation and that alone would make them valuable. With gold for eyes Joe couldn't even guess at their monetary value.

The Falls inhabitants made their living from the sea he wondered if maybe they had dredged them up at some point. But why would statues like this be off the coast of Scotland?   Perhaps they were stored here only recently, after being shipped in, illegally maybe, ready to be moved on. Then the storm had come. Hadn't Melanie said that smuggling had once been a big part of the economy around here?

Joe couldn't convince himself of this sequence of events but it had some elements of sense so he left it at that for the time being. He mulled over heading back to the hotel. The store and the statues had crept him out already and he wasn't sure that he was ready to deal with more of what Winter Falls might have to offer.

The snow had started to become a little more intrusive as well. Instead of just constantly falling it had begun to switch direction and dart about in little squalls. The wind was beginning to pick up.

Despite all of this Joe decided to press on. He had the whole of the afternoon to spend sat in his hotel room, worried and probably scared. If he continued to investigate the town at least it would keep him busy. He left the covered army of little monsters and continued on the path.

The rest of the journey was much of the same. Someone had walked by on the opposite side of the street but because of the snow Joe couldn't make out a face. The person, whoever it was, had seemed stocky and walked with a familiar, awkward shuffling gait.

When he finally reached the far side of the harbour one building stuck out from the rest. It was taller by an extra floor than the two-storey units that flanked it but unlike them it was built from large solid bricks rather than decaying wooden planks. The frontage reminded Joe of the Masonic Lodge in London. It had tall pillars either side of a grand set of double doors but there the art deco similarity ended. The rest of the building was plain and dreary.

Joe approached it looking for clues as to what its purpose might be, but this was made difficult by the increasing strength of the wind forcing snow against him and a substantial amount of it already covered the building.

What was clear was that it had been used recently. The snow leading up to the door was much lower than everywhere else. A lot of feet had walked up those steps and turned the snow to slush. Only today's flurry had settled on top of it.

Melanie had said that her father had to gone to worship on the other side of the town and Joe wondered if this might be the place. As he neared the entrance he looked for anything that might indicate its purpose or confirm that this was the Doctors place of prayer. There were no signs or notices set against the walls, at least none that were obvious with the snow cover. He listened carefully but could only hear the wind.

A couple of feet above the door a concrete lintel ran around the front and sides, and perched on these were various small statues or gargoyles. Joe couldn't fathom what they represented as age had desiccated the stone and their features had crumbled away leaving only squat stumps. He considered trying the handle of the door but knew that if it opened he still wouldn't go in and so let it be.

Something about this building more than any others disturbed Joe deeply. It felt *wrong*, as though all of the decay and degeneration of the town emanated from behind its walls. Joe knew that he was being fanciful, that the effects of the morning were still with him but he couldn't shake a feeling of dread here.

No, not only would he not try to open that door he wouldn't stay here any longer. He started back along the street the way he came.

After a short walk saw that he was near the second jetty and decided to take a look at it before he finished his reconnoitre. The other jetty, further down, had been obscured by the 'local shop' but the route to this one was clear other than the snow-covered mounds of fishing gear. Along the both sides of the jetty boats gently bumped against tyres that dangled down on ropes which were almost rotted to threads. Like every single thing Joe had seen so far in Winter Falls the boats looked old and unused. They certainly didn't look seaworthy.

As he carefully walked the length of the jetty he could see that some rudders and masts were chewed with rot and others had completely fallen away. Snow covered the decks but Joe imagined missing timbers and dangerously weak patches that would collapse into the deck below if any weight were put upon them.

At the very end there was one craft that looked as though it might be serviceable, a motor boat. There were only a couple of inches of snow inside it.

This appeared to be the only boat in this whole fishing port that had been in use recently, and it was the only one Joe would have trusted to sit in should he have to. He looked out at the sea but the snowfall only allowed ten or so yards of choppy dull water to be seen. As he watched the torrent of snowflakes assault the water, only to become a part of it, Joe felt like he might be standing on the edge of the world.

He turned and made his way back to the hotel, this time without stopping to examine any more of the town's attractions. He felt he had not learned much from his adventure but some things had become apparent. The *Falls look* was real enough, and it was more advanced in the shopkeeper than it was in Henry. He had also met another person, another girl who shared none of the physical effects Kevin had listed, just like Melanie.

The weird statues were puzzling. How could such items, possibly priceless artefacts, be left outside under a tarpaulin, and where did they come from? The state of the waterfront and jetties suggested that other than the lone motor boat there wasn't a single sea-worthy vessel in the harbour.

Joe would be the first to admit that he knew very little about the sea but he was certain that three foot tall sculptures didn't come up from the sea easily if you were working from a little boat. More questions poured into his thoughts and he welcomed them if only to keep the scenes of the horror in the forest out of his mind.

As he approached the hotel he checked the time. It was three thirty and already the sky was darkening. The wind had begun to intensify, the new storm front was almost upon the town and the snow was dancing wildly as if in anticipation of its arrival. Joe picked up his pace as best he could and although not pleased to finally see the hotel door appear he was a little relieved.

He entered the reception and brushed snow off his shoulders, stamping his feet onto the worn carpet as he did so. Henry was sat at the reception desk and stared blankly across the room. Joe wondered if he had moved at all since he had left. He approached the desk and only as he drew to within striking distance did Henry appear to notice he was there. Automatically Henry reached below the counter top as before and produced the key to Joe's room.

Joe took it. 'Thanks.' He said.

As he moved away from the desk Joe paused and turned back to Henry. He felt that he already knew what the outcome of his question would be but decided to give it a go just for completeness.

'Is there a pay-phone or just a telephone I can use?'

Henry stared at him as though he was speaking in a foreign language, his mouth slightly cracked open. Joe raised his hand to his ear, thumb and little finger stretched out to perform the universally known 'telephone receiver' gesture.

'Telephone...' Joe said, as though he were communicating with a simpleton.

Henry shook his head slowly. Joe dropped his hand.

'So this is a hotel in the middle of nowhere and there isn't a phone? I'm supposed to believe that?'

Henry's expression didn't change but he tilted his misshapen head a little to the side and attempted a look of sympathy. In a breathy retort he answered, 'Phones not working, lines are down.'

Joe nodded and returned an equally mock smile. 'Of course they are. The storm I'm guessing?'

Henry nodded and shrugged his shoulders apologetically.

'Thanks again.' Joe said, and marched off to his room.

He pushed the door open. All seemed fine. The iPhone was still on his bed with the power cord snaking from it to the wall socket. His bags looked undisturbed. He had angled them in a way he thought would be difficult to copy had they been moved. He closed the door and locked it.

Once again he removed his boots and denims but when he went to the radiator to his surprise it was warm. In fact it was approaching hot. It was only then he realised the room itself was much warmer than it had been. He placed his denims across the top of the radiator and his boots beneath to dry them out.

He thought this over for a moment. Why had the heating had been turned on? To what end?

He decided that it was likely that the conclusion had been reached that Joe was going to be in the town at least until the storm stopped and the road out could be cleared. They were keeping him comfortable or at least relatively so. Trying to keep him calm and probably indoors. He slipped on his trousers and trainers, which were now dry. He checked his phone for a signal but there was nothing.

Sitting on the bed he realised how hungry he was. He hadn't been offered breakfast, dinner-time had passed him by while he was exploring the harbour and he guessed that Henry would bring his MacSedative Happy Meal up at around eight as he had done the previous night.

Joe thought there must be a kitchen in the hotel as Henry had been ordered to rustle up food by Macgregor. Joe decided to give Henry a job to do.

He made his way to reception where Henry upon seeing him reappear at the bottom of the stairs audibly sighed.

'I'd like something to eat please.' Joe said 'What's on the menu?'

'No menu.' Henry responded. 'Meal at eight. I'll bring it.'

'Well I'm hungry now. I've had no breakfast or dinner. Do I need to go out into the town? Shopping for my bloody food?

Henrys big eyes almost narrowed and Joe realised that he had managed to get under the skin of the odd looking man. He liked the thought of this, it felt like a little revenge against Winter Falls for putting him through hell.

'What you want?' Henry responded grudgingly, his voice both sloppy and rasping at the same time.

'How about some chips, an egg, some beans and sausage?' Joe said and having come up with it really did want that particular combination right now.

'Got beans.' Henry replied. 'Got mash.'

'Beans on toast?' Joe countered.

Henry shook his head. 'No bread.'

'No bread?' Joe asked and as Henry began to speak Joe mirrored his words.

'The storm.' They said together.

'Yeah, yeah.' Joe said dismissively. 'Ok I'll take the beans and mash, any chance you can make it from actual potatoes?'

Henry stared at him.

'Ok. Beans and Smash. Thanks. I'll be in my room.' At this he left the harassed receptionist to it. Half an hour later a light knock on the door indicated that Henry had arrived with the goods. Joe took the tray and thanked him. Henry shuffled off and Joe watched him all the way to the stairs.

He placed the plate of food, a mountain of instant potato mash covered with what he assumed was a whole tin of beans, onto the table. There was a chance it was drugged, but if they did it now, this early, he might wake in the night so he figured it probably wasn't. Joe sniffed at the food although he wasn't sure what smell he would need to detect for the presence of drugs. His stomach growled fiercely and he tucked in regardless.

After thirty minutes had passed Joe thought it was a safe assumption that there had been no drugs present in the food. He felt better having eaten, even if it had not been a spectacular spread. He cast his thoughts to the rows of brown boxes in the Satanic Lidl. Everything was processed in there, or dried or salted or in some other way preserved. Nothing fresh.

Kevin had said that men from Winter Falls would occasionally come into the village and buy stores. Clearly they only bought goods that would last a long time. They kept their contact with the real world to an absolute minimum. This tied in with their fear of him working for the government. If the town was involved in some kind of cult, if they were murdering people for bizarre and horrible rituals of worship, the last thing they needed was government interest.

'By Christ they will get some interest when I get out here.' Joe thought. *'I'll bring the fucking army.'*

The sound of the storm blowing outside interrupted his thoughts of leaving. He wasn't going anywhere while a foot or more of snow was added to the roads each day. The Winter Falls townsfolk didn't need to have a wall built around the place to keep him here, not while they had the weather. He had never felt so remote from his real life.

He thought of Melanie. She would be coming to him later and it lifted his spirits a little. They would get out of Winter Falls together and head to London. This place would be all over the papers by the weekend. He closed his eyes and pictured them cruising along the banks of Loch Lomond in the Nissan. London signposted a mere few hundred miles away. She touched Joes hand as it rested on the gearstick and looked up at him with her beautiful hazel eyes. Joe was asleep before he knew it.

He awoke to knocking on the door. It took him a moment to realise he had been asleep and wondered if he had actually been drugged again. His watch stated that it was slightly after eight. No he had just dozed off. The knocking came again, a little louder.

Joe got up and approached the door.

'Yes?' He said

'Got your meal.' Henrys flat voice answered.

'Right sec.' Joe said and turned the key in the lock. He opened the door revealing Henry, stood before with a tray once again. There was once again a bowl of soup and a plate heaped with bacon, beans and mash.

'Excellent.' Joe said, taking the tray. 'Please compliment the chef on his diverse and wholesome selection for me.'

He didn't bother checking for Henrys reaction to his sarcasm he simply turned and pushed the door shut with his elbow. He wasn't entirely sure that he needed to keep up the 'Southern Wanker' persona with Henry now, but he was enjoying it.

'I'm just staying in character.' He thought.

He placed the tray onto the table, having to move the plate from his earlier meal aside to accommodate it. There was no way he was touching this meal, not this time.

He now had three hours to kill before Melanie would be here. He picked up the iPad, plugged the charger in, his phone was at 100%, and started to go through the documents again.

There had been two very distinct Black Holes in his data, 1914 and 1939. The most obvious thing about the dates was that they were war years but for the moment he couldn't see any other relevance.

He skipped to the 1939 documents and began to examine them. Once again the format was familiar. No Doctors scribble, no notes from the mid-wife, except this was not wholly true. He bookmarked a number of images and then swept back to the 1914 entries. He started to go through them again this time highlighting the female births rather than the male.

Joe found something that brought the two dates together. Whereas the male birth records were just the parent's name, the child's name, date of birth and the signature of the attending Doctor, which he couldn't read anyway, the female records had all of the missing information. Some bore notes haphazardly scrawled in corners or across the 'particulars' section. The name of the mother and father were listed but also the father's occupation was stated as well.

For each period the births of the boys had been faked but the girls appeared to be accurate. Why hide the births of the male babies? Joe thought that maybe the *Falls look* might have something to do with it. Perhaps they did it to hide incest or disease or whatever it was causing the problems in the children.

Both Melanie and the girl he saw in the store bore no signs of the look, but then Macgregor, Peake and the thuggish looking man, Billy Duggan, all looked normal too. He dropped that as an explanation and considered the dates alone.

The war years might be the thing. Could the records have been misplaced or not reported, a clerical error due to the upheaval of the war. It was possible. But why only the males for both periods. Joe dismissed this. It didn't feel right.

He turned his thoughts reluctantly to the religion of the place. Whatever it was these people were involved in they weren't above mutilating men on slabs in the forest. Possibly the connection was here. They were hiding the births of the men of the town, or perhaps it was only the men who had the *look* they wanted to hide but did them all wholesale anyway. He knew he was making a huge leap of faith in deciding that the women didn't suffer the disease. But this would then explain why they felt no need to change their records for them. However, they did hide them. The data he had received in London had indicated *no* births at all during these periods and in Glasgow the records were absent.

It made sense that it was a 'job lot' decision though. Although the girl's records were not faked the records were not passed on to the authorities to keep the consistency. Joe tut-tutted to himself. His logic was shaky here at best. He was leaving too much to guesswork and there were some gaping holes in his theory. It was the best he had though, for the moment.

He decided to copy the data from the pad to his phone as a backup. The phone was also easier to carry around. *'If I have to run for it.'* Joe thought grimly. As the phone was now fully charged he thought it wise to power the iPad to its maximum as well. Meanwhile he transferred the files via Bluetooth.

After he had set the pad to work he decided to make the most of the heating situation and have a good wash. He tested the water from the tap on the little sink and it was hot. He perked up a little. In his travel case was a bag with his toiletries. He stripped, stood on the small towel he had packed and rinsed himself down.

Once he was washed and dried as best he could Joe clutched at the bottom of his denims. They were warm and dry. He slipped on his underwear, jeans and sweatshirt and waited for Melanie to arrive.

A little after eleven a quiet knock sounded at the door. Joe didn't ask who it was he simply unlocked the door and quietly pulled it open. Melanie stood before him, her coat dribbled water onto the carpet and her huge boots still had a small hill of ice on each toecap. A backpack was slung over her shoulder.

She smiled at Joe when she saw him. He gestured for her to come in.

'Is Henry gone?' Joe asked in a low voice. Melanie nodded and Joe closed the door.

'Henry, Dad, Macgregor, they will all be at worship now. Are You Ok?' She asked as she removed the backpack and slipped out of her coat. Joe helped her with it and draped it next to his near the window.

'Yeah fine.' He said. He felt awkward standing so close to her in the small room and put his hands into his pockets. Melanie appeared to be unaware of any such tension and sat on the bed. She noticed the untouched food on the table.

'We will need to get rid of that.' She said. Joe nodded. He had already decided to take the plates to the back door and to tip the food into the snow.

'What have you been doing today?' She asked.

'I went for a stroll.' Joe said

'You left the hotel?' Melanie looked shocked and a little scared.

'It's Ok. I kind of set it up so that Henry would be convinced that I have no idea what's going on.' Joe said to reassure her. 'Although actually I don't have any idea what's going on.' He added.

'You have to be careful Joe, things are tense here and not just because of your visit.' Melanie said.

Joe could see that more was about to come. He decided to be bold and sit by her on the bed. Currently he understood that his life could be in danger, that the people who might wish him harm were capable of staggering brutality, but all he could think of was how much he wanted to kiss Melanie. As he sat Melanie turned to him seemingly unfazed by their proximity.

'I'm going to tell you everything that I know or at least how much I can make sense of what I know.' Melanie placed her hand on Joes which was resting on his thigh. The skin on his throat and neck felt like a fire was spreading across it. He hoped that Melanie couldn't see his blush as it threatened to colour his entire face.

'Ok.' Joe said normalising his voice as best he could. 'I want to hear it all.'

Melanie's hand gripped his fingers, not tightly. She curled her fingers around them slowly, they were smooth and warm and Joe couldn't hold the stirring of an erection. His trousers were made from thin cloth, they couldn't hide spontaneous 'awakenings' like a pair of thick denims could. Joe was so concerned that Melanie might see his arousal he didn't notice that she had moved her head closer.

As he turned his attention back to Melanie she was so close that his nose almost rubbed against hers. He had been about to say something regarding the town, anything at all to keep her attention from the obvious effect she was having upon him but the words were lost. Instead he found himself staring into her eyes, brown, '*like ginger biscuits.*' Joe thought. Her lips were slightly parted and Joe had never wanted lean forward to kiss anyone so much in his life, but he was too late for that. Melanie leaned forward and took the kiss instead.

Her lips pressed against his firmly for a few moments and then her free hand reached up to his cheek and caressed it, pulling him in even more.

Joe recovered from the shock quickly and began to take part with more confidence. Their mouths opened a little and each took turns with a movement of lips or tongue, testing and probing, reacting to the sensation by repeating what the other had done.

Joe couldn't help but detect what he thought might be a lack of experience in Melanie, her kisses were simple and light but she pushed at him as though her passion was a force battering at a door, demanding to be unleashed. Joe began to gain more boldness. He broke the kiss and began to nuzzle her neck, she groaned quietly as he ran his tongue up the length her throat and then kissed his way back to her mouth.

She moved her hands across him, exploring his body. Her palms pressed up and down his arms, following the contours of his biceps. Joe was still conscious of his erection, now embarrassingly obvious, and as he tried to lose himself in the pleasure of the moment he was held back by the polite reserve he had always maintained with women.

He knew that he was going to break the moment. He cursed himself but he couldn't help it, he had to apologise for losing control in such a way, in such circumstances. But as he started to draw away Melanie sensed his conflict. Her hands gripped his arms more tightly, she drew her leg up and let her knee slide across his thigh slowly and then in one fluid and sensual move she was straddling him.

She let weight of her body push down onto his hips. Joe leaned back on his elbows, looking up at her. She reached out with one hand and gently took his wrist. Pulling his hand up to her left breast she pressed it down firmly.

Joe moved his hand in a small circle, he could feel her nipple, hard through the bra.

'Please.' She said and began to unbutton her blouse.

Chapter Nine.

They left via the back door of the hotel again and ditched Joe's drugged evening meal. Melanie then led Joe toward the upper part of the town, away from the harbour. The snow blew hard and the wind pushed them around like a schoolyard bully.

'We have to keep off the path and out of the lights where possible, even with this snow we can't risk being seen' she told him once they had reached the top of the road.

'Aren't they all at the church thing?' Joe asked. He found that he had to raise his voice to be heard over the wind.

'They don't all go.' she said 'None of the girls will be there, Macgregor and Duggan don't usually attend although Macgregor is there tonight.'

'Your Father?' said Joe.

'Oh yes, he will be there, he has to be there.' She said.

They ducked into an alley just off a street that wasn't far from where Joe's Nissan was parked. He had insisted on seeing that the car was still there before they could carry on. It hadn't moved and was sat in a field of crisp snow that was almost up to the windows.

'Where are we going?' Joe asked.

'To the church.' Melanie replied. She produced a small torch from her pocket and tested that it was working.

'What?' Joe said, alarmed.

'Not that one.' Melanie replied and pulled his on his hand as she increased her speed through the snow.

Joe soon saw what Melanie was referring to. Ahead, away from the street lights and houses, set in its own grounds that were covered with untouched snow, was an old and dilapidated church. It wasn't a small building. Joe estimated that the grounds in front and to the sides covered about half the size of West Ham's football pitch.

The church roof came to a point at around thirty feet. There had been a spire at one time but now it was a broken thing, the brickwork finished in a ragged stump about five feet above the roof. Every window was boarded and the arched doors at the front had a large rusted and padlocked chain doubled around the handles.

'Are we going in?' Joe asked. He hoped they weren't.

'Yes, but we need to go around. We can't let anyone see footprints going in there.' she said leading him around the rear of the church.

There wasn't any light at the back and Joe saw that the low wall surrounding the grounds had crumbled here. Together they cautiously walked up the hill the snow had made over the rubble. It was only a few feet but the uneven bricks beneath the snow wobbled as Joe's weight fell upon them.

The cemetery took up all of the grounds except for the wide pathway at the front. Where Joe now stood was dotted with crosses and arched tombstones that leaned at tired angles. Melanie was moving towards the church trying to keep close to the stones and Joe did his best to tread in her footprints.

He could see that there was a thick door in the side of the church but it hung away from the frame. Only the bottom hinge kept it fixed there and Joe thought that a strong tug would pull the whole thing away completely yet it had held fast in the storm.

Melanie slid her backpack off. She stepped through the open doorway and waited for Joe to join her. As Joe entered she illuminated the area with the flashlight. He saw rows of wooden chairs that were in various states, some upturned, some with parts missing, some stacked on top of others. Towards the front of the church there were five lines of pews. Two of these were broken and had fallen or been pushed over.

'Could I take the torch?' He asked.

Melanie handed it to him and as Joe swept it around the church she opened the back pack and began to take items out of it.

The entire church was in total disorder and looked as though it was ready to collapse. The windows had all been smashed, the boards on the outside clearly visible. Where the altar would have been was a pile of broken timbers, rags and glass. As Joe turned full circle a light sprang up next to him. Melanie had lit a kerosene lamp and as she increased the flame its light softened the harsh revelations of the torch.

'Wow.' Joe gasped. 'I guess Christianity really isn't a big deal here these days.'

Melanie checked the strength of two of the wooden chairs nearby and then brought them over to the lamp. She sat and Joe followed suit.

'No one comes here.' Melanie said. 'We should be able to talk'.

'Good.' Joe said but he wasn't sure that he meant it. He was beginning to think that ignorance might just be bliss. *Just stay quiet, let the roads clear and then get as far away as possible. Let the police come and sort this place out.*

He looked at Melanie. The fear she carried inside was visible in her eyes, as she spoke they darted around looking for things in the shadows. He found it hard to believe that no more than an hour ago they had been making love, naked and wanting each other desperately in the small room, on that small bed.

Melanie rummaged in the bag.

'Do you want a drink?' She said.

It caught Joe by surprise. 'I'm sorry what?' He raised his eyebrows. 'Did you say *drink*?'

Melanie pulled out a silver flask and two tin mugs 'I made coffee.' She handed him a mug. 'I didn't bring any sugar though.' She said apologetically.

'I don't take sugar.' Joe replied, accepting the mug. They were silent as Melanie poured out the drink. A cloud of steam rose between them and in the cold, dank church, the strong aroma smelled divine to Joe. Melanie took a few sips and Joe mimicked her.

He could see that she was building up to say whatever it was she had brought him out here to tell him. He didn't want to hurry her and he felt that the longer he didn't know what it was the better for his sanity.

Melanie turned the mug around in her hands, her attention on the coffee as it circled inside, until finally she looked up at Joe and began.

'I don't know everything Joe, in fact I'm not really sure that what I think I know is real. I could have mistaken some of it, misheard, misread. But I know what I've seen.'

Joe didn't speak. He gave a slight nod and listened.

'First you need to know about the town, about Winter Falls, or at least as much that I know is true. You must already know where the name comes from, from what you saw. In Victorian times this was a fishing port, not big business but it kept the town alive and was a hub for all of the villages in the area, but the Falls were a quite a popular attraction.

Of course the phenomena only occurs when the weather is just right so you have to be very lucky to catch it. Apparently it was quite a talking point for any Victorian gentlemen who had made the trip all the way up to see it and was successful.'

Joe couldn't dispute that the sight of the frozen waterfall really was something, had it not been for the awful taint inside it and of course what followed afterwards he was sure it would have been amongst the most breath-taking things he had ever seen.

'In 1895 a man arrived in the town from America, his name was Jacob and he claimed to be a preacher, an evangelist of a new religion that was bringing prosperity to the Americas. He was ignored by virtually everyone. The Falls was a very Protestant town and it's said that on a couple of occasions Jacob had to flee to nearby villages as the Winter Falls residents were getting angry at his attempts to convert them.'

'But things started to go bad for the town. The fishing became very poor, boats were coming back with empty nets, and sometimes they wouldn't come back at all. Jacob Blake had managed to find a few followers, there was some talk of him having a great deal of money and that he had used it to bribe some of the fishermen who were struggling to feed their families. However it came about Jacob's new religion started to gain ground and anyone who converted began to prosper.'

'Where did you get this information?' Joe asked incredulously. 'I must have spent half a day searching the net for even a sentence about the town and all I got was a sixty year old map.'

'You have to let me finish Joe.' Melanie said placing a hand on his knee. 'I'll answer that shortly but you will have a lot more questions so, just listen Ok?

'Yeah, I'm sorry.' Joe placed his hand on hers by way of apology. Melanie smiled a little and withdrew her hand back to the heat of the mug.

She continued her description of the town's history. 'While the new group continued to do well, they called themselves 'The Order,' the rest of the townsfolk fared badly. Soon the catches were practically non-existent, empty nets were the norm. Worse still people were going missing more frequently, some boats never returned and the crew couldn't be found.'

'Fingers were pointed at Jacob Blake and his followers. Word had got around that they met late at night and prayed to 'other Gods', but there were too many of them by the time that some people had the guts to face Blake.'

'He did his best to drive anyone who clung to the old faith out of the town. The sheriff for the region had been called in at one point but he found nothing amiss and left, never to return. The rumour was that he had been bribed with a bag of gold coins so heavy he could barely carry it.

By the 1900's the town was almost totally under the influence of Blake. Visitors were not made welcome and the ridge and surrounding area of the Waterfall was fenced off. Travellers were told that there were wild dogs in the forest and that they risked being mauled. The number of tourists began to drop and after a few years no one came at all.

The trouble at Winter Falls seemed to spread through the region like a plague. People started to go missing on the moors and hills. Not long after, children vanished from their beds. Cattle and sheep were found in a terrible state of slaughter and out of pure fear entire villages were left deserted.'

Melanie took a few sips of her coffee. Joe could see that she was preparing to deliver an even more difficult part of the story.

'There are only a handful of people aged over forty in Winter Falls Joe, probably five or six.' She said and waited for Joe's reaction.

'Over forty?' Joe repeated. 'In the whole town?'

'My father who is fifty six, I think, and Macgregor, whose age I'm not sure of but I suspect he's older than my dad.'

'And that's it?' Joe asked, as though he may have misheard.

'There are a couple of other men, they are called Wardens, and if that seems at all odd you should know that there are no women over twenty-five here either.'

'You can't be serious.' Joe scoffed.

'I'm twenty-three. I imagine the girl you saw in the store was Rosalie Kames, and she's twenty two. The store keeper? That's Mr Dunne and he is, as far as I'm aware thirty-eight years old. He's getting slow and hard to understand, like Henry but more so. In two years he will never be seen in the town again, at least, not in any recognisable way.'

Joe desperately wanted to start questioning Melanie. This last information was vague and cryptic. It also made no sense unless he hadn't followed the thread or misunderstood what she was saying. Melanie drank a little more coffee, taking in more than before as though it were a shot of spirits to stiffen her resolve.

'By 1913 the whole of the town had succumbed to Blake's religion.' She said. 'Something happened that cleared away any resistance to him.' Melanie looked at the lamp for a moment and then at Joe. She fixed his eyes with hers as though daring him to question her truthfulness.

'Some things, some creatures came from the sea. They walked like men but were anything but. They murdered all of the men not under Jacob's leadership and most of the women. With the exception of a few women that were in thrall to Blake any female over twenty-five was killed. The remaining ones that were old enough to have children were raped by the things. While they did this Jacob and his followers looked on as they performed some kind of ritual.'

Joe saw Melanie shudder. She gripped the mug so tight that her knuckles whitened against already pale skin.

'After this the women were kept locked up and out of sight until they gave birth. Any that didn't fall pregnant, mostly the really young girls, they disappeared. Once the babies were delivered the mothers also vanished. Looking after the babies was the job of the remaining girls. Those who were completely in thrall to Blake. Most of the children were boys and they bore the signs about them. It's not so apparent when they are young but as they grow older the condition gets worse, more pronounced. A handful of the babies were girls, a few of them had the condition but most seemed normal.' Melanie paused to take a breath before she could deliver the next part.

'Twenty-five years later the same thing happened again.'

She remained silent now. Joe could tell that she had more to say but was offering him the chance to ask his questions.

'I'm not entirely sure that I'm getting this Melanie.' Joe said trying hard not to sound patronising. 'First off how did you find all of this…*history*? I mean it sounds like the sort of thing that wouldn't be spread around if it were true.'

'The source is my father, although of course he doesn't know that I know.' She said. 'He keeps a journal. I don't know why. I do know that he fancies himself as some kind of big shot in the Order. It was thanks to him that the records for the town are, as far as you would be aware, accurate for births and deaths for every year since nineteen sixty.'

She searched Joes face for a sign that this might have pinched at his pride but he only continued to stare at her.

'He realised that questions might be asked if they weren't kept up to date. The only reason he didn't do the others, the ones you were after was because they were the war years and he figured no one would be able to unravel the mess from that period, of course he didn't take into account computers and data analysts.' She smiled weakly at this. 'I think the journal is meant to be like a gospel or something. A record for future generations to marvel at how wonderful he was.'

'So what is the Order? Is it like a fundamentalist group or something?' Joe asked.

'It's not Christianity Joe, or anything else you think of as religion. This is older, much older. The Order is a cult I suppose. They hide their Gods and they keep their practices secret because if the outside world finds out things will go very badly for them.'

'The guy in the forest.' Joe said. 'Obviously, that is part of their... practice?'

'Oh Joe.' Melanie said in a sympathetic tone. 'That is just a taste of what is happening here. The Order is not just some group of idiots worshipping some pathetic God in the sky. What they pray to is real, what it can do for them is real.'

'What do you mean *real*?' Joe asked suspiciously.

'I told you that there were townsfolk killed by Blake and his follower's, right?'

'Yeah, and you said *something* came out of the sea too.' Joe said, trying to avoid sounding cynical.

'That's right. Blake and his people couldn't have overwhelmed the townspeople alone, even with their numbers growing there were too few of them for a war. These were men of the sea Joe, the Winter Falls men strong, tough and very willing to fight. So Jacob called on his God and his call was answered.

'Answered how?' Joe interrupted.

'The things from the sea came. They came and tore those who wouldn't follow to pieces. Any that tried to escape the town were blocked by Jacob and the rest of the Order. The Deep Ones soon got to those and finished them off.'

'Deep Ones?'

'Aye Joe. That's what the Order calls them, the things from the sea. The brood of the Sea God, Father Dagon.' She stopped now. She knew that this was the point where Joe would begin to doubt her sanity, her honesty or both.

He didn't say anything at first. He appeared to be in a state of conflict, she could easily see his feelings for her. They were written into his face, his eyes, and the turn of his mouth. He stroked at his chin and looked surprised that he found stubble there.

'Do you want me to carry on Joe?' Melanie asked after he had remained silent.

He breathed deeply. 'Yes...please.' he said quietly.

'Joe, I'll tell you as simply as I can because no matter how I explain what goes on here you will think I'm crazy. The reason that there are no men over forty here, none other than my father and his lackey Macgregor, is because they *change*. They change into those *things* and go into the sea. There are no girls over twenty-five because every twenty-five years those same things come ashore and rape them. If they become pregnant they are locked up until they give birth and then they are killed out in the forest. The girls who don't get pregnant are kept for a while, to raise the children, eventually they are disposed of. I'm twenty-five in two years Joe.'

Joe hadn't drunk any of the coffee. Instead he had just wrapped his hands around the mug and let the heat warm him. His eyes left Melanie's he and looked into the coffee. The poor light made it look much darker than it was, like a pool of ink.

She hadn't said 'monsters' but he knew it was what she was trying to describe. Creatures, things, Deep Ones. All the same thing, monsters.

He could buy the cult, psychopathic leaders and deluded followers, even the murders, the rituals, and the strange look of the males in the town. It was all within the grasp of Joe's belief system. Monsters were not. Nothing came out of the sea to rape young girls, adult men didn't turn into sea creatures.

Melanie reached out a hand and lightly gripped Joe's thigh again. 'I know you can't believe this Joe, but look around you. Look at this church, the body in the forest, the Falls. All of this is because of what Jacob Blake started and what my father is continuing to do.' She placed her mug on the floor and pressed her hands around Joes.

'I told you that they were concerned about you working for the government, my father mentions this in his journal. I'm not entirely sure what happened but sometime in the 1930's a place in America, a place like Winter Falls, was assaulted by government agents and the military. My father says that Jacob had family there, it's where he travelled from.'

'To stop it happening again the Order invested a great deal of effort into performing a great ritual to protect the town from outsiders. That's the reason it's impossible to find your way in or out without the key. It took twenty years to complete the ritual, this is why so many people went missing. The Order needed them to be offered as sacrifices to their God. When the spell was complete no one entered, or left without the Orders approval.'

This was too much for Joe, he pulled his hands away from Melanie's touch and placed his mug on the floor next to hers.

'Monsters and spells Melanie? Seriously, don't you think that there is enough crazy in this fucking town without that as well?'

He stood and shivered a little as the cold material of his trousers brushed against his skin. The light from the lamp only illuminated a few square feet of the church and Joe began to walk up to its limit where the yellow glow faded into the dark.

Melanie pleaded with him, looking over the pew to where he stood. 'Joe you have to listen to what I'm saying. My father will have you killed in an instant if he realises that you are a threat to the town.'

Joe turned to face her, in the poor light shadows pooled in his pale face and made him look ghostly and scared. He *was* scared.

'Melanie I don't want to hear any more of this to be honest. I get that this town is in one way or another, fucked. I am fully aware that someone or some people, probably that slimy bastard Billy Duggan is capable of murder.'

Melanie interrupted 'You met Billy Duggan?' She sounded shocked.

'Yeah, he came to my room with a message from your dad. I think he was just pissing up the wall, making sure I knew he was around.' Joe waved his hand dismissively, 'I don't give a fuck about him anyway, or your dad or anyone in this shithole to be perfectly honest. I just want out.'

'What about me Joe, don't you give a fuck about me?' Melanie rose from the pew. 'I've risked my life to make sure you know what's going on, to try and protect you. I've given you everything I have Joe.' She walked up to him and touched his face. 'Everything.' She said quietly.

Joe swallowed. Guilt poured into his system quenching his adrenalin.

'I'm sorry,' he said and took her hand, holding it against his cheek. 'I'm really sorry, Melanie.' He struggled to find a way to express the frustration inside him. He looked into her eyes, they were wide and frightened and he thought close to tears. 'I don't understand. This is a nightmare. I feel like I'm actually in a fucking nightmare and I can't wake up.'

'How do you think I feel Joe?' Melanie wrapped her arms around his waist and laid her head onto his chest. 'I *live* this. Day in, day out. I have had to hide myself from them for years, they don't know that I can read and write, that I have seen what it's like outside, that I've seen them and what they do.'

Joe put his fingers into Melanie's hair and massaged them into the luxurious strands. He closed his eyes and let his head rest on hers. Melanie felt his fingers stop their gentle motion.

'How do you know what the outside is like, I thought you couldn't leave?' Joe asked.

'My dad has a computer, he doesn't know that I have his password.' Melanie rubbed her face a little on Joe's coat and squeezed him gently. 'He's not as smart as he thinks he is.'

Joe gripped Melanie's arms and gently pushed her away so that he could look at her.

'Your Dad has a computer.' He said, slowly.

'Yes.' Melanie said, a puzzled look drawn upon her face. 'In the guest room. It's locked but there's a key on top of the tall clock. I used to stand on a stool to get at it when I was little.'

'Can it access the Internet?' Joe asked quickly.

'Yes.' she said.

Joe's knees almost buckled. Melanie could feel him sway. 'Are you Ok?' She asked.

Joe regained his balance. He had been overcome by the sheer weight of Melanie's news, his head spun as the possibilities rushed into his mind.

'Jesus fucking Christ, why didn't you tell me this sooner?'

'I...I didn't think...' Melanie stammered.

'Didn't think what?' Joe's voice was excited and angry at the same time. 'That direct communication to the outside world, outside of *this place* would be useful?'

'H...how...how would you do that?' Melanie asked as a child would ask an adult how a combustion engine might work.

Joe stared in stunned silence. 'Fucking...email, Skype, Facebook. Jesus Christ I could add this fucking place to Foursquare!'

Melanie stared without any glimmer of comprehension. Joe tried to calm down. He found himself rubbing his hands up and down Melanie's arms as he spoke.

'You know this stuff, right? If you have been on the net you know this stuff?' He said.

'I know the news.' She answered. 'The BBC and the Microsoft Explorer, there's news on that too.' She said, her eyebrows raised a little.

Joe tried to picture Melanie at the machine. What she would see or understand if she had never seen a computer before. 'So when you use his computer all you hit is the big blue 'E' I'm guessing. Is that right?'

Melanie nodded. 'And I put the arrow on it with the...thing, and then Microsoft comes on, with the news.'

'Microsoft comes on with the news.' Joe repeated. He shook his head and smiled a little. He smiled at the absurdity and the sadness of it. 'I need to use that computer.' he said. 'Right now.'

'But Joe I need to tell you...' Joe cut her off.

'You've told me enough for now.' Joe walked back to the pew and began to pack the flask and lamp. 'What we need to do now is get to that computer.' He fastened the straps, loosening them so that they would fit over his shoulders. 'Melanie, do you get the weather reports...on your Microsoft?'

'Yes.' She replied. 'I don't think it's very good though, they are usually wrong about the weather here.'

'Right Ok, but what did they forecast about the storm for tonight, tomorrow?' Joe asked.

'Oh. It's bad.' She said

Joe sighed. 'I suppose that should come as no surprise.' He looked toward the hanging door, solidly fixed into the snow, the storm roared outside slowly adding to the drift building up against it.

'How long do we have?' He asked.

'They will finish around five.' Melanie said. 'We have a few hours. How will the computer get us out, do you think it can?'

Joe thought she looked doubtful, with the lamp off there was only the harsh light of the torch and it painted them both with the same ghostly aspect.

'It will help us Mel. I can get word out to friends, to the police maybe.' Joe realised that he had shortened her name. It was something he only did with close friends, people he knew well. His mother had always frowned upon nicknames. He had always been Joseph to mum and dad, although when mum wasn't around his dad would occasionally call him 'Joey.'

Mum had been gone for eight years now, taken by bowel cancer. His dad had been stalwart, stronger than Joe could have ever imagined. He had told Joe that what was happening was a horror and that Joe could be scared, because he was scared too. He explained to Joe that all horrors ended and that when Mum passed the horror would be gone for her, so it should be gone for them. 'Remember how brave your mum was son.' He had said. Joe wanted to be brave too, as brave as his mum and dad had been.

He took Melanie by the arm and with the torch lighting the way guided her out of the church and back into the storm.

Chapter Ten

Billy Duggan watched as the couple exited the ruins of the church. Following them had been easy although they had taken a circuitous route, avoiding houses that might be occupied by those who would not be at worship this evening. This was clearly the girl's involvement.

The hardest part had been waiting for them to reappear. He had taken refuge by sitting inside a partially collapsed sepulchre that faced the side door of the church. Ideally, he would have liked to have gotten close enough to hear what she had told him. He knew that she was up to something with the outsider, the government man Joe Clarke. The storm had prevented this though, even if he had stood right next to the broken door the howl of the wind would have covered any sound they made. So he had sat and waited.

As they left the church he stayed low until the bobbing of the torch was all that could be seen and emerged from his hideout. Once again they cut through the town, with purpose in their direction, which Billy knew was due to the girl guiding the way. They were not going in the direction of the hotel, or Joe's car. Billy believed he knew where they were headed.

Peake hadn't been happy when he had returned with news of a government man asking about the town in Roscregan. His beady eyes had turned to coal and he had flitted off to Macgregor as fast as his legs could carry him. He always sought out the big man when there was likely to be trouble from the outside. Contacting *them* about it was a last resort.

And he had to hand it to the old bastard, he had a plan all ready to go. He had foreseen this kind of thing happening and done something about it. He had just not done enough. It took two days for Peake to prepare the records that he had neglected to ready the first time around. Billy had seen him in the surgery scribbling away, name after name, copying from the parish records.

Now there was a problem of course. The government man was still here, still snooping around the town and perhaps fucking the Doctors daughter? Billy couldn't be sure but there was something going on between them that was obvious. He had a gut feeling that she had dropped her knickers for him. She had never done that for Billy, no one was allowed to fuck the girls anyway. It was a trip to the Falls for anyone stupid enough to pull that stunt. There were other pleasures than fucking though and Melanie knew how to work it to her advantage.

Billy bought her stuff in from the other side. Usually books, sometimes sweets and fresh food like bread and vegetables. Now and then she wanted batteries, he wasn't sure why she would want batteries but he didn't really care. She sucked his cock if he got her the right stuff and Billy liked that a lot.

It was more satisfying than the paralysed sex he got from the girls he snatched off the streets in the cities, gutting those girls was a better climax than coming on them. Of course, if Peake found out about his little deal with Melanie he was done for. He would have Macgregor twist his head off and then the big bastard would probably fuck his neck. He would enjoy it too, the mountainous prick had a thing for the young boys they found and he especially liked to put his cock in 'special openings' that he made. Billy had no doubts that murdering him would give Macgregor a great deal of pleasure.

Billy didn't care for Macgregor anyway. They would always go their separate ways for a while when they visited the cities for offerings, then meet up later to hunt. Sometimes Macgregor would have some young thing in a bag, which he would amuse himself with as Billy drove them home.

While he had no time for Macgregor's kind of antics with boys the thought of what the girls in the back must have going through their minds, as they watched him cut and fuck the little lads, got him very hard. Occasionally they would return with one less girl because he had gotten so turned on that he had to 'use one of them up.' Macgregor kept his silence and a happy accord was reached between them.

Perhaps it was because daddy was the big noise in the town that Melanie had the confidence to cajole Billy, she was a determined one alright. They had each other in a vice, neither could break the confidence as they would both suffer. The government man though, he was a different matter. If she wanted out of the town, which Billy had long suspected, then she might just fuck him to achieve her goal.

He saw the flashlight disappear around a corner on the street ahead. He knew where they were going now, only one place of interest lay on that street. Melanie was going home. Billy picked up his pace and closed in. If she was taking him to the Doctors house she had almost certainly broken the Oath, she was fair game and Billy could take it to Peake. Without daddy to protect her and the Oath broken Billy could fuck her till his cock bled. Then he could take her to the Falls and open her up like a can of peas.

The Doctors house was a grand Victorian pile that stood in its own grounds. A few other homes flanked it but none had the same presence. Its magnificence lay only in its size and architecture however, it still wore the same makeup of decay and abandon as every other building in the town. The wall that marked its perimeter was an erratic pile of rubble, much like that of the church. Under the snow lawns were tangled knots of weeds and brambles. The brambles were everywhere in Winter Falls in some places thorny canes sprawled across the pavements and into the road.

Billy arrived on the street in time to see Joe and Melanie enter the house, disappearing quickly inside. He leapt over the snow covered rubble and hastened towards the building. The lights had been left on downstairs so he couldn't tell which room the pair had gone to. He skirted the property, boosted a little higher by the steep snow which enabled him to peer into the windows on the ground floor.

Every room had its curtains drawn, another tradition of Winter Falls homes, but he looked for shadows that might move in the faint light cast through them. He made his way around and stopped when he came to the back. Above the kitchen, on the first floor, a light came on.

Billy cursed and looked around for a ladder or some other method of getting to the upper floors. He could see nothing but also reasoned that he wouldn't be able to hear anything over the sound of the storm. He would have to get in. He made his way back to the front door and carefully tried the handle. Melanie had locked it. Billy couldn't fault her caution, *'always on her toes'* he thought.

He wasn't going to risk disturbing the worship. This was something that everyone in the town understood, you never, ever interrupted the worship. Macgregor would be attending tonight as well, there were offerings and his presence was required to keep them in good order.

He was on his own for this. Billy had no doubt that he could handle Clarke. He was a city boy, a weak little child that would cry for his mother when he got to have a go at him. Clarke didn't know real pain or fear yet, but he had taken and delivered it in bucket loads. He fancied showing the Government man what pain really was.

Billy knelt and withdrew a long thin knife from his boot. The lock on the door could easily be jimmied but it would also break it. Billy figured that it was a small price for the Doctor to pay to catch the Government man before he did something that could hurt them.

He inserted the blade into the keyhole and angled it carefully before applying pressure. There was a satisfying 'chink' as the as lock broke. Billy tried the handle again and eased his shoulder against the door, which slowly opened.

Upon entering the house Joe was immediately struck by the paintings that lined the long, wide foyer. Each framed a stern looking individual, most of them had sat for the portraiture although a couple were pictured standing against a wild and natural backdrop. The seated gentlemen all held a Bible in their right hand. The paintings set in the countryside featured both hunting dogs and horses.

'Who are these guys?' Joe asked as Melanie walked ahead of him

'I don't know.' She said. 'They've been here since before Oath I think.' She stopped sharply but Joe picked up on it.

'The Oath?' He caught up to stand by her. 'What the fuck is the Oath?'

'I'll explain it all later, you wanted the computer, right?' She said impatiently. Joe studied her for a moment. He had started to grow wary of Melanie. They had made love not more than two hours ago. He had wanted her so much then, he still did, but something was gnawing at him, warning him of a danger that he hadn't considered, something that he couldn't see coming.

'Yeah, the computer where is it.' He said.

'First floor, towards the back of the house. I'll need to get the key.' She led him to the bottom of the stairs. 'Wait here and I'll fetch it.' Joe nodded and Melanie disappeared into the house. While she was gone he examined the rest of the foyer. On a plinth, topped by a flat square of marble was a telephone, an old thing like he had seen in black and white movies. He quickly moved to it and lifted the receiver.

There was no dial tone. He turned the dial, 9...9...9 but nothing happened. He had been under no illusion that it would be that easy. Melanie returned as he was dropping the receiver back onto its cradle.

'There's not a working phone in the whole town.' She said.

'I thought that might be the case.' He saw that in her hand she gripped a key, holding it between her thumb and forefinger. 'Is that it?' he asked.

'Yeah.' She said.

Joe took it. It was unremarkable, just a standard Yale key. He had half expected an ancient wrought iron thing. 'Ok, let's go.'

Melanie pressed a switch to her side and a light at the top of the stairs came on. She climbed the stairs and Joe followed. At the top she led him down the corridor, which had four rooms leading off from it. At the end, facing them was a plain looking door.

Melanie inserted the key and turned it. There was an audible click. She pushed down the handle and the door swung open to a dark room. On entering she flicked a light switch immediately to the right of the door. An un-shaded bulb revealed the room.

Joe thought it small, even for a Victorian servant to sleep in and guessed it was probably a converted linen closet or something similar. There was a single chair and a table which had a bulky PC tower underneath it and on top of it a monitor, an old CRT.

Joe squeezed past Melanie and looked at the tower.

'How does he get access to the internet?' He asked.

'What do you mean?' Melanie asked.

'When you turn on the PC and you press the big blue E does the browser load up immediately with the latest news?'

Melanie stared at him with a blankly.

'The Microsoft, does the Microsoft come on. Is it up to date news?' Joe asked slowly.

Recognition crossed Melanie's face. 'Yes, well it comes up with the news but sometimes it's not...fresh, you know, it's a day or two old.'

Joe took out the torch and got on his knees to get a good look at the back of the tower which was in shadow. There were no cables leading to a router or modem line. He spied a small plastic adapter protruding from one of the USB ports. He quickly accounted for the mouse and keyboard which left the adapter as the only possible connection device.

If there was no router then Doctor Peake's connection was mobile and if it was mobile then it had to have a method of connecting.

'Does your dad have a mobile phone?' He asked Melanie from the floor.

'Yes he does. It will be in his room. He doesn't take it to worship.' Melanie replied.

Joe stood. 'And can he make calls on it, you know, use it normally here and around the town?' Joe asked.

Melanie nodded. 'He calls Billy and Macgregor when they are on the outside, he's always shouting at them because they spend too long away.'

Joe rummaged inside his pocket and pulled out his phone. No signal.

'Fucking Vodafone.' He cursed, convinced now that the lack of signal was not some technological conspiracy dreamed up by pagan zealots. 'I'll bet Virgin has five bars from Roscregan to the fucking moon.'

'I'm sorry Joe I don't understand.' Melanie said nervously. 'Is there a problem with the computer?'

'No, it doesn't matter now. I just need your dad's phone and I can sort this mess out with one call and an email.' He put the phone back into his pocket. 'Which is your dad's room?'

Melanie moved into the corridor and pointed, 'The second door.'

Joe walked quickly to the room and as he did so slid the call lock off his phone. If Peake's phone had a signal then he should be able to make an emergency call from his own. If his phone wouldn't play ball then he would use the Doctors. All the angles were covered.

He tried the handle and the door opened without force. He fumbled on the wall to the left for a light switch which he pressed when his fingers found it.

Peake's room was huge. A large king size bed commanded the far side of the room and all around it was what could only Joe could only think of as an Aladdin's Cave of works of art, paintings, furniture and draped over plain wooden boxes were finely illustrated cloths.

Closer inspection of the surfaces of cupboards that stood against the other walls revealed small piles of gold coins, gems and jewellery. He forgot about his phone for a moment.

As Joe moved in to the room he saw various weapons, a rapier with precious gems set into the pommel, a dagger with what he thought might be an ivory handle, these and others were cast around the room without rhyme or reason.

'Jesus Christ.' Joe said in wonder. 'It's like Pirates of the Caribbean.' He stepped further into the room, treading on more coins and gems. The reason he had come here came back to him. 'Where does he keep his phone?' He said to Melanie who stood in the doorway.

'By the bed on the right, there's a shell' she said.

Joe stepped over valuable detritus to reach the top of the bed. There inside a large clam shell, which whilst tarnished was clearly gilded with gold, lay a mobile phone. It looked new and therefore totally out of place, a Samsung, a Smartphone. Peake was clearly using it to connect to the internet.

Gingerly he picked it up. If it was powered up, if there was no lock in place, he could call the police and this nightmare would be over. He experienced a small sense of joy as he thought that he could bring the cops down on this place with Peake's own phone.

He pressed the small button on top of the screen and a colourful array of buttons flashed into being on the touch screen. At the top right of the screen a tiny transmitter icon sat next to five bars three of which were fully illuminated.

'Oh thank God.' He said and turned to Melanie.

The dark figure of Billy Duggan stood behind her. His hand, clutching a thin but vicious looking knife was resting against her chest, the blade's edge pointed up, lying against her throat.

'Hello Joey.' He said.

Chapter Eleven

Kevin turned the business card over in his fingers. The chances of the lad not wearing the coat were extremely slim, there was no way he wouldn't have discovered the pistol. He was convinced that just moving the coat from the front of the car to the back would have alerted Joe to the weight in the pockets.

But the lad hadn't called. He hadn't called to shout at him for putting a loaded gun, covertly in his possession, nor had he called to thank him.

Dynamic Systems, flashed in red text, appeared as the card turned, it was then replaced by the blue scribble that was Joe's mobile number as it turned over again. He had called the number from his landline of course, a few times now but he had been transferred straight to an answer service. He dropped the card to the table and took a look at his watch. It was 1pm. The bar was empty but for Tim Buttress who had fallen asleep at a table next to the fire.

Kevin picked up the card again. The name on the front, just under the bold company name was of Michael Stone CEO, there were three methods of contacting Michael, an office number, a mobile number and an email address. Joe had explained that as a junior in the firm he didn't get his own card just yet. Kevin stood and walked over to the bar. He pulled the phone out from under the counter and dialled Michael's mobile number.

It rang for a while. Kevin thought it may switch to an answer service as Joe's had done but just as he thought it would go that way the line clicked and a muffled, grunting sound could be heard.

'Hello?' The voice was deep and tired.

'Hello.' Kevin said. 'Is that Mr Michael Stone?'

There was a pause as though the person on the other end wasn't sure, but the tired voice answered. 'Yes, who is this?'

'My name is Kevin Smith Mr Stone. I'm the landlord of the pub your employee, Joe Clarke stayed at.'

'Joe? What...what's the problem, is he alright?' Kevin thought he could hear a faint voice in the background. 'It's ok, go to sleep.' Mike said, away from the phone.

'I take it he's no returned to London yet then?' Kevin asked.

'No. He's not been in touch for two days, do you know where he is?' Mike sounded more awake now, more alert. Kevin thought he had moved out of his bedroom.

'Well he was headed to a town not far from here but we have had some terrible bad weather on and off up here' Kevin said, laying on the accent and simplicity in his language, 'most likely Mr Clarke is having to sit it out there as the roads will be closed for days.'

'Well he's not called in and I can't contact anyone at the town...what's the damn place called again?' He asked somewhat sharply.

'Winter Falls is where I believe he said he was going,' Kevin answered.

'Shit, yes. I keep getting it confused that...fucking TV show,' said Mike. Kevin couldn't add to this having no clue what he was talking about, but Joe had not returned, this was what mattered. 'Do you think I should call the police? Technically he's been missing for over twenty-four hours.' Mike said, concern clear in his voice.

'Och no, I don't think so Mr Stone. I'm going to be headed out that way tomorrow, so long as the weather holds off a little. We have a vehicle that can negotiate the roads well enough so I'll see if I can't speak to Mr Clarke and make sure that all is well.'

'Right, that would be good thank you...Mr Smith?'

'Aye, that's right. Sorry about the late hour as well Mr Stone, I'm afraid all of the lines have been down and I thought I should call while I had the chance, they can go down again must faster than they can be repaired.' Kevin knew that the lie was weak but Stone was tired and confused.

'Oh no that's fine, thank you for being so considerate Mr. Smith. I'll make sure that you are compensated for any inconvenience.'

'Ach, its nae bother,' said Kevin. 'I'll let you away back to bed Mr Stone and I'll be in touch once I have word from Mr Clarke. Good night'

'Thanks again, good night.' said Mike.

Kevin replaced the receiver. 'TIMMY!' he shouted across the bar.

Tim Buttress stirred and slowly lifted his head from the table. 'Aye, aye, I'll take a pint o' Steam Kev,' he said automatically.

'There'll be no Steam Tim but I'll stand yeh a shot of whiskey, you're going to need it.' Kevin said fetching a bottle from the back.

'Oh aye?' Said Tim as he slowly emerged from his sleep. 'How's that then Kev,'

'I want you to go and fetch Harry, Angus Flint, The Tunny's, Big George all the lads who know the score, get them here now. Tell em its Falls business.' Kevin said as he placed a shot glass of whiskey in front of his friend. Tim already looked pale but what little colour was left in his face drained at the mention of the Falls. His eyes widened and he stole a glance toward the door to the bar.

'Are there folks in the village Kev?' Tim asked quietly.

'No, not in the village Tim, this time we are going to them.' Kevin didn't wait for Tim's reply, he turned and walked behind the bar. From underneath, below the spirit glasses and half pint pots he produced a twin-barrelled shotgun and placed it on the counter. He rummaged again and pulled out a box of cartridges. The gun had been his father's, it was a good weapon but Kevin knew that he was going to have to bring out a good deal more firepower than this.

Tim looked on aghast at the gun. He immediately understood what it meant.

'Away now Tim.' Kevin said, 'Get the lads, and we are going to need Sally firing up.'

Tim blinked and brought his thoughts away from the shotgun. 'Aye Kev, I'll do her ma self when I have the lads.' He downed the whiskey shot and left the bar.

Kevin poured himself another, a double measure with a little extra besides. He didn't down it quickly, instead he took a few mouthfuls and let each stream down his throat. It tasted good and strong, and reassuring as the warmth of it spread through him. He took a deep breath and looked at his watch again. Time was running on and he had work to do.

Chapter Twelve

Joe stood with the mobile clutched in his hand staring at Billy as though he was some kind of apparition. He had appeared from nowhere and now held Melanie fast with the blade almost cutting into her skin. He had no idea what to do, every situation so far had seemed absurd and awful and not once had he been able to react with resolve or a practical attitude. This was no exception. He stood, waiting for instructions.

'Why don't you throw that phone over here Joey.' Billy said with a deliberate, well-practiced menace. Joe looked at it, he had no choice. He chucked the phone towards Melanie's feet.

'Good lad, now move away.' Billy indicated with his eyes, shifting them away from the bed. Joe took a few slow steps away. Billy suddenly pulled Melanie to the side a little and raised his foot, immediately bringing it down onto the phone. Joe could see the unit was destroyed, snapped across the middle and the screen obliterated.

He had kept a tiny hope alive inside him that Billy didn't realise he had his own phone in his Jacket pocket but the hope was extinguished.

'And now for yours Joey, let's have that fucker.' Billy said.

Joe looked at Melanie, she was slightly off balance as Billy held her, almost suspended at the neck by his knife. A slip of her footing and she could well cut her own throat. He pulled out his iPhone and tossed it carefully towards Billy.

'Any chance you couldn't smash that. It's on a two year contract.' Joe said.

Billy's smile widened and he stamped on the iPhone, twisting his boot into it for good measure. He put his mouth to Melanie's ear.

'Perhaps now your Daddy will realise how dangerous it is having this kind of shit in the town.' He resumed his position, fully covered by Melanie and Joe was at least pleased to see her balance return.

'Ok, now here's what's going to happen.' Billy moved into the room a little, nudging Melanie forward, the knife didn't leave her throat.

'You.' Billy jabbed the word at Joe, 'are going to lie face down on that bed and this treacherous cunt.' He pressed the knife harder against Melanie's throat and Joe saw it cut into her skin, 'is going to tie your hands.'

Joe nodded. 'Ok, I will. Please don't hurt her.' Joe said meekly. Billy was enjoying this. Joe could see it painted across his face and the bastard couldn't drop the smile that seemed to have permanently edged itself onto the corner of his mouth. His dark eyes were bright and full of malice.

'Hurt her Joey?' Billy moved the knife back and forth a little, a trickle of blood snaked down the blade and ran across his fist. 'I'm going to fuck her six ways from Sunday, I'm going to fuck her with every piece of the good Doctors treasure you can see in this room.'

He pushed Melanie forward again which caused the knife to bite a little deeper, she made a quivering 'Oh!' sound and tears spilled from her eyes.

'And when I'm finished Joey, when I've torn her cunt up so bad that it's like a bowl of chopped liver I'm going to open her up and fuck her inside too.'

Joe hadn't realised that Billy had Melanie restrained in no other way other than having the knife against her throat. It was usually enough for Billy, in fact it was always enough to ensure the total compliance of the city girls. The whores and strays froze like rabbits in a full beam when his blades sharpened edge bit them. But Melanie wasn't a city girl.

Joe had thought the tears were Melanie's fear manifesting itself physically. He felt sick and hollow, gripped with a numbing dread. But the tears were only an unwelcome by-product pain, her skin reacting to the cold, cutting steel, forcing unwanted streams out of her. Melanie was shocked only that she had not heard Billy approach.

He was quiet, as a stealthy as a cat but her ears were sharp and sensitive. It was Joe's ramblings about her father's cache of goods that had distracted her.

She coughed a little, nothing too heavy, just a couple of small lurches of her chest to prepare Billy's attention. As Joe began to turn Melanie coughed again, forcing her throat to press harder against the blade, its cut was hot but she ignored it. Instinctively Billy eased the pressure, not alarmed or suspicious of Melanie's movement as it was natural to him, allowing her a moment to act.

She swept her arm up in an arc and in almost the same instant spun on the spot. The desired effect of pushing Billy's clenched fist away happened and she came face to face with him. Surprised, Billy gawped at Melanie as her large brown eyes flared right in front of him. Melanie brought her head back and then butted him on the bridge of his nose. She then brought her knee up sharply into his groin and he dropped heavily to the floor.

Billy let out an animalistic grunt as he fell but his instincts kicked in quickly. He lashed out with his knife hand and got lucky, the blade sank into Melanie's calf. She screamed out and staggered backwards, her left leg gave way as a searing pain shot through it sending her to the floor next to Billy.

Joe watched the scene unfold with his mouth open, his legs felt as though they were filled with lead. Billy lifted his head up, his face wore a snarl and his teeth were bared as he whipped the knife out of Melanie's leg and raised it to strike again. The heel of Melanie's foot smashed into his teeth, pushing the front row clean out of his gums. A second thrust caught his nose and mashed the cartilage. Instantly blood cascaded from it

'Arrrgh...you *cunt*!' Billy screamed. His free hand cupped his broken face and he slammed the knife down hoping to pin Melanie's leg again. This time Billy was not so lucky, the knife rammed into the wooden floor. Melanie kicked again as she used her elbows tp drag herself backwards but she had already moved a sufficient distance for her flailing foot to strike at empty space.

Joe finally found his guts. He ran across the room, nimbly avoiding Melanie as the struggled back towards the bed, and delivered a full force kick to Billy's head. He struck with the front of his boot, catching the hapless Billy across his eyes which were already smeared with blood and tears. There was a gargled 'Ooof!' as Billy's head snapped backwards, he then fell face forwards onto the floor.

Joe reached down and tugged the knife free, having to wiggle it to pull it out. He backed away from Billy as he feebly writhed in the doorway.

'Kill him.' Melanie screamed at Joe. 'Stick that knife in his fucking head.' Joe turned to look at her. She was trying to pull herself up to the bed, her eyes were wild and her hair was matted with sweat against her face, she almost looked insane.

'What are you waiting for, fucking kill him.' She screamed at Joe.

Billy continued to squirm, trying to push himself up from the floor. His hands slipped on blood that was pouring from his face. He groaned but tried again, this time managing to raise his head and lift his torso up, supporting himself with one hand on the doorframe. His face was a ruin, both eyes were already swollen and tightly shut and from the bridge of his nose down Billy's face was a mass of bloodied pulp.

Joe heard Melanie shouting behind him, to kill Billy, to shove the knife into the fucker, but he couldn't do it. He couldn't even bring the thought of killing the man into his mind.

'Shut the fuck up.' He shouted back at her, almost at the point of screaming it. 'I just need to...stop him, uh...restrain him.' He looked about the room, *'there must be a rope or cable amongst this shit,'* he thought.

He started to push things off the cabinets, opening drawers. There were more golden coins and Jewellery; he was surprised when he found a set of drawers that contained only clothes. Shirts sealed in packets, multi-packs of socks and underpants. Joe kept looking back at Billy as he searched, he was groping around now, just outside the room, blood still poured from his face.

Melanie had managed to lift herself onto the bed and lay on it taking deep breaths but she seemed to be Ok. Joe moved to a wardrobe and pulled it open. He found a selection of ties dangling from a hanger. He snatched a few of them and went to Billy.

He didn't want to touch him. There was blood everywhere and Billy was still trying to crawl away, to the stairs. The shock of Melanie's assault was wearing off and Joe knew that his strength would soon return smashed face or not. He gritted his teeth and placed his foot in the centre of Billy's back, he then put his weight onto it and Billy was forced back to the floor.

Quickly Joe pulled each of Billy's arms towards him and fixed the thugs hands at the small of his back by kneeling on them. Billy squealed and shouted undecipherable curses. Joe's ability with knots was not at scout standard but he could make sure that he bound Billy's wrists tightly at least.

Satisfied that the hands were secure he took off Billy's boots and performed the same task with his feet. When he was done Joe stepped back from Billy and debated with himself how secure the ties would be.

'I'll bet you will get out those in ten fucking minutes won't you, you bastard.' He said, more to himself than Billy. A faint chuckle issued from Billy, muffled as he lay with his face to the floor. 'Yeah, well fuck you. Let's see how funny you think it is when the police get here.'

He went to Melanie. The left leg of her denims was soaked with blood from just beneath the knee.

'Jesus Mel. I don't know what to do.' Joe said in a quiet voice.

'Just get it bound, its deep but I don't think he hit the bone, went right through the muscle,' she said weakly. 'There are bandages and painkillers in the kitchen. The cupboard by the oven, look in there.'

'Right, Ok. I'll be straight back.' He said. He exited the room, checking that his knots still looked solid on Billy's wrists and feet before dashing down the stairs and through the house in search of the kitchen. The house was large and featured many rooms but Joe pressed on towards the back of the ground floor. His guess proved right and he found the kitchen.

The light switch was once again on the left of the doorway and as he entered and he flicked it on. The kitchen was, like most of the rooms, very large and looked as though it saw very little activity. As he made his way to the oven, a large cast iron range, he noted that there was dust and grime in the corners and on most surfaces.

A row of cupboards above the oven stretched the length of the room. Joe opened the nearest door to the range and was surprised to see only a few ancient looking bottles, a pack of bandages with their own coating of dust and a box of Nurofen that looked new. He snatched the box and put it into his pocket. He took the pack of bandages and polished dust off the wrapping. He was fairly sure that bandages didn't have a sell by date.

To his surprise a roll of tissue kitchen wipes stood near the sink. That any cleaning product could be found in the town at all seemed odd. He pulled a number of sheets from it and dampened a few under a tap.

He ran back to Melanie. When he reached the top of the stairs he could see that Billy had managed to roll over onto his back. His blood appeared to have stopped flowing but his face had puffed up so much it looked like it had been inflated with a foot pump. As Joe stepped over him he heard Billy mumble something through his shredded lips.

Joe looked over to Melanie, she looked as if she was asleep. '*The pain and shock knocked her out.*' He thought.

Billy mumbled again. Joe lifted Billy up by his side up a little to check that his hands were still bound. He was fully prepared for him to suddenly lash out. He had seen too many Wes Craven movies to fall for that one, but the knots and binding still looked good. He moved to Billy's head and crouched near to him.

'I'm getting out of here Billy.' Joe said quietly, 'and then I'm coming back with the police, the coastguard and the fucking Salvation Army.'

Billy gave another of his guttural chuckles, his mouth moved a little and fresh blood began to drip from the wounds. 'Y'ain...' He gasped a little, 'y'ain go... enwhere ...ucker, ya canna leave...ere.'

'Well I guess we will see won't we.' Joe said defiantly.

'See ya ...ucking whore girl...end eh? She'll cut your...ucking throat...irst chance she gets.' Billy let out another chuckle, he tried to open one of his eyes but could only manage to flutter the swollen eyelid.

'*I did that.*' Joey thought and found that he had a sense of pride about it.

He stood and went to Melanie, stepping over the remains of the crushed Mobiles. A small pool of blood had spread across the blanket. Although it looked as though it was congealing Joe was unsure whether he should attempt to bind the wound. Melanie stirred as he hovered over her.

Her eyes opened. She looked pale, the boldness of her hair exaggerated the lack of colour in her skin. When she saw Joe standing over her she gasped a little but memory rushed in to bring her back to the scene and she reached up a hand and touched the pack of bandages in Joe's hand.

'Fix it up Joe, quickly.' She said.

Joe nodded and moved his attention to her leg. He pushed up the denim until the cut the knife had made was clear. Melanie closed her eyes and made no sound. The whole of her calf was caked in blood and near the top Joe could see that the wound was capped with blood that had already begun to blacken. Using the damp kitchen towels he cleaned around it as best he could and then lifted her knee a little, allowing him to bandage the leg.

When he was done he drew down the jeans leg again. He looked at Melanie, the reason she hadn't stirred at this was because she had passed out again. Joe sat on the bed next to her and took in the surroundings and his predicament.

He was sat amongst a treasure hoard with a stabbed girl and a trussed up, badly beaten psychopath. The remains of the two phones lay scattered about the floor. There would be no calling the police, no emails, no Facebook.

He looked at his watch. It was almost twelve thirty. If what Melanie had said about the townsfolk worshipping until four am was right then he had a three and half hour head start to get away from the town. Of course that was if he went alone. Even if Melanie could walk when she woke up how fast could she possibly travel in two to three feet of snow? He looked over to Billy Duggan. He lay quietly. He too may have passed out but he still managed to appear threatening.

A thought occurred to him. Peake used his phone to call Macgregor and Duggan when out of the town, so there was at least one other mobile. He walked over to Billy, carefully checked the knots that tied him without getting too close and then, satisfied, crouched next to him.

Billy must have sensed that Joe was near and smiled with his broken mouth but said nothing. He obviously hadn't passed out. Joe began to search the pockets of his jacket. Finding nothing he patted down Billy's trousers not wanting to put his hands in the pockets, the revulsion he felt was simply too much. Nothing was apparent. No phone, no keys or a wallet. It appeared that when in the town all this psycho needed was a knife.

Billy gurgled a little, it could have been one of his chuckles. He said something incomprehensible. Joe stood and shook his head. 'Maniac.' He said.

Melanie stirred. Joe marched over to her side. 'Melanie!' She took a deep breath and puffed it out. Her fingers wiped at her eyes.

'God, how long have I been out?' She said, Joe detecting a hint of panic in her voice.

'Just a few minutes.' He indicated her leg. 'I bandaged you and I guess you blacked out.'

Melanie pushed herself up, wincing a little but not pausing. She then slowly swung her legs over the bed until she sat upright.

'He doesn't have a phone on him.' Joe said

'What?' Melanie asked, a little vague.

'The other phone, he doesn't have it I searched him.'

'No, he wouldn't have it. Macgregor has the other one. Billy doesn't agree with the modern stuff.'

She called over to Billy. 'You're a traditionalist aren't you Billy Duggan?

Billy didn't reply but once again issued a deep chuckle.

As Melanie slid off the bed and attempted to stand Joe held her, giving her support. She was strong, as strong as any person he had ever met. She had seemed to be unafraid of the murderous entity, now trussed up on the floor, when he held a knife to her throat. Whereas he was still nervous even with Billy secured.

'Kill him.' She had said. Without hesitation she had told Joe to 'stick the knife in his head.'

Something nagged at Joe, deep at the back of his mind where he kept his doubts and fears, something was trying to talk to him. It was a sane and rational voice unlike the panicked shriek of his conscious. It told him to 'be careful', that he had to 'take it easy' with the girl. And he had.

Joe hadn't told Melanie about the gun. It still lay inside his deep pocket, not loaded but still, a gun and the bullets were only another pocket away. He hadn't pulled it on Billy because he hadn't even thought about it. The pressure of the moment had been too great. He also didn't want to shoot anyone. Not ever.

For now Melanie didn't need to know about the gun. Billy was unaware of it too. Joe decided that this was the best state of affairs concerning it.

'What are we going to do?' He asked, almost like a child might. He was beginning to feel ashamed of his weakness.

'We have to get out right now.' Melanie said without hesitation. 'We need to leave the Falls before my father is done at the Order house.'

'There's three feet of snow out there and that's just on the road, you can't walk through that.'

'We can use your car, it should make it through.' Melanie replied but Joe shook his head.

'I don't know Mel, it's a tough car but that depth of snow...'

'It's that or we wait here for them to find us.' She indicated Billy with a nod of her head 'For them to let him loose, you would prefer that?

'No.' Joe said emphatically.

'There is still a problem though, even if the car can get through the snow. We can't get out of the town without a sigil.'

'A sigil?' Joe asked.

'It's a like a key or a pass, without it there is no way to find a way in or way out of the Falls.' Melanie began to limp over towards Billy. Joe supported her and was happy that at least he was strong enough to easily carry her weight.

'Mel, I'm not sure what you mean, what key?' He asked.

Melanie stopped moving. She looked at Joe, 'How did you find this place Joe?'

'I Googled it.' He said. Melanie stared back at him with her 'what the fuck are you talking about look.'

'A map, an old map. I found one with the Falls on it.' He said.

'And it brought you straight here?' She asked

'Yeah, well no it wasn't easy to find I spent a couple of days taking the wrong turnings on these roads and...'

'So you couldn't find it with your map? Melanie said sharply.

'Well...no but I was going the wrong...' Joe started

'So how did you really find Winter Falls Joe? She repeated.

Joe thought for a moment trying to see where she might be going with this then explained to her the first time he received instructions on how to get to the Falls. 'Your father gave me directions.'

'*Gave* them to you?' Melanie asked

'He sent a letter...and a list of landmarks.' Joe replied.

Melanie nodded. 'Yeah I'll bet he did.' She said. 'Anything odd about that letter, any symbols or odd words?'

Joe remembered the two lines with the spiral, the reddish brown colour of it.

'There was a picture or icon of some kind, on both pages.' He said.

Melanie nodded again, slowly. 'He was very keen to make sure you brought at least one of those pages with you, yes?'

Joe felt as though he was being reprimanded as a schoolboy would for not knowing the answer on the blackboard. He cast his mind back to the letter.

'He told me to hand over the letter at the Police Station...to introduce myself.'

'The thing on the page Joe, it was ward, a *sigil*, just think of it as a key that unlocks the door to this place.'

'I still don't follow.' Joe said.

Melanie sighed and shook her head. She moved her leg a little to adjust the weight on it.

'Joe we haven't got time to go through all this and I don't know how much you are prepared to accept even now, but this is not a normal place.'

'No shit.' Joe said.

'I mean it's not just different from other places because of people like Billy Duggan or the Order, or Henry. This town is *protected* Joe. From you, from the outside world. Without the letter that my father sent you would have *never* found Winter Falls.' Melanie looked into Joes eyes and cupped her hands on each side of his face. Joe held her close to maintain his support of her.

'The rituals that are performed here, that body near the Falls, it isn't just an offering to our Gods, it has significance and purpose in the real world.' Her hands closed tighter on Joes face and she moved her face in towards him.

'Our Gods move upon the face of the Earth. They are not impotent like the Christian God, their actions are tangible and their threat is real.'

'*Our Gods.*' The words spun in Joes mind as Melanie spoke and the small calm voice at the back of his fear said, '*be careful*' once again.

'My father placed a ward on the town. It took him ten years to perform the ritual and so many offerings that Macgregor was rarely seen in the Falls for most of that period. It's a powerful spell Joe. Without the correct sigil, the correct key, no one gets in and no one gets out.'

Joe looked into Melanie's eyes for even the slightest sign of hysteria or panic, but there was nothing. Only a calm and determined woman who had more control over this situation than he did.

'Melanie I...' Joe couldn't finish the words. He was lost now, the boundary of a natural and physical fear had been broken and he found himself utterly out of his depth.

Psychopaths and weird cults were on his radar, they were tangible threats although they lurked only at the periphery of his thoughts, alongside nuclear war and Al Qaida. Magic and spells were for the realm of Harry Potter and Gandalf, it was for fairy stories and Hollywood CGI extravaganzas.

Melanie let her hands slip from his face. Joe could see the frustration lining her expression.

'Check his forearm.' she said bluntly.

Obediently Joe walked to Billy and once again crouched near to him. He pulled Billy over a little to get at his arms. Billy grunted, 'All over ...or you soon laddie.' he giggled.

Joe pulled up the sleeve of Billy's right arm, there was nothing but pale skin.

'The other arm,' Melanie said. 'Always the left.'

Joe hauled Billy onto his stomach. He pulled back the second sleeve and there, in great detail and stretching the full length of the inside of Billy's forearm was a tattoo, was the symbol he had seen on Peake's letter.

'Look familiar?' Melanie asked.

'That's it.' Joe said. 'That's what was on the letter.'

He could see that the spiral was a snake of some kind, a twisting serpent that writhed around two pillars. Runes featured at the top and bottom of each one.

'Macgregor has one too, and my father of course. One or two of the men who can handle the outside world are trusted with it, they fetch supplies in to the town.' Melanie said as she limped towards Joe.

'Without that mark we don't go anywhere, you can choose to believe it or not Joe, it's up to you but you should know that any idea you might come up with, that doesn't involve having that symbol with us means we are going to die.'

'Okay, alright well that's fine, if that's what you think we need we will take one with us. I'll draw one okay, just get me a pen and paper.'

At this Billy started to laugh. His body shook a little as the laugh became a roaring thing. Joe could see that tears spilled from his eyes as his mouth stretched wide and fresh blood began to ooze from his cut lips.

'I'm afraid that won't do it Joe.' Melanie said over the drone of Billy's laughing.

'It would have taken a couple of days to prepare the sigil on your letters, the effect will last a few weeks. Billy's tattoo took few months as its permanent.'

Joe sighed. 'Okay, then we find the letters Macgregor had them off me when I arrived.'

'There's no time Joe, they could be with him, with my father, they might be destroyed...there's no time to find out what happened to them.'

'So what do you suggest?' Joe asked.

'We take him.' She said indicating Billy. The laughing died down.

'Is that wise? The fuckers bound up with neck-ties, which he's clearly going to undo while he's in the car and then he'll strangle us with them.'

Joe felt that this was how his luck was going now. 'And he's bound to slow us down anyway.' He added to try and appear more rational.

Melanie waved her hands in front of her to stop him, 'Okay, okay fair enough. Look, go get the car, bring it here, it will be much quicker than trying to walk me over to it.'

Joe thought about this. The logic was sound. 'Will you be ok with him?'

Melanie nodded. 'So long as your knots are good there's no need to worry, besides he's not in any fit state to start another fight I think.'

Again Joe concurred, the thinking was faultless. Time was against them and they needed to move quickly. 'Okay, I'll get the car. You grab some food and drink in case we get stuck or have to move on foot. I'll be back in ten minutes.' He said.

Melanie moved to him as he stood up from Billy and wrapped her arms around his neck. She kissed him passionately. Joe didn't want the kiss to end but she eased him away.

'Don't worry.' She said. 'Just get the car and come straight back, I'll be waiting at the front of the house.'

Joe said nothing. The small voice at the back of his mind was drowned out by the noise of his desire. He stepped over Billy and made his way out of the house and into the night.

Chapter Thirteen

The hall was filled with a steady, low murmur of chanting. Peake stood at the head of the assembled townsfolk with his head bowed in quiet contemplation. The robes he wore were heavy 'heavy with the weight of responsibility' he often quipped. The cloth was strong cotton, dyed to a very deep crimson. Not to hide the blood. Most of the front of the robe was darkened almost too black by staining. Years of offerings had taken their toll.

This past week had been extremely trying for him. The arrival of the Government man into Roscregan had merely added to an already challenging set of circumstances. Duggan, as usual, was the problem. He had almost got himself caught during a foray into Edinburgh and had it not been for Macgregor, and he supposed Billy's own brand of vicious cunning, he may not have escaped. They had however left behind them a bloodbath.

The larger part of the problem was that they had been required to despatch two policemen as well as two girls, both prostitutes, and a boy that Macgregor had probably got in tow for his own pleasure on the return route. Peake was very clear about anyone who caught sight of the men in action, they all had to be destroyed immediately. No living witnesses.

This had upset the supply of offerings. The police forces across the country were now on high alert and as The Great Father had been very demanding lately, the blood that Peake had delivered was not enough and punishments were to be had should he not quench the thirst of his master soon. There was no explanation of why such a rise in demand had occurred but who was he to question The Dweller in The Deep, praise be unto him.

As if this was not enough many of the men were due to Return. The next two years would see them take their place with the Great Father. They would be at his side, finally after forty years of living with the wretched filth that is humanity. As Patrician he wouldn't see this day until he was in his eighties, a lifetime eaten up inside a dirty and fragile skin. Ah, but the glory that would await him would be reward enough, a just reward for his devotion and personal sacrifice.

He had given his entire life to the Father and soon he would offer the bounty of his own seed. That day couldn't come quick enough in fact. Peake's thoughts darkened and moved from reflections of praise and duty. The girl had been a problem even from her earliest days. Questions, curiosity, rebellion and defiance had been her gift to him for creating her.

He wished he could have offered her up sooner. But no female child born of the human men of the Falls could be given until the Great One allowed it. None could even be shared as gifts of their sex to deserving members of the faithful. *They* were very specific about this. The punishments for transgression were terrible even to him.

The chanting began to rise up from the monotonous rumble to an excited chorus. The faithful nodded their heads lightly and repeatedly as they uttered the words, '*Ph'ngluim glw'nafh Cthulhu R'lyeh wgah'nagl fhtagn.*' Peake breathed deeply and let his thoughts disperse, he pictured only a deep and dark place and within it a city, a vista of cyclopean structures worn by time and tide.

'Great Father and Lord Master Dagon. Guide us. Bring us to you. Open the gates of R'yleh so that we may gather and give ourselves to He Who Dreams. You who stand at his side, you who are his power in the depths.

The chanting rose yet another octave, the nodding became faster. Peake lifted his arms, spreading them to accept the whole of his Masters will. In the dark city, his mind's eye moved through to the centre to where he saw the Temple, which dwarfed all around it. A vast construct of basalt hewn by ancient sculptors into a worthy throne for Great Father Dagon.

Peake felt his body begin to shiver, he almost vibrated as the power of Dagon began to flood into him, such gifts his master would give, and such rewards.

He no longer heard the chants, only the impossible noise of an ocean of water filled his ears. Dagon would speak soon. He would guide his acolyte and make his demands. Peake shouted with an excited glee in his voice, 'My Father! My Master! Bless us your faithful, we wish only to bow at your feet.'

Abruptly blackness replaced Peake's vision. He felt as though he was moving backwards at an incredible speed. His heart threatened to burst as he tore through the darkness. He was being pulled, sucked violently backwards, away from the Temple, away from the city and his Lord.

He eyes opened. Startled and dazed and he staggered back, falling to the floor as his foot trod on his flowing robe. The townsfolk ceased their dirge, heads stopping their nodding simultaneously. They looked to Peake and then at each other in confusion.

Peake gasped and tried to stand. The hulking form of Macgregor appeared at his side and took his arm, lifting him with ease to his feet.

Peake gasped. 'One of ours is gone.' He pushed Macgregor away and turned to his flock. 'Brothers, something has happened in the town, one of ours is fallen!' There was no mistaking the break. The community was tightly woven into the rituals that bound the town. Each of them gave a portion of their *Essence* to the ward that protected them, to the demands of the Great Father. The rituals bound them together, they were sewn into the very fabric of the place. When a follower died, when a part of the weave was unpicked, it struck at the very centre of Peake's being as all of the rituals were channelled through him and this in turn, although to a lesser extent was felt by the others.

Grunts and gasps flooded the room at his words. Peake pulled the robes over his head and dropped them to the floor, he was naked underneath. Scars and tattoos covered his chest and back. Sixty years of worship written upon him.

'Get my clothes.' He ordered and Macgregor lurched off to a side room. Peake approached the book upon the lectern and began to flip over pages of it until he found the section he was looking for.

The men quietened and waited, all eyes on their naked leader as he mumbled words over the book. He had to call *them*. The instructions were clear, precise. Should a bearer of a sigil be lost without reason they must be called. Yet Peake hesitated. To call them was surely to be seen as a weakness, even after all of this time, even though they couldn't have a doubt of his loyalty to the Father they might question his suitability to be turned.

He laid his hand on the page he had stopped at. A little blood and the words would bring them. Macgregor returned with his clothes. He accepted the pile of clothing but put it to one side, remaining naked for the time being. Peake instructed his lieutenant.

'Macgregor, bring him up, it's his time.'

The big man nodded and left the room.

Peake raised his arms and called out to his gathering. 'Brothers and sisters, a rite of calling must be made. Macgregor is bringing our offering to the Father so please prepare yourselves.'

At this the gathered men began to pull off their robes. Those who were too stiff in body due to their advanced stage of returning were assisted by younger members. In a tidy, practiced order they formed a line which moved toward the rear of the room where a table contained an assortment of objects.

In a large basket were dozens of slim metal spikes, each a foot in length. One by one the worshippers selected a spike and brought it to their lips, kissing the middle of it lightly as they walked back to their position in the hall.

Macgregor reappeared but not alone. He pushed forward a well-built man, tall but not as tall as or as burly as the Policeman. The man was naked but for a dirty, bloodied gag that was tight across his mouth. His hands were tied behind his back and a short rope hobbled his feet. He had a thick beard that was matted with filth.

Macgregor grabbed his hair, put his boot into the back of the man's knees forcing him to kneel.

He looked to Peake who nodded. Producing a large knife from his belt Macgregor cut the gag loose and the bearded man gasped and spat onto the floor. Still holding on to his prisoner's thick hair Macgregor yanked his head back.

'You're all going to fucking burn you heathen scum.' The man shouted, his accent was foreign, strange to the worshippers, as the last one had been. Macgregor jammed a worn wooden cylinder into the corner of the man's mouth and with a deft flourish of his fingers and the knife cut his prisoners tongue out with one slice. He tossed the severed piece aside and dragged the screaming man by his hair to Peake's feet.

The prisoner shook his head in agony and his body heaved up and down on the floor. The gathered men began to chant, the ritual was started.

Now that the man's mouth was empty of a human tongue Peake could fill it with the items required to send the call to his brothers in the deep, but first, as the outsider was unfit to see the Great Fathers symbols his eyes would have to also be excised. Peake knelt and Macgregor offered his knife to the Doctor.

Trond whipped his head from side to side until Macgregor knelt behind him and clamped his huge arm around his neck.

Chapter Fourteen

Joe noticed the wind that had been driving the snow so viciously an hour ago had begun to drop. Instead of a wall of blinding ice there was now only a sprinkle of flakes lazily drifting down. Even with the large coat and warm boots Joe's legs were cold, the snow had settled to a depth of three feet at its lowest and it soaked into his denims as he pressed through it. It amazed him the speed at which the wind could switch from a frenzy to gentle an almost gentle, if freezing breeze.

When he reached the street mild panic flashed through him when he couldn't see the Nissan, but as he closed the distance it became apparent that the snow had drifted heavily here. The car was still parked outside the Police House but snow had covered the near side almost to the roof. Joe increased his pace as best he could, the snow was a least a further foot deeper on the street.

Upon reaching the car he moved to the driver's side and found there was no drift on that side. He pulled out his keys and brushed snowflakes and ice away from the lock.

'*Don't be frozen.*' he thought.

He pushed in the key and turned it. There was a satisfying 'clunk' as the central locking did its job. Joe pulled on the door, easily dislodging the soft snow that clung to it. A light at the top, centre of the windscreen frame illuminated the inside.

'Hello baby.' Joe said and climbed in.

For a reason he couldn't explain he had expected it to be warm inside the car, but it was far from it. The windscreen was a mess of patterned ice and his breath appeared more visible inside. He put the key into the ignition, not allowing himself any time for pessimistic thoughts of the Nissan not starting. The engine immediately hummed into life and the dash lit up.

Joe hadn't realised how much he had missed colour. Bright blues and greens appeared on the fuel gauge and speedometer.

'The snow is too deep though,' he thought. *'I'm not being negative here, it's just too fucking deep.'*

He turned the heater on and tried the windscreen wipers, which he thought would be stuck to the screen. To his surprise, almost as if to prove him wrong, the wipers immediately kicked into life and began to push the snow away. He pulled out his wallet and slid a Costa Coffee loyalty card from it. The air-con was not yet strong enough to move the ice so Joe scraped at it with the card creating a little ice storm across the dashboard. The street ahead became visible. Joe put the Nissan into gear, the tyres bit into the snow and ice and moved steadily forward.

Negotiating the unfamiliar streets proved more difficult than getting the car to work its way through the snow. Fortunately, he was able to follow his own tracks, the only ones visible and soon saw the Doctors house. He could see that the door was open, wide enough for someone to look out and see a car approaching.

As he pulled up to where he thought the kerb might be the door to the house opened wide and Melanie appeared. By the time Joe had climbed out of the Nissan and made his way towards her Melanie had already managed to hobble halfway towards him. Joe ran as best he could to intercept and help her.

'What about Billy?' He said as he reached her. He looked toward the house half expecting to see Duggan appear in the doorway.

'He's not going anywhere, don't worry. We will be long gone when they find him.' Melanie mirrored Joe, putting her arm around his waist and tightened herself up to him.

Joe eased her down the steps. Although she appeared to be managing the injury well he allowed her full weight onto his shoulder.

'I should check those ties before we go.' He said

'Joe it will be fine.' Melanie insisted 'He's tied up and half blinded. Even if he got loose he would have to wander around in the snow. Leave him for my father, we need to get out of here *now*.'

'Okay, okay.' He replied feeling a little chastised.

He pulled open the door and Melanie climbed in. Joe pushed her door shut and returned to the driver's side, taking a final look at the doctor's house before getting in. He pulled away from the kerb, the Nissan slid a little as he negotiated turning in the snow but it regained its strong traction as he straightened up and moved forward.

The engine was powerful, the tyres were well balanced and the thick tread bit into the snow allowing it to power though the constant blanket that lay ahead. But Joe knew that it wouldn't be able to make it, not all the way. There would come a point where snow had drifted to four or five feet. The Nissan would build up a wall of snow in front of it as it resisted being pushed it to the side, and it was that, if it wasn't a skid into a wall, which would bring them to a dead stop. The question wasn't whether they would be stranded, but when.

But he had a plan. When the town psychos found Billy and saw that the Nissan was gone they would come after them. Trying to get back to Roscregan, through the snow would be impossible. It was too cold and Melanie would slow them both down. The townsfolk knew where they were going, he didn't and Melanie had stated that she had never left the town so she couldn't help so the answer was simple, if he could pull it off. He had to make them think that they had already escaped. At least for a while.

The road Joe had taken into the Falls and to the street on which he had found the Police house had been straight. Once he was out of the street in which the Doctors grand house stood he recognised that this was the wider road that he had come in by.

Melanie said nothing from the moment he had started to drive. When Joe stole a glance at her she looked to be in a state of sheer terror. The high beam of Nissan's headlights reflected in the snow as it showered the windscreen, ploughed up by the car as it pushed through. Beyond this only a couple of metres of the road or at least where Joe assumed the road should be was visible.

Is this the first time she has been inside a car? He wondered.

'Don't worry, I just need to get some distance,' He said hoping to reassure her. He found he had to shout over the noise of the engine and the pelting of the shredded snow against the windscreen. Melanie nodded, not taking her eyes off what she could see of the road.

Joe had a destination in mind but he wasn't sure that his landmark would be visible. He became certain it wouldn't as he passed the last of the cottages with large gardens that marked the edge of the town.

The drifts had built up to the middle of the side windows. He had vainly hoped that the bicycle would show up perhaps as a bump or even dark handlebar sticking out, prominent against the white background. It didn't, however he found his spot through other means.

He recalled that the bike had been propped near to a stile and as Joe drove along he noted a sudden dip in the snow bank, indicating a gap in the wall. He gently braked, only shooting past his mark by about three feet and turning the wheel slightly so that the front faced where the wall would be in a graceful and deliberate slide.

'Why have we stopped? What's the matter?' Melanie asked. The panic in her voice made her sound a little shrill. Joe reached between the seats and grabbed the bag of supplies she had brought.

'We need to get out here.' He said.

'Why? What's the problem?' Joe had unbuckled his safety belt and Melanie, seeing this, did the same.

'The car isn't going to make it much further, I'll guarantee it. Plus the further we go the more dangerous it's going to get. It's not just the snow either. If we get lost out there, and trust me we will, they will easily catch up by following the tracks we leave.'

'What are we going to do?' She asked.

'We're going back into town.'

'WHAT! Are you out of your mind?' Melanie's eyes were wide and her mouth hung open. Joe thought she looked angry, she also looked scary.

'Mel, there is no way we can go forward but we *can* go backwards. The forest is really close to the road here.' He pointed to the dark tree line that the deer had vanished into after almost causing him to crash. 'We are going to make tracks into the trees then double back and then do the same in the tread marks of the car. We can get off the road when they approach and let them pass us. By the time they have figured out that we haven't gone into the forest we can be in the town.'

'Why would we be any safer in the town?' Melanie said. 'We can't hide there, and you can trust me they *will* find us.'

'We aren't going to hide in the town. We're leaving this shit hole tonight and I don't think they will be able to follow us. We can take....'

Joe was interrupted by a sound that carried through the air and grew steadily in volume. It was a deep tone, so low that as the sound wave enveloped the car a vibration ran through its body.

'What the fuck is that?' Joe asked. He looked through each of the windows to see if there was anything visible.

Melanie slumped in her seat and stared out once more at the wall of snow lit by the headlights.

'It's a call.' She closed her eyes and let her head drop. 'My father has called them.'

'Called who? His phone is trashed.' Joe paused. 'Macgregor's phone I guess, who has he called? What's that fucking noise?'

'It's not who it's what, and he wouldn't use the phone even if he had it. There's no one he needs to call on that phone.' She said flatly.

The sound continued for another minute, fading a little and then blasting again. Joe listened until it appeared to have stopped completely.

'They'll be coming now.' Melanie said in an emotionless tone.

'Then we need to get going, whoever it is that's coming.' Joe said firmly.

He had to push heavily against the door, forcing a wall of snow away from it. Once the door was open he stepped down into the drift. He left the engine running and the lights on to allow him to see the tracks they would make towards the forest, at least as far as was possible. No doubt the townsfolk would have torches so he wanted to make sure they couldn't see through his ruse to soon.

He went around to the passenger side to help Melanie in case she struggled with the door, but she was already out of the car when he got there.

'Okay, so the plan is we head to the forest. Make as much of a mess in the snow as you can. Do you need me to help you across?'

Melanie shook her head. She looked down, she no longer looked scared but rather depressed. As she went to where the dip in the snow bank indicated the location of the stile Joe helped her anyway. If there was anything more likely to cause someone to fall than a climbing over an iced stile he didn't know of it.

Melanie pushed her hands into the snow and felt the cold wood of the stile. Using only a faux memory of where the struts 'should be' she attempted the step up and over the platform and then through the gap. She managed it without issue although the drift on the far side was deeper due to a drainage ditch that ran beneath it. When Melanie stepped into the snow came to her chest.

Joe quickly followed. The climb also presented no problem for him but he lost his footing as he stepped off and fell into the drift behind Melanie.

'Jesus!' He cursed as snow poured over him. He wasn't hurt but ice dropped onto his neck and melted instantly, the freezing trickles finding their way down his spine.

Melanie didn't look back. She trudged slowly through the blanket of white, a couple of feet deep past the drift. Joe regained his footing and as much composure as he could and took a few long strides to catch up to her. He walked at her side, taking her hand. Hers was cold to him and he squeezed it as if to put a little of his own heat into her.

It only took a couple of minutes to reach the edge of the forest. Joe scanned the perimeter to try and find a suitable entry point. Just along to Melanie's right the brambles were low to the ground. Joe moved to the spot and peered into the gloom. The Nissans lights added nothing to the visibility here and Joe could only make out more snow albeit less deep.

'Come on, we'll walk in a little.' He said.

Melanie dutifully followed, remaining silent and looking glum. Joe stepped onto the brambles and felt them snap and crunch under his boots. He moved ahead of Melanie so that she could follow his path. The forest was still and it was silent except for the noise of Melanie's awkward steps towards him. He was barely inside the line of the first few trees and visibility was now practically zero.

Suddenly the area ahead was bathed in a cold light. Joe was a little surprised until he gathered that Melanie had turned on a torch. She swept the beam back and forth revealing only more trees and snow.

'Do we have to go deeper?' She asked quietly.

'No, I don't think so.' Joe replied. 'This should confuse them enough. He pointed at the brambles. 'The snow is thinner here and the brambles mess up the tracks enough to keep them busy at for a few minutes at least.'

He put his hands on his hips and took a final look around. He thought of the deer crashing through here, its home, and wondered if perhaps they should try to press on through the forest. Getting lost was the problem. Fall over here and when you stood you would have only a trail of your own footsteps to guide you, a trail that would be followed by the townspeople. No, he would stick to his plan.

'Let's head back now.' He said gently to Melanie, who turned and began to follow the trail they had made back to the car. Joe couldn't help but notice that she walked surprisingly well considering she had not long ago had a blade rammed into her calf.

At the Nissan Joe turned off the engine and closed the doors. Melanie waited for him, she stood in the deep tread mark left by its large wheels. Joe stepped into the parallel furrow and together they began to head back towards the town holding hands across the snow barrier created by the perfectly good car they were leaving behind.

Chapter Fourteen

Peake hadn't wanted to call them but he really had no choice. Someone in the community had died and if a community member died they had to be called. He now he had to find out who it was and what had happened. There were a few of the men awaiting the call, incapable of movement until their hardened skin finally cracked and they were reborn. They were sat in their homes counting the days until the Return.

Duggan was out there, and although he knew that Macgregor and Duggan were more than capable of looking after themselves he couldn't shake the idea that it was one of his lieutenants that succumbed in some way.

It had to be the Government man, Clarke. Somehow, he was involved and of that he had no doubt. Killing him would bring unwanted eyes upon the town but they would have to deal with that situation when it happened.

Once he was dressed he assembled men capable of participating in a search before him while the rest were told to return to their homes. There were not many that could handle a search in this weather and an even greater number could barely move. It was a bad time to be having trouble in the town. So many of the men were close to returning, even some in their early thirties were advancing in the process much faster than he had ever seen before.

Peake wondered if the power of his master had grown so great that its effect was being seen in the speed at which he was able to bring his children home. A small bubble of excitement rose within him. Surely if this was the case then his time was at hand. So long as he didn't fuck this up of course.

Whatever the answer to the problem it wasn't going to be those about to return that could help with it. They unable to contend with snow and ice, they were strong but they were slow and awkward in movement.

They looked at him with their bulging eyes wide, blinking. Peake could feel their fear and vulnerability. This was the most dangerous stage of the return as they were virtually helpless.

Fortunately, his contingent of Wardens was fit and able. He looked out at the faces of those scattered amongst the assembly, those who had not received the blessing of Dagon at birth. Outwardly they looked like the other humans, like Clarke, like himself he supposed. They could pass through towns and cities without attention, collect supplies and pay off certain individuals.

While Macgregor and Duggan were his lieutenants, the most experienced, the others could handle themselves. They still had the blood of Father Dagon running through them after all. These were the Wardens of the Brood.

'Brothers.' He called to them all. 'As you know a Government Man has been here for two days. We had hoped to give him the information he required and send him on his way, but this has been undone.'

A gargled murmur ran through the crowd. 'I will need some of you to assist Macgregor in locating the Government man.' Peake jabbed his finger into the crowd, indicating four of the Wardens. 'You will come with me to find Billy Duggan. We need him.' As one the heads nodded. 'Andrew, open the cache and give each man a firearm.'

The man called Andrew broke from the crowd and left the room. Peak instructed Macgregor to get his guns as the policeman had his own cache at the Police House. He was to go after Joe with as many men as he felt he needed to ensure the job was done.

'Finish it there and then.' He advised Macgregor. 'Don't fool around with him either.' He added, giving the big man a sharp look.

'I'll get it done.' Macgregor replied and turned to leave, pointing to some of the gathering to accompany him.

'Not them.' Peake called out. He indicated the Wardens that Macgregor chosen. The big man said nothing and instead nodded towards a number of the men who were less advanced towards returning. They shuffled out behind him.

'Fucking coward.' Macgregor mumbled. He knew that Peake was saving the most able men to protect his own sorry skin instead of giving him the resources to tackle of the problem at hand. He led his band out of the lodge and into the snow with dark thoughts of what he would do to the Government man once he had him in his hands.

Chapter Fifteen

They had seen the first beam of torchlight sweep through the snowfall together. Without hesitation Joe lifted Melanie into his arms, she gave a mild gasp, he then walked with her into the snow drift to their right. The drift gave in to him easily as he pushed through it until he reached the wall. He carefully set Melanie down and held a finger to his lips.

'Stay quiet.' He said as low as he could over the storm. He then moved back to the road and began to push to snow back into the gap he had made. Joe knew that it was a poor attempt at camouflage, one that would fool no one on a clear day, but with the dark of the night and the blinding dance of flakes it would be difficult for the townsfolk to notice the disturbed snow.

If it didn't work all he could do was go over the wall and head for the forest. He knew that he would have to leave Melanie behind if that was the case.

For at least a minute all he could hear was the wind but then the deep tones of male voices were carried upon it. They were close. Only a small wall of snow hid them from the roadside and Joe held Melanie tightly as the voices grew a little more in volume.

A shaft of light reflected in the snowfall above them but the beam didn't appear to be directed at their location.

The voices quickly began to fade. They had passed by.

Gingerly Joe released Melanie and she let her arms slip from him. He crept through the gap he had made and pushed away his makeshift wall. He looked to his left, he could see beams of light probing ahead but couldn't make out the men who carried them.

It had worked. He felt Melanie move up behind him and he reached for her hand. He stepped back onto the road and pulled Melanie to him.

'Ok, we have to move now. With any luck that's the only group looking for us out here. We get into the town and head to the dock.'

'The dock?' Melanie said surprised. 'Why the dock?'

'There's a boat there, a small motor boat.' Joe said. 'We can use it to get around the coast.'

Melanie looked at him with incredulity. 'A motor boat in this fucking storm?' She said and then stopped abruptly, realising that she had raised her voice.

Joe gripped her shoulders. 'I have no better idea Mel, not a one. Yeah, it's going to be rough I know, but if we can just get out of the bay and make some distance around the coast we can make it. I'm fucking positive.' He gave her a little shake as he said the last, just to show his conviction.

Melanie stared at him, eyes wide but looking tired. 'That's the worst fucking plan I have ever heard.' She said, 'But as I don't have another I guess it's all we have.'

Joe smiled gravely. 'Let's go.' He said.

The men of Roscregan gathered in the bar of the Silent Piper and Kevin looked at the assembly with a mixture of sadness and pride. There was not one of the remaining villagers of the parish who had not answered his call.

'This needs to be quick and it needs to be clear.' Kevin said in a confident and strong voice. 'This is it. The end of it. I'm sick of watching this place decay under my feet. I'm sick of letting good people wander off from here and probably never be heard of again.' Some heads bowed, shoulders swayed a little. 'You all know that there is an evil out there and I'm as afraid of it as you are. Where are our kids? We've sent them all packing, safe, away from here. By doing that we have condemned this village to an early end, our legacy to them will be a few acres of land that no one will buy and homes that no one will live in. Unless we do something and do it now.'

Kevin turned and placed his hand upon a large wooden crate that rested upon two tables that had been drawn together.

'There should be enough in here to go around, at least one to every man. You all know how to use them, we have practiced enough for this moment.' He patted the lid. 'I don't know what the consequences will be if we succeed. A lot of questions are going to be asked you can be certain of that, but I do have a good idea of what will happen if we lose. Roscregan will be one more village that disappears off the map.' He turned his back to the crowd and lifted the lid of the crate off revealing a collection of assault rifles.

There was no indication of surprise from the men as they were all well aware of existence of the guns. Sending children to the best schools and university's cost money, second homes in the south cost money.

Kevin looked down at the array of hardware before him, M16's mostly, some AK47's. Each one a token of appreciation, or a way of meeting a payment, from gun smugglers that operated on the remote coastline. Kevin had often wondered how much the silence and complicity of this village had contributed to the spread and implementation of evil generally.

The IRA once had a well-established supply line that ran through Roscregan and into the south during the eighties and while Kevin had no truck with their politics, having served a term in Ireland his father had not shared his view.

Yet even Kevin had to admit that living near to the port of Winter Falls made the idea of having a cache of firearms available more attractive than not.

There were fifteen rifles and a half dozen Beretta pistols. Each weapon had enough rounds for four reloads. On occasional weekends he had run through general tactics, what to do in the event that the village came under attack. He had only halted the practice runs when rounds had begun to become limited. He had refused to deal with anyone hoping to run gun through the village once his father had died and this made acquiring more ammunition too risky.

He turned back to face his fellow villagers.

'If you have no stomach for this I don't blame you, and I'm sure that not one of us here will lay blame on any man who chooses to walk away. If this is what you would prefer to do then do so now and have nae bad conscience about it.' Kevin waited. No one moved.

'I'm wi' ya Kev.' One of the men called from the group and at this a few more, 'Here mate' and 'Ayes' were issued. Kevin nodded.

One of the Tunny brothers, Joss, stepped forward. The Tunny lads had refused to leave their father even though he had offered a good deal of money to them, to set up a life away from Roscregan. Instead they had stayed to continue working on the family farm.

Their mother Patricia was also one of the few females left in the village. A tougher, more loyal family would be hard to find in the whole of the region.

'Are we away for the London boy Kev? And the foreign lads?' Joss Tunny asked.

Kevin nodded. 'Aye, although I dunna hold out much hope for the Norwegians, but the lad has only been gone a couple of days.'

'It doesnae really matter Joss.' Brian Tunny called out to his brother. 'I'm happy just tae be going over there to shake those weird bastards outta that place.'

A few of the men laughed a little at this and even Kevin managed to smile.

'Ok lads.' Kev lifted an M16 from the crate. 'It looks like we are to be away. Let's get geared up.'

Woolly Brown, a diminutive dairy farmer whose holding lay the furthest north from the village stepped out from the assembled men and Kevin presented him with the rifle.

'McDowdal will sort out your ammo mate.' Kevin said and Woolly nodded. The rest of the men formed a line to take their weapons.

Chapter Sixteen

Joe was surprised at how quickly the town came into view. The buildings hampered the flurry of snow enough to increase visibility and he could see that they were back on the outskirts of it. He clearly had not driven as far as he had. Now he wondered if there would be enough time for them to get away if Macgregor figured out that they had doubled back sooner than anticipated.

'How are you holding up?' He asked Melanie as they passed by the cottages that had marked his initial entry to the town.

'I'm fine.' Melanie replied and that did appear to be the case. She only limped a little and was not leaning on to Joe for support. He marvelled at her resilience and strength.

'Is the quickest way to the dock this road?' He asked.

'No.' Melanie replied. 'If we cut across the town just down from here we can save some time.'

'Right, let's do that then.' Joe said and allowed himself a small moment of hope. They had made it back to the town and it was highly unlikely that anyone had thought they might return. Duggan was out cold and even if they had found him, as Melanie had said, he was in no fit state to fight. Macgregor was with the gang looking for them and he felt sure he could take Peake down if it came to it.

Obviously there was a town full of others to contend with but all they had to was avoid them and they had a chance. Unfortunately, Melanie was also right about the plan, the boat *was* a shit idea but he told himself that it did have some merit. He hadn't seen another boat in the docks that would have a chance out on that sea, so they couldn't be followed. He tried not to think of it being smashed to pieces against the cliffs. That was another bump in the road of his plan.

The snow's depth inside the town was nowhere near as deep as it was outside and the going was much easier. Melanie appeared to be completely unhindered by her wound and easily kept pace beside him, to the point that Joe began to move a little faster.

He was pleased that he could do so as the cold was starting to bite into his skin. His jeans were soaked through and his feet felt like ice. What protection the jacket had offered was now lost as it had also succumbed to the wet, although not yet as badly as his jeans.

As they had crossed the town the wind had also begun to ease although the snowfall hadn't, this was another good sign for his plan he thought. Less wind meant a sea that might not try to smash them to a pulp added to this the snow would further hide them.

Emerging from an alley that Melanie had led them through Joe realised that he recognised the road they were now on, despite the knee-deep snow. About four hundred yards to the right and across from them was the Satanic Lidl, this was the road adjacent to the dock. They had made it.

Visibility was still poor due to the curtain of drifting flakes but not as severe as before, when the wind had turned them into a twisting living curtain. He couldn't see anyone. This was by no means proof that no one was watching but his plan was almost at its point of completion so Joe decided to go for it.

He grabbed Melanie's hand and darted across the road with her in tow. They moved quickly past unlit shops and homes and past the recesses where the fishing equipment was stacked under snowy hills. Finally, they came to where the road turned into the jetty entrance, where he had seen the boat.

'Brilliant.' he whispered to himself. The sea was moving with strong swells but didn't appear to be too violent. He couldn't see the boat, but that was Ok, it was at the far end and they had to cross the length of the Jetty to get to it. To his left, at the top of the road, was the lodge building. He stared at it and his mouth went dry, his mind dug at him with insinuations that faces were pressed against its boarded upper windows, watching him through the gaps and knot holes with cold black eyes. He shuddered and dismissed his paranoia.

'Let's go.' He said. Still gripping her hand he led Melanie along the jetty until they reached the boat. He had harboured a cold fear that when he got there the little vessel would be gone, but as they approached the end of the jetty he could see it rising and falling with the swell.

Joe looked back. Still no one was in sight. All they had to do was get in the boat, start her up and they were away, out of this nightmare. A thought struck him and he felt he should ask even though he was not wholly convinced that it needed to be considered.

'We can get out right? The thing with the symbol, you said we would need it.' Joe stuttered over the words, not just because he was cold but because the idea seemed so ridiculous.

'It's ok, we can get out. I have what we need.' Melanie replied.

Joe nodded. 'Ok, good.' He looked down at the boat and followed the rope that secured it to the jetty. He grabbed it and pulled the boat against the rotting tyres.

'Get in Mel.' He said, and she stepped into the little boat.

They both suddenly stopped what they were doing and listened, Mel had one foot on the jetty and one on the floor of the boat. A sound, distinct despite being distant had carried on the wind and bounced around the town.

'Was that a gunshot?' Joe asked, his face wrinkled up as blast of wind leapt up off the sea and the cold of it burned his skin. Before Melanie could answer a further report came and then like firecrackers on November the fifth the air was punctuated with reports. Somewhere a lot of guns were being fired.

'Jesus. What now?' Joe said.

'I don't know and I don't care Joe.' Melanie said sharply. 'Let's get the fuck out of here.' At that she carefully finished her climb into the boat. Joe unravelled the last of the rope and made a little hop to get on-board. His feet splashed into about three inches of water that had collected inside the bottom but he paid it no attention. It was floating, that was enough.

He turned to the outboard motor. He had never used one before but had seen them on the TV and in movies enough to judge that they all started by pulling on cord. He looked for it but couldn't see one.

'What's the matter?' Melanie asked.

'I don't know how these work.' Joe said, angry at himself.

'Are you fucking kidding?'

'No!' Joe whipped his head around to face her. 'I'm not fucking kidding. Do you know how they work?' He said, surprised at his own vicious tone.

'No.' Melanie said, shaking her head. More gunshots dotted the air, they still sounded far away. Joe looked over the motor, for buttons, levers or switches that might make the thing come to life but nothing he did caused the motor engage.

He let out a frustrated grunt and slammed his hand onto the top of it.

'Fuck!' He ran his hands through his sodden hair.

'Ok...ok,' He said. He stood straight and looked around. Melanie watched him. Silent. Joe leapt back on to the jetty, the rope in his hand, and secured the boat once again.

'Joe?' Melanie called to him.

'It's Ok.' He shouted back. 'Plan B.' He ran back towards the start of the jetty and a few moments later emerged from the snowfall with two oars held before him.

'We'll just have to do it old school.' He climbed back in to the boat and released the rope once again.

The boat was immediately pulled back a few feet by the current. Joe fixed the oars into their hooks and began to row them into the dark. Seeing the edge of the town get more distant by just a few feet put a little fire into his heart and he hauled at the oars with vigour.

'Fuck you all you creepy bastards.' He said quietly. The darkness swallowed them.

Chapter Seventeen

As Peake made his way to the hotel he had no expectation of finding them there. The moment he had discovered Duggan he realised that he had been betrayed. His lieutenant's throat had been cut from ear to ear but this was of no importance other than to prove that either his daughter or the lad had the ruthlessness to dispatch a defenceless man, regardless of how dangerous Billy was when not trussed up like a hog.

He didn't think that Clarke had the spine for that kind of work so it was most likely Melanie. The fact that Billy's sigil had been flayed from his arm further underlined her involvement. She meant to leave the town and the government was her ticket out. With Billy's sigil she could do it too. Just walk right out the fucking town, except she wouldn't be walking would she. If she had Clarke under her spell he would be trying to drive them out. Macgregor would take care of that.

There was no chance that anything other than a snow plough could make it on the road out of the Falls and even that was doubtful. He looked down at Billy and the deep ragged trench that almost separated his head from his body. He was no longer concerned about the Government man. He was as good as dead already. What was important now was that he stop *her* from escaping the town.

The men behind him shuffled as they tried to peer over Peake's shoulder and catch sight of Billy. As Peake turned to face them they stepped back as one.

'We're returning to the lodge.' He said and led them out of the house.

It was as they reached the end of the path that the sound of gunfire echoed across the town. Macgregor and his men were armed with shotguns and hunting rifles and there was no mistaking the sound of automatic fire, not the reports of the weapons his men were carrying bursting through the air. Something was happening out there that was not in his script.

Peake's lips pulled back from his teeth, he almost snarled.

'Quickly!' He snapped and strode off back towards the lodge. The others followed.

Chapter Eighteen

Once Kevin was satisfied that every man was armed and that they all carried enough ammunition to reload their weapons at least twice he had them file up onto the back of the truck that Tim had parked outside The Silent Piper. The vehicle was an old but sturdy Leyland and the front had an impressive plough fixed to it. Although the flatbed was sizable the men were mostly stocky and bunched up on the narrow shelves that passed for seating on either side. There was a strong canvas fixed to a frame that protected the men from the wind and snow but it couldn't stop the cold.

They talked in low voices and flasks with potent contents were passed around between them which helped to combat the chill. Once they were all settled Kevin gave those that looked at him with concerned eyes a nod to indicate that he shared that concern but also that this had to be done. He moved to the cab and climbed inside, glad to be out of the snow which was blowing hard.

'This is going to be a hell of a ride Kev.' Tim said

'Aye, I imagine it is.' Kevin replied, his tone neutral and his expression offering no opinion. Tim waited for a few seconds in case his friend added anything to that but Kevin said nothing and stared passively out into the blizzard ahead. Tim flicked the Leyland's headlights to full beam and pressed the accelerator. The truck shuddered a little, as though it was waking up in the cold, and began to push through the snow with ease. Her engine was loud and growled as it powered the huge wheels. The Leyland was well travelled on roads and nights like this.

Tim guided her through the tight roads as though it was a dry summer's day. He could navigate the journey with his eyes shut as far as Dunbannon where the land began to sweep up into the hills that enclosed much of the coastal region and to where Winter Falls was nestled beyond Ardach Coille. The road past Dunbannon was a mystery to him though. He had never attempted to go any further on that route and had thought that he never would.

He wanted to ask Kevin how he was going to find the road that led to Winter Falls. No one had ever found their way there, at least no one that had ever returned to talk about it. But Kevin was still silent. He decided to drive until Kevin told him to do otherwise.

Kevin didn't speak until they reached the Cenotaph. Tim hadn't realised that they were so close to it as after passing Dunbannon he had been required to concentrate more on the lay of the unfamiliar road ahead. It was a blessing that the wind at least had begun to drop and he could now see the twists and turns a little more clearly.

'Hold here Tim.' Kevin finally said and Tim immediately eased off the accelerator to bring the Leyland to a safe stop. Kevin unbuttoned his jacket and reached inside it. He withdrew a small padded envelope and lifted the flap which didn't appear to have been sealed.

'What do ya have there?' Tim enquired.

'I think it's a key Tim.' At this he pulled out what looked like a folded piece of paper until he opened it up and Tim could see that it was made of either stiff cloth or some sort of old parchment. He reached up and turned on the interior light of the cab.

'A key ya say? Tim said craning his head to try and get a better look at the strange paper. 'Looks like a drawing'

'Aye, it is a drawing, but I think it's more than just that.' Kevin now turned to face Tim 'Ya remember those lads that came by a few weeks ago.'

'The Swedish lads?' Tim asked.

'They were Norwegian but aye, those two. They were headin to the Falls they said. Said they had business there.'

'Oh, not tourists then? I thought they were tourists. They asked me some questions about the place but, well you know, I told em there was nothing out there now, best to head over to Lochniver.' Tim looked a little concerned, as though worried that he had not done his civic duty.

'No Tim, those lads weren't tourists and don't worry, they knew what they were doing or at least they seemed to think they did. We got to talking, we talked about the villages that are gone now, about the missing people and we talked about the town that no one could find and they told me they knew how to find it.'

Kevin lifted the paper up to the light and turned it so that Tim could see the symbol that was imprinted upon it. 'They gave me this. They said that they were going to take a look around and that if they didn't come back in a few days that I was to call a number one of em, the big fella with the beard, wrote down for me. They said that people would come and that I was to give em this,' Kevin waggled the page a little. 'Said that it would help them find the town.'

The picture, that appeared to be burned on to the page somehow, looked to be a spiral with a line running through it.

'I'm no following Kev, is that a map o some sort?'

Kevin shook his head 'No mate, like I said I think it's some sort of key. The lad Joe had a letter from there with the same mark on it' He brought the letter back and placed it on his lap, pressing it flat. 'And those weird bastards that come from the town to buy stock from the village, I've seen this same thing on them, when their sleeves have ridden up I've seen it on their arms.'

'Like a password then,' Tim said, 'Like a secret code'.

Kevin pushed his lower lip up 'Maybe it's something like that.' He said.

'Anyway, how many times have you driven past this Cenotaph?' Kevin asked Tim thinking that the men must be getting concerned and very cold.

'Oh...I don't know,' Tim replied. 'A few times I suppose, a long time ago. I try not to come out this far.'

'Aye.' Kevin said, nodding. 'That's understandable, but tell me now have you ever seen that turning up ahead?

Tim looked at Kevin in puzzlement for a moment and then his own eyes turned to where his friends gaze appeared to be focused. To his absolute surprise, barely visible in the headlights that were invaded by swirling snow was a junction. A road that went off from this one and lead off he supposed towards the Ardach Coille.

'Fuck me.' Tim said. 'Where the fuck did that come from?'

'I think it's always been there mate.' Kevin said. 'Let's get going.'

Chapter Nineteen

Joe's biggest concern about his escape plan, accepting they had actually got to the boat had been that the sea would be so rough he would be unable to avoid being thrown on to the rocks around the cliffs, and thus smashed to a pulp. He hadn't considered the sheer freezing cold that now clung about him.

His powerful rowing strokes had kept him warm at first but after the jetty had begun to retreat from sight it was as though any heat there had been inside him had left his body. His hands felt frozen to the oars and he didn't think he would be able to easily release his grip on them. His teeth chattered and there was a dull ache in his legs and feet.

He had tried to talk to Melanie, who didn't seem to be affected by the arctic conditions at all but found that it was too difficult to breathe and make intelligible words at the same time. He was so cold that he had stopped worrying about the sound of the waves breaking over nearby rocks, which he tried to keep to his right so that he could be certain of staying on the coastline. One thing he was certain of was that if the boat tipped and he hit the water he was dead.

But this aside they *were* escaping. The wind was now only an occasional bluster and the snow was rapidly thinning. Even with the numbness of his hands and the slow paralysis of his legs he was rowing with strength and speed. His estimate of how far he would have to row to get to a suitable place to put ashore was nothing but pure guesswork but he figured that no more than thirty minutes of hugging the coast would take him far enough from Winter Falls to continue the journey on foot. He almost managed to smile at the thought. And then he saw Melanie do a strange thing.

She had been looking back towards where the town would be if it were visible in the dark and were the snow not obstructing the view for most the trip so far. Then he noticed her lean forward a little. Her head was lifted almost as though she was sniffing the air, her eyes narrowed. She then took off one of her gloves and reached over the side of the boat and allowed her hand to move through the water.

He wanted to exclaim, 'What the fuck are you doing Mel, the water is fucking freezing!' But all he could manage to say was 'The fuck?'

She appeared to ignore him, her attention at least was elsewhere until she suddenly looked directly at him and shouted, 'Put to shore Joe, NOW!'

Joe blinked at her as though he couldn't make out what she meant. She couldn't mean what she had said, or what he thought she had said, because it would be suicide to row the boat towards the cliffs. He wasn't even sure that he would be able to control the boat nearer the shore when the time came with the force of the waves easily besting his diminishing strength. He was too cold now. He only hoped that the tide would carry them onto a beach, preferably a beach of sand and not bone breaking rocks.

Melanie stood and ran her hand through her hair. Joe could see that she was thinking hard. He said nothing and continued to row, more carefully so as not to unbalance her. She didn't repeat her command to head to the shore, instead, to his absolute shock, she began unbuttoning her jacket and then shrugged it off. Following this she quickly pulled off her sweater and that too was dropped onto the floor of the boat.

Joe stopped rowing. 'Mel, what the fuck are you doing?' He gasped, barely getting the words out through chattering teeth. Melanie remained silent and continued to remove her clothing. Her breasts bulged a little within the lace bra she wore. Joe didn't feel any arousal although he would have welcomed the heat. She sat and began to remove her boots.

'Mel...' Joe tried to bring the oars in so that he could go to her but his fingers were fixed on to the wood, his muscles refusing to unlock.

'Don't Joe.' Melanie said, as though he had tried to offer an unwanted kiss. She pulled off her final boot, the socks she had worn had come off with them. She then artfully slipped out of her jeans. She was naked all but for her panties and bra.

She stood again and reached down for her coat, tugging something out of one of the pockets. It looked like a thick cloth and when Melanie opened it out flat Joe could see that it was patterned on one side. Melanie tossed it to him and it landed on his lap.

'Don't think I'm not grateful Joe, you gave it your best shot.' Melanie said. She stepped forward and knelt in front of him. Her breath was warm on his face. She appeared to be completely unaffected by the terrific cold, her face was ruddy rather than the tinge of blue that coloured Joes cheeks.

As Joe tried to speak again Melanie took the back of his head in her hand and pulled it to her. She kissed him hard on the mouth. Her touch was cool but not cold. Joe couldn't stop tears running from his eyes, the heat of her causing him mild discomfort. Melanie pulled away and stood again.

'Try to stay alive for a while and if you manage to somehow make it to the shore that will get you out.' She pointed to the cloth on his lap, and then, as though stripping to her underwear had not been surprise enough Melanie turned and dived gracefully into the sea.

Joe's eyes goggled. Finally finding some strength and flexibility in his frozen limbs he lurched to where she had been and looked over the edge of the boat and into the black swell of the ocean.

'Melanie!' He shouted, his voice was cracked but he still screamed out her name as he desperately stared into the dark around him.

'What the fuck?' He said, abjectly confused. With effort he stood in the boat but couldn't keep his balance. Melanie had managed to strip with ease and yet Joe found that he could barely stand for more than a few seconds before the motion of the waves forced him to sit.

He was glad that he had sat down for shortly afterwards the boat lurched violently. The wind hadn't changed that he had noticed and he thought for a moment that a sudden squall or current had tugged at the boat. He realised that he was moving, quite rapidly, back in the direction he had just come from.

He shook his head as though to shake up his thoughts. Quickly he took his position once again and began to row to counter what must be a tidal current. The boat continued to move forwards, back towards the town.

'Jesus fucking Christ.' Joe grunted and hauled at the oars using all of his remaining strength. The paddles splashed at the sea with each furious motion but the boat continued on its unwanted course. It was now moving faster towards the town with him fighting against it than it had been when Joe had been rowing away from the place.

He let go of the oars and they swung back, hanging uselessly in the water. The boat continued to move forwards at speed.

Very soon the lights of the jetty came into view and shortly after that Joe could make out figures standing on the edge of it. Waiting for him to return. What Melanie had said about the rituals, about magic and spells started to seem less like ignorant superstition. Was it magic that was propelling the boat back to the town?   A spell of some kind?

He remembered the pistol.

He felt its weight against his chest. Deep inside the chill of his fear a small spark ignited at the thought of the gun. He would shoot Peake, perhaps with him shot, hopefully dead, the crowd would run for cover. He would have to shoot Macgregor too, he had no problem with that, in fact if the giant policeman was there he would shoot him first and then Peake. Then he would take a hostage or even just run, they would be panicked so he could probably just blitz through them, brandishing the gun, shouting 'GET THE FUCK DOWN! MOVE AND I'LL FUCKING SHOOT YOU!'

It was a plan at least.

His shaking hand retrieved the pistol and then pulled bullets out from his other pocket. His hands shook so badly that a couple of them immediately fell into the pool of water at the bottom of the boat. He ignored them. He still had enough to load the gun. He repeatedly blew on his fingers so that he could manipulate the little brass shells. When the last bullet was chambered he snapped the pistol shit and checked the safety catch was off. He had seen enough movies to not fuck that up.

He flicked the little lever down. 'Ready.' He said.

He wouldn't let them see it until he was close enough, until the boat was almost at the jetty. If he was too close they might hit him with a pole, throw a net or even shoot him with their own guns so he would wait until he could see Peake and Macgregor and then blow them away. He put his hands into his pockets and his right thumb cocked the hammer back.

Chapter Twenty

Macgregor had been suspicious of the abandoned Nissan as soon as he had seen it, and Joe's escape into the forest seemed foolhardy but had already decided that the boy was half-witted and chose to see where the tracks took him.

It was probable that the vehicle wouldn't have gotten any further than another mile but that would have been a mile less on foot. He supposed that the forest might also offer some cover for him and girl but as his men all had strong torches that wasn't going to help them too much.

He instructed his men to head into the tree line and to be careful not to disturb the tracks. Once inside it became case of following the disturbed snow. They had clearly tried to hide their path by crossing over brambles. Morons. They would soon be in his sights. But when the tracks abruptly stopped Macgregor immediately knew that he had been duped.

'Fuckers'! He said.

Macgregor stood over the final footprints that had been left in the drift. He shone his torch into these and then at those that preceded them. A closer look revealed that there were footprints inside, facing the opposite way.

'Little fuckers.' he growled.

His men stood around him looking confused.

'Which way they go?' One of them asked, still looking around for more prints.

Macgregor lifted the torch up, into the speakers face. He was returning but wasn't yet at an advanced stage, his eyes bulged a little though and in the harsh torchlight Macgregor thought he looked like a Mackerel that lay on a fishmonger's tray of ice.

'They doubled back you fucking imbecile.' He snarled. He wanted to smash the man's vacant face to a pulp. His rage was building but he had to keep it in check, it was forbidden to cause harm to a returning male and the consequences were dire even by Falls standards. Macgregor cursed again and then headed back to the road with large forceful strides.

It was as he reached the Nissan that he saw the full beam of a vehicle's headlights sweep across the sky, then the noise of a heavy engine became apparent. Macgregor stared ahead towards the crest of the hill where the road continued on and out of the town.

His face was a picture of confusion. No one from the Falls should be out tonight. No one from outside of the town should be able to get through the ward. Had the boy somehow got so far ahead that he had raised an alarm, bought help? Impossible. He hadn't enough time, not even if he had been in the Nissan and managed to get further than was probable.

'You lot! Get the fuck over here.' He shouted to the remaining men who struggled with the deep drift at the stile. He turned to those already waiting for their instructions.

'Right, you.' He pointed to one of the youngest men, a youth in his late teens who everybody called 'Coop' and who only bore slight signs of returning. 'You can drive, right?' Coop nodded. He had learned to drive a year ago but had yet to be allowed to travel out of the town. It would be a few years before he would receive his marks and training for the outside world.

'Bring the van up and park it next to this.' Macgregor flicked his thumb at the Nissan. Coop didn't need to be told twice, he turned and quickly made his way to the vehicle.

Macgregor looked up to the top of the road again, there were no lights but the sound of whatever was coming, it sounded like a strong engine, was closer.

'Everyone, get your fucking weapons ready and turn your torches off. There's something going to come over that fucking rise and when it does I want yeh to all direct yeh lights at it and let those fucking guns go. D'ya understand me?'

All heads nodded and the townsmen took up positions around the Nissan and the van after Coop had pulled it around.

Macgregor went to the Jeep to fetch his rifle. As he was pulling the Remington from its canvas cover the space behind him was illuminated and a volley of shots thundered through the air.

The drift either side of the road was deeper than Tim had encountered on the route to the Cenotaph and a couple of times a substantial volume of snow was forced under the plough, causing the truck to swerve dangerously. Even over the roar of the engine Tim could hear a chorus of curses from the lads in the back each time they were thrown across each other.

Kevin peered through the windscreen and tried to garner some idea of how close they might be to coast. The Ardach Coille loomed up to the right of them, but it wasn't a good point of reference as it easily covered a good fifteen miles.

A minute previously he thought he had seen a light of some kind as they had taken a long bend that followed the forests edge, but it had vanished and he wasn't sure it wasn't just a reflection of his own trucks headlights. His scrutiny did allow him to see that the road was about to take a dip.

'Take it easy here Tim, from the looks of it the road drops up ahead.' Kevin said.

'Aye mate.' Tim replied and eased his foot off the accelerator. He didn't want to let the truck slow too much as a loss of momentum could cause it to struggle in the drifts.

As Kevin had suspected the front of the truck bowed as the road became a fairly steep descent. Snow cascaded on to the windscreen as it was forced upwards by the plough and suddenly the whole cab was lit by lights from somewhere beyond.

There was a sharp crack as the windscreen fractured almost at its centre. It was followed by the noise of distressed metal and the shattering of one of the headlights.

Memories of side street ambushes in Afghanistan came quickly to Kevin's mind and he ducked down, pulling Tim with him.

'HIT THE BRAKE! Kevin shouted, and Tim fumbled for it with his feet. His hands still gripped the steering wheel and the sudden jolt made him swerve the truck. Before the Sally had finished her graceful slide Kevin opened his door and pushed it wide. As soon as truck stopped he dove out into the snow.

'LADS GET OUT! GET OUT NOW AND GET TO COVER.' Kevin shouted as loudly as he could.

The men had first thought that Tim had run them over another lump of snow, but as they heard Kevin bawling and the sound of gunfire that punctuated his cry, they all jumped out and made for the side of the truck.

Kevin looked into the cab. Tim was lying low and signalled that he should get out of the way. Kevin nodded and scrambled behind the truck to the lads. More shots rang out. There was the odd 'DUNK' as a bullet hit the cab of the truck but most appeared to go wide or high.

'Well, looks like we were fuckin expected.' Kevin grunted.

'Is Timmy Ok? One of the lads asked anxiously.

'Aye he's fine.' Kevin said, and he believed it was so. The shots coming at them were mostly shotgun rounds and if the range was what he judged it to be they hadn't a hope of penetrating the metal of the truck. There were at least two to three rifles out there as well however, it would have been one of them that cracked the windscreen, but Tim was safe so long as he kept his head down.

'Ok fellas, I admit, that came as a bit o' a surprise.' Kev wiped away a film of perspiration. His cold hand revealed how hot and flushed his face was. 'I don't know how many we have doon there but I think at least six or seven. They've got shotguns and a few rifles and from what I can gather most of them couldn't shoot a fucking elephant if it was sat in front of them.' There was a low murmur of agreement.

'Barney, can yer see oot?' Kevin asked the he little tailor who was peering around the side of the back of the truck.

'I can see em movin aboot Kev,' he replied.

A few more shots rang out and Barney ducked back. 'I don't think they are coming up the road though.'

'Ok Cheers Barney. Give me a second lads.' Kevin moved back around to the open cab door. Tim had turned off the engine. He looked across at Kevin as he lay on the seat.

'Fancy meeting you here Kev.' Tim said, as his friend had appeared at the door.

'Very good Tim.' Kevin said dryly.

He pulled his M16 from the foot well where it had dropped. 'In a minute we are goin to light those fuckers up so much that they will think we are saving Private Ryan. As soon as we stop, fire up the engine and try to get this bitch straight.

'Nae bother Kev.' Tim replied. Kevin made to move away.

'Kev!' Tim called to him. Kev turned. 'Yes mate?'

'Could yer get a fuckin move on, I'm getting a proper cramp.'

'Cunt.' Kevin said.

He returned to the rear of the truck and as he did there was the sound of a harsh deep voice shouting in the distance. Shortly afterwards another volley of shots rang out. A few more picked at the cab but still most flew harmlessly into the night.

'Right lads they are getting bold, some cunt's shoutin the odds down there so I think it's about time we showed em what we've come all this way for.'

He was acknowledged with stronger murmurs of agreement. 'We are goin to unload into those lights, doesn't matter whether we hit anything, let em just see what they are up against and that should be that.' At this there were clicks and the shuffle of metal as weapons were cocked.

'We give em a half fucking clip, then wait. Tim is gonna start up the truck and swing her round, keep her arse in front of you just in case they have a spine. And in case they do, we then deliver the rest o' the clip to make sure they get the message. Right?'

A series of 'ayes' and 'right kev' followed and the men took position as best they could on each side of the truck.

'Ready em lads.' Kevin said. He waited until the lights from the torches swept across their position. He brought the M16 up to his shoulder and gauged the drop off, the snow had become lighter and the wind had eased considerably. 'God help you.' Kevin said quietly, and squeezed the trigger.

Chapter Twenty One

As the little boat neared the Jetty Joe imagined he would see Peake stood at the front of a group who were gathered about him like evil little elves around Santa. An electric lamppost, Joe hadn't noticed it on either of his previous two visits to the Jetty, was illuminated, and it cast a wash of bright light over the crowd.

Peake called out to him. 'Welcome back Mr Clarke. I see you and my daughter decided to take in the Bay this fine evening.'

Joe realised that the old bastard couldn't yet make out that Melanie wasn't on the boat.

Joe's hand had warmed a little in his pocket and he delicately ran his thumb over the outline of the pistol. Other than a few minor scrapes at school Joe had never been involved in violence at any level. An hour and a half of free weights at the gym every other day was the only period of aggression he had really had experienced in his twenties, but right now he strongly desired to watch Peake and Macgregor drop to the floor screaming.

Torches sprang into life and blinded him for a moment. The snow had stopped all but for a few flakes that vanished as they hit an almost peaceful sea. The storm had dropped faster than Joe had thought possible. He couldn't know that Mother Nature could pick the wind up just as quickly and because of this began to think that more of Melanie's sorcery crap might be at work.

Once his eyes had accommodated the initial glare of the torchlight the Joe could make out individual figures and sure enough there was Peake, almost has he had pictured him, stood with a gaggle of his henchmen gathered about him. He couldn't see Macgregor but he dismissed this, it was something to deal with when required. For now, Peake was stood right there at the front a the shit eating grin pasted across his face. Which remained until he could see that Joe was alone.

'Where is she Mr Clarke?' Peake shouted out to him as the boat moved steadily towards the Jetty. Joe could see one of Peake's men had a rope curled in his hand ready to tie the boat down. He wasn't surprised to see that at least a couple of the men had shotguns. Joe said nothing.

'Did she abandon you once she had poor Billy's skin?' Peake smiled. 'I'll bet she's giving old Macgregor a run for his money right now eh?'

Joe collected his thoughts for a moment. Peake was fishing, he was sure of it. '*He must mean the gunfire, but we were together, here when we heard that.*'

He considered, that being the case, what Macgregor might have been firing at. He took another look into the group Peake stood in front of. There was still no sign of the giant Policeman. Joe gripped the handle of his pistol and prepared to draw it out and shoot at Peake until he dropped.

'*Got to be close enough to the Jetty to climb out of here fast.*' He thought. '*Shoot Peake, climb out, shoot more if needed, run. Get to a vehicle. Shoot Macgregor if he appears.*'

It was the sum of his plan and his execution of it went perfectly only up to the point that he pulled the pistol out and pointed it at Peake, who was now a mere three or four feet away.

He stood up once the boat was only an arm's length from the jetty. The man with the rope, balding and with bulging eyes had knelt to toss the hooped end of it over one of the hooks in which the nearest oar was slotted. Peake had leaned forward with his hand outstretched, still with the shit eating grin, he meant to help Joe up onto the platform. Joe reached out his right hand which Peake didn't realise held the pistol.

Joe paused. His finger had tightened on the trigger but had stopped. His mind screamed at him to pull, to fire the gun directly at Peake's chest. The bullet would surely pass straight through whatever passed for a heart at this distance.

He couldn't do it. He felt as though he were in a Peckinpah movie, time had slowed, his vision expanded, movement on each side of the boat caught his attention. Peake's shit eating grin dropped, his eyes widened and his thin lips formed a cavernous 'O.'

As Joe failed to find the courage or at least the violence within him to kill a man, something launched itself from the water to his left and grasped the wooden frame of the Jetty. Something with slick, blue grey skin, something that looked human but wasn't.

As it climbed the timbers the men, who couldn't see that Joe's outstretched hand held a pistol directed at their leader, stepped back to allow the thing room to clamber up to them. It turned its head to the side, to look directly at Joe and its large, bright eyes, set aside a batrachian head stared balefully at him, it opened its maw which was filled with small needle like teeth, and issued a low, guttural snarl.

Time suddenly snapped back to its proper position in space and Joe found that he had lost microseconds during the event. He saw that he had swung the gun away from Peake and towards the thing that had emerged from the water. His conscience didn't demand pause or debate as it had with Peake, who was human, instead his finger immediately twitched at the trigger and the pistol blasted out two bullets in rapid succession.

The first shot was true and entered the things skull just above its right eye. Matter blasted up and out from it and the eye rolled upwards in its socket as though trying to see what had just entered its brain. The second shot went high and wide but the thing was already falling back into the ocean.

Joe screamed and brought the pistol around, it was as though firing the gun had released his own safety catch. He fired two more shots at anything that was in view. Neither struck anything but air. He heard himself shouting as the deafening blasts began to fade but had no idea what words were coming out.

He gripped the pistol with his other hand as he had seen in cop movies, bracing the weapon and steadying his aim. Peake was still close but was trying to push past the panicked men. Joe fired again, three shots roared from the pistol in quick succession, but the Doctor was already falling as he had taken aim. Peake had tripped and been sent sprawling, an accident that saved his life. Instead the man whose legs Peake had fell against caught all of the rounds from Joe's shots in his chest, neck and head. Joe roared in panic.

He took a firm step across the boat and launched himself at the Jetty as the thing had done. The pistol dropped from his hand and into the black sea.

He had been right about the men fleeing from him, even though he hadn't taken out Peake. The plan was still good. He didn't want to think about the creature and blanked it from his mind.

His leap to the Jetty had been sound and he pushed himself up, lifting a leg over the side, he could see Peake, the fucker was scrambling along on all fours, trying to get away from him.

Then there were more gunshots and they couldn't have come from his pistol. Joe almost fell from the Jetty as he ducked thinking that they were shots coming at him from the townsfolk.

He saw that the group of Falls men was backing up towards him, their heads were switching back and forth from him to the street and back again as though they didn't know where the greater threat lay. More shots sounded and Joe saw at least two of the mob near the front drop.

Macgregor appeared. He was hard to miss as he towered over all of them. The big man was taking aim with a rifle but it wasn't pointed towards Joe, rather there must be someone or something at the end of the street.

For a moment it appeared that Joe was forgotten and he recommenced his climb up and on to the Jetty. He hoped it was the police, the real police or even better the fucking army had come to flush this turd of town into the sea. This brought his thoughts back to the thing that he had shot.

Something pulled at his jacket. Something had emerged from the water beneath and grabbed at him. Joe felt himself be pulled violently backwards and then went into shock as ice cold water filled his world.

Chapter Twenty Two

Macgregor tried to catch a sight of who was behind the truck. He recognised it. It belonged to one of the Roscregan lot, but even with the strong torches fixed on it he couldn't see anyone clearly although at least one had been skulking around by the cab. His men were appalling shots and he began to wonder if there was any chance of them hitting anything even if they moved closer. No return fire had come from whoever was taking cover but he couldn't be certain that they didn't have firearms. There wasn't a farmer worth his salt in the highlands that didn't own at least a shotgun.

He was considering his options, they couldn't stand about here all night that was certain, when sheer hell erupted around him. In an instant he was deafened by the sound of dozens of bullets that tore into the Nissan and his men. He hit the floor as blood, teeth and brains sprayed across him and the snow. It must have only been a few seconds but the onslaught seemed relentless. Caught completely by surprise the others had looked on in shock as an invisible wall of death descended upon them.

Instinct took over Macgregor and he began to crawl across the slush to the Jeep. The volley ended although a few occasional shots still rang out. He climbed in to the driver's seat, Coop had left the keys in the ignition. He didn't think to look where the young man might be, he had no interest in the condition of any of them.

A second volley pummelled the position and Macgregor thought that the attackers must have merely re-loaded. He dropped down below the dashboard and waited out the barrage.

He thought that a couple of shots might have been returned by his men after the second attack from the top of the road subsided but he didn't really care. He sprang up, turned the ignition and as soon as the engine kicked in slammed the jeep into reverse.

He didn't turn on the headlights so that he presented less of a target but as he reversed torches began to appear from the behind the truck and a few shots whizzed by him. One bullet passed through the windscreen leaving a hole the size of a golf ball and turning the glass into a fractured mess.

Macgregor reversed as far as he dared and then hit the brake and turned the steering wheel as far over as it would go. The Jeep almost turned back on itself but it was enough for Macgregor to hit the accelerator and get it headed in down the road without driving straight into a drift.

At the top of the road the truck's engine roared into life.

'Ok lads get in.' Kevin yelled. The Roscregan men quickly returned to the back of Sally and Kevin ran around to the cab and clambered in.

'We good to go?' Tim asked.

'Aye.' Kevin replied. 'Fuckin go fer it'.

Tim had to steer carefully to bring the big truck around and not get stuck in the drift either side of him and so kept his upper body as low as he could as he turned her, meanwhile Kevin leaned out of the window with his M16 braced and ready to fire at any sign of movement. Finally, the truck was back in position, Kevin took his rifle from the window but held it ready to fire if needed. Tim recommenced his journey down the road.

As he approached the Nissan, which looked as though it had been through a shredder Tim frowned.

'That was the boy's car no?'

'Aye.' Kevin replied.

'You don't think...'

'No.' Kevin interrupted.

Tim saw a figure running across the snow towards the woods. He looked to Kevin. 'Let him go.' Kevin said, 'I want to see where that Jeep is going.

Tim nodded and steered the truck carefully around the SUV.

'Christ almighty.' Tim gasped as he saw the bodies of their attackers sprawled around it. 'Fucking hell Kev, we did that.' It was almost a question.

'They shot first.' Kevin said. And that ended the conversation.

Chapter Twenty Three

Macgregor had almost crashed into the swarm of bodies as they scrambled off the Jetty and into the road. He jumped out of the jeep and grabbed one of the men to find out what the fuck was going on but heard the truck's breaks squeal to a halt not far behind him.

He dragged the man, who had a shotgun in his hands, to the side of the Jeep and bawled at him as he pushed him to a kneeling stance. 'Keep your fucking eyes open and if anything moves down there you shoot, do you understand me?' The man nodded. Macgregor turned to the rest of the group who were staring back towards the Jetty.

'You lot, what the fuck are you doing? Get your weapons and get into cover.' Macgregor stormed into them and pushed each man into a defensible position. Peake had taken the best of the town's men for himself, which was only natural for the arrogant, cowardly fuck, so these would at least have a chance of shooting in the right direction.

Peake couldn't understand how it had all gone so horribly wrong. He lay flat behind a stack of crates that were marked with a faded stencil that read 'WEIGHTS'.

The Government man had killed a brother, right in front of him, his thoughts reeled. 'Clarke had a fucking gun POINTED RIGHT AT ME!' His mind had shrieked with shock and disbelief.

He had to get away from here, get to the lodge. The others would be here soon and would take care of it all. He had no clue where Clarke had gone, no idea where Melanie was but at least Macgregor was here now. Peake looked out from his hiding place and along the Jetty but nothing stirred at the end of it.

They were coming though, the scouts had arrived and that fucking imbecile Clarke had killed one of them, but they were coming and they would tear that fucking London retard to pieces.

The thought of this relaxed Peake a little, he even managed to etch a grin onto his face. He heard Macgregor shouting orders and thought that it seemed to be quiet and under control, enough for him to make an appearance, but he had come to this conclusion too soon.

No sooner had he stood up than the air was filled with gunshots. One of the crates near to him was struck, sending up a shower of splinters.

He heard Macgregor roar at the men, 'Take em, kill those fuckers.' He bellowed. Peake raised his head so that he could see over the crate that defended him and saw Macgregor standing with a rifle aimed down the street. He fired two shots in succession then got to his knees as fire was returned. He couldn't help but notice that there was considerably more coming back at them than his men were firing out.

'Was it the army?' He thought. If it was it was all was done, it would be Innsmouth all over again and if he didn't die now his masters would make him die a thousand times over. He crawled around the side of the crate, trying to ensure that it shielded him as best he could and shouted to Macgregor.

'Macgregor, over here, Macgregor! Here man!'

His lieutenant turned and seeing Peake crawling behind the crate scowled.

'What the fuck is going on?' Peake shouted. 'Is it the army?'

'No!' Macgregor shouted back and then, after looking towards the attackers, sprinted over to Peake. Even crouched Macgregor was enormous and Peake felt safer with him in front of him than when he was behind the crate filled with iron weights.

'It's the fucking Roscregan lot.' Macgregor spat. 'Armed to the fucking teeth.'

'Ok.' Peake said. 'Don't worry, they're coming, just keep them busy and they will be taken care of once our brothers get here.'

'Keep them busy?' Macgregor snarled. 'They are shooting at us from five hundred yards down the road with assault rifles, our shotguns can't penetrate a fucking tee-shirt at that range.'

'Just do your fucking job Macgregor and I'll do mine.' Peake snapped. 'Do it or explain to *them*.' Peake cocked his head towards the sea. 'Explain how you let a bunch of villagers get past you.'

Macgregor stared at Peake with sheer loathing painted into his expression. He wanted to grab Peake's greasy skull and crush it in his hands. He spat at the floor as though speaking to Peake had left a bad taste in his mouth and returned to his position.

Peake retreated behind the crate. Macgregor just had to keep the Roscregan men tied up for a short while and then, then they would hear the Roscregan men screaming and it would all be fine again.

Chapter Twenty Five

As Joe awoke he struggled to open his eyes, the lids were heavy and felt sore. He could tell that his hair was wet but the rest of him seemed dry, and he was warm. He tried to sit up but his body ached too much to allow that just yet.

Someone was talking. No, not talking, more like praying, as there was a gentle, sensual sound to it and he thought there was repetition. It was almost certainly a female voice he could hear and as the only female voice he had heard in a week belonged to Melanie he recognised it almost instantly.

'Mel...' He tried to call out but produced a weak whisper. The praying voice continued. Joe used what strength he had to turn on to his side, it hurt, but he managed it. He closed his eyes tightly for a few seconds and then slowly forced his eyelids to open.

He was in a large room lit only by flickering oil torches. At its centre was a circular wall of brickwork about a foot in height and from within it an eerie blue light reflected off the sides. Stood before the ring, naked, with her profile presented to him and head bowed was Melanie.

He almost smiled at the sight of her but then his eyes focused on something else lying nearby. A man, with a thick beard and tattered clothes, typical of a hill walker. He lay dead, very dead. His eyes were gone and his open mouth was black with congealed blood.

'*Christ almighty.*' Joe thought. '*Does this never stop?*'

He croaked out her name again, it was a little clearer but she continued her prayer. Finally, Melanie lifted her arms up above her head and said more loudly and in a language Joe couldn't comprehend, 'Iä! Iä! Cthulhu fhtagn! Ph'nglui mglw'nafh Cthulhu R'lyeh wgah-nagl fhtagn.'

Her arms dropped to her sides and she remained still and silent. Joe didn't call now. It felt wrong to interrupt her, as though he had spied her in church in deep reflection.

At last she turned to face him and could see that he had woken. She walked towards him. To Joe she looked almost serene.

He realised that he was wearing a long heavy cotton robe and he was naked underneath it. He supposed that Melanie had removed his wet clothes and put this on to him to stop him dying of hypothermia. How she had stopped him from drowning, from being drowned, he couldn't reason.

Suddenly he began to spasm. His mind had visited the moment when, as ice cold water had filled his throat, he had seen a huge glassy eye next to his face as he thrashed in the water, he felt the hand, large and powerful that gripped his face as it pushed him deeper into the dark depths.

But no, that was a nightmare, hysterical dreams, the hand that had grabbed him had been small and soft. It had drawn him through the water and to the shore. He had seen pink skin, a slim body.

Melanie's cool touch that brought him out of his panic.

'It's Ok Joe, you are in shock, relax.' She stroked his forehead and then trailed her fingers down his cheek.

Joe coughed a little and then felt his mouth and throat lubricate a little as his body began to produce saliva again.

'What happened...there were things...in the water' He said.

'Deep Ones.' Melanie said as naturally as though she were naming a breed of cat. 'Peake called them.'

'I don't understand.' Joe eased himself on to his back, enough strength had returned to his limbs to allow him to bring his hands to his face and he covered it rubbing gently at his eyes.

'It doesn't matter Joe, this is the end of Winter Falls, at least for us.'

'Us?' Joe said.

'For me, for Peake and my brothers, for Macgregor. It's over, here at least. Those who survive today will have to move on, some won't be able to of course, they are too far gone in their returning but not close enough to change. They must be taken care of. The Wardens will scatter, those that live, and they will find other broods to protect.

Melanie's words meant nothing to him. He couldn't understand, Wardens, broods, the things were... Deep Ones, he remembered those? He shook his head.

'Who's he?' He nodded towards the dead man.

'I'm not sure but I think he knew what was happening here, the man in the forest, what remained of the man you saw in the forest, he was with him. Father will have used this one to call the Deep Ones.'

'What, another ritual? Jesus this place needs burning to the fucking ground.' Tears began to well in Joes eyes.

'It's Ok Joe. It will make sense soon. But you will need to be brave. Mother is coming, she is coming to take me home. I am her first child in a long while to be able to speak to her and she will protect me.'

'I don't... Mother?' Joe said. He managed to move to a sitting position with Melanie's aid and was able to look at her face to face. She looked different. Not markedly so but her eyes were a little bigger he thought, as though pressured a from behind.

'Joe, I told you that there are no women in Winter Falls over twenty-five years old and the reason for this is that they are all murdered, sacrificed.' Joe opened his mouth to speak but Melanie placed a finger on his lips to silence him. 'Every twenty-five years Deep Ones come ashore to breed with human women. They do this because a pure bred Deep One has little to no attunement to the *Essence*. This is a powerful force through which the stuff that you would call magic is projected. However only the female offspring of these unions can utilise the essence fully, males can only tap the shallowest depths of it.

This is anathema to Father Dagon, he who rules the depths while the Great Old One sleeps. Father Dagon is the strongest of all Deep Ones but this is only because he won't allow Mother Hydra, a sister of sorts, to claim her own brood.'

Joe couldn't hide his confusion. It was visible in every crease and line of his face, in his trembling lips and wide eyes.

'They are here now to protect their secret and to destroy us Joe.' Melanie said.

Joe had made nothing of anything that she had said but a question crossed his mind.

'Is Peake really your Dad?' He asked

Melanie shook her head and smiled a little 'No, he isn't.' Some women are brought in to give birth to human daughters and they will be raised to look after the brood. All of the girls born of Deep Ones will not, they are taken to the Falls and offered to the Father as sacrifice. But my mother switched me out with another, a human child, Peake's child.'

'If this is true then, if the monsters out there...' Joe stopped, if Melanie truly believed what she was saying then technically she was one of them, those eyes. He decided to alter his question 'If the things that attacked me are here so that all of this can be kept a secret then why tell me?'

The smile that had appeared on Melanie's face faded.

'Mother Hydra can see what will come, she has seen what Dagon cannot because she can see into the Essence. It is a gift that very few of the Elder Gods possess.

The Great Lord is dead, but eternal, and when the stars are right he will rise again, this is prophecy. Dagon is in thrall to him and obeys his every command but Mother Hydra has seen what he will bring to Earth, to time and space, and seeks to aid mankind Joe. Only with mankind as allies can she stop his return. This is her home as well as yours.'

Joe gazed at her, he let his eyes fall from hers and sweep over her naked figure, '*How can someone so beautiful be so fucked in the head.*' He thought.

He felt a vibration through the floor and looked down. 'Did you feel that?' He asked

'She is here.' Melanie said.

'She?' Joe said 'Mother Hydra?'

'Yes.' Melanie replied.

'Ok.' Joe said, feeling his old self return. 'So what do we do now? I assume that Macgregor and his band of merry men are still out there somewhere. Where are we by the way?'

'We are inside the lodge you saw when you visited the town. Macgregor is busy with your friends, the Deep Ones have come ashore and are attacking them."

'My friends?" Joe said.

'The village men, from Roscregan. Somehow they got through the ward and assaulted the town, but the Deep Ones are strong and they are legion, your friends won't stand a chance.' Melanie replied.

'So, that's what they were looking at when I was pulled under, what was going on down the road.' Joe said, 'I've got to help' He carefully got to his feet.

Melanie stood and steadied him by his elbow. 'You can't help, you are in no fit state and besides they have guns and they still won't be able to hold back the Deep Ones.'

'I've not heard shots.' Joe said.

'The lodge is sound-proofed.' Melanie said. Joe looked at the dead Norwegian and thought that at least made sense.

'I've got to help Kevin if he's out there, he tried to help me.' Joe looked around the lodge to find an exit. There were two standard doors set either side of the wall closest to him and at the far side a large double door.

'Is that the way out?' He said

'Your friends are already dead Joe, just stay until Mother is ready for me.'

Joe ignored her and walked stiffly towards the door. Another vibration ran through the floor and this time the walls shuddered sending down showers of plaster. Melanie kept pace with him.

'Can't you put some clothes on?' He said.

'I don't need them.' Melanie said

'I was thinking more of me than you to be honest.' Joe replied. When he reached the double door he pulled on the handle and one side swung open. He found himself in a large foyer that was empty except for a few big but simple wooden chairs. Directly across the room was an ancient looking door, obviously the other side of the one he had examined when he had first seen the lodge.

He walked over to it and turned the handle. As he did so Melanie's hand closed over his.

'Nothing you have seen comes close to this Joe.' She said.

Joe turned the handle and opened the door.

Chapter Twenty Six

Once past the remains of the Nissan and the spectacle of the corpses Tim focused on chasing after the Jeep to try and shake the terrible sight from his thoughts. The head start the driver had got was quickly lost as it skidded and ploughed into a drift. The Jeep was undamaged but it had cost the driver valuable time as he had reversed out of the verge and back on to the road.

The truck was a beast to control on the ice but Tim had negotiated worse, he had been through mud and rock falls with the old girl and knew how to handle her. Watching the Jeep's lights swerve violently showed that he was in pursuit of a man who didn't know how to get the best of out such a vehicle.

When they entered the town proper Kevin observed the outlines of the buildings ahead as best he could. It was obvious that the driver would go to wherever he could find support and Kevin didn't want to run his men into an ambush. Whenever the Jeep hit a corner and vanished from sight Kevin instructed Tim to 'go easy' and reluctantly Tim gave up a little of the ground he had made.

The snow had ceased falling with any real strength and visibility was now as good as it was likely to get with only the widely-spaced streetlights to illuminate the way. They had come to a long wide road when Tim and Kevin saw the Jeep slide to a halt ahead and Kevin told his friend to hit Sally's brakes.

Tim performed a manoeuvre like the one he had done at the hill, hand-braking the vehicle so that its back end skidded across the road and presented instant cover for the men who promptly jumped out of it and took position. Once again he felt the mild buffeting on the cab as the men seated on the left side took a small dive into their friends on the right. Tim managed to grin a little.

Kevin saw a man, a huge man quickly exit the Jeep and at the same time a crowd suddenly emerged from the right hand side of the road. His first thought was that it was an ambush, that the big man had radioed ahead, but he realised that that there was some altercation taking place behind the fellow. Some looked down the road towards the truck others back to where they had appeared from. Kevin couldn't know that because of the noise of the truck he had missed the sound of Joe firing at the Deep One but as he observed the confused crowd there were three loud reports that sounded to Kevin suspiciously like those his own pistol might make.

He leaned out of the cab and braced his rifle to his shoulder, drawing a bead on the big man. At this range it was unlikely he would hit but it would be close enough to cause a scare. If that was Joe firing the pistol a distraction might be the difference between life and death.

He opened fire with a short burst and saw the whole crowd duck as one as the shots tore into a stack of crates to the right of the big man. Unfortunately, as he had neglected to inform the Roscregan lads of his intent to simply draw the crowd's attention suddenly the whole street was filled with the roar of automatic fire.

The lads had taken it as a cue to begin an assault and from either side of the cab orange bursts of flame punctuated the air. The people at the top of the road scattered and the Jeep shook as rounds impacted on its frame.

'Stop firing, Stop firing!' Kevin bawled. The shots rapidly dwindled.

'Fucks sake.' Kevin shouted from the cab window. He opened the door and jumped down to them. The lads all waited for instruction.

'Don't fire unless I say, or you really feel you have too. Alright?'

They all nodded. Kevin looked back to the top of the road and could see that the men there were taking defensive positions. He could tell that some of them at least had guns, rifles and shotguns which sat well with him, this meant that his men had not just fired on an unarmed crowd.

He was worried however that none of them appeared to be concerned with whatever had made them run to the road. Had they killed Joe? Was that why?

He harboured a wishful thought that as they had just lost people up on the road, the big man would have told them what kind of force they were up against, and they had just experienced a pretty powerful volley, surely they would just give up now. They would just hand over Joe and let them leave. Kevin stepped around the cab a little.

'Bring the lad out to us, let him go and we'll leave.' He shouted. There was no reply. Kevin looked at Tim who had shuffled around behind him. 'You think they heard that?' He said.

'They heard. 'Tim replied.

Kevin moved further around the side of the truck and kept his rifle held low. 'This won't end well for anyone if it goes any further, give us the lad, and we'll be on our way.'

This time a reply came by the way of a volley of shots. The shotgun blasts were loud and the rounds unleashed fell well short, however the rifle shots whizzed through the air and a couple hit the cab forcing Kevin to duck back to safety.

'Told you they heard.' Tim said.

'Aye, thanks.' Kevin replied.

'What do we do now?' Tim asked

'I'll be honest, I hadn't really thought this far ahead.' He looked at the buildings around him, at the rotten signs and dark alleys filled with unused sea fishing equipment. Even with its layer of snow the town gave off an impression of being in decay. 'This place is fucked, I've never seen anywhere like it.'

'Like old wild west towns.' Tim stated.

'What?'

'It's like those gold-rush towns that are abandoned in the Westerns.' Tim replied

Kevin nodded. It was a good comparison. 'What are they hiding here?' He said quietly.

'Kev, they are moving mate.' Curly Bateman, a tall and serious looking villager spoke. Like Kevin he was ex-military and he indicated with a nod of his head that Kevin should take a look.

Kevin returned to the edge of the cab and observed the group. They appeared to be backing up, retreating further down the road. He couldn't see the big chap but someone was barking orders to them and he assumed it was probably the same man.

Kevin thought hard. A standoff wasn't going to work as they could be flanked, plus they were all going to get very cold soon. They could assault, the rifles had a huge range advantage and this would push the Falls men back, but to what end? They wouldn't talk with him so the odds were not good for negotiation. Perhaps if he could take down the big man...

A startling cry of pain rang out from one of the men on the other side of the truck and as Kevin whirled around to see who it was a shot was fired close to him. Suddenly there were figures converging on all of them, charging in and jumping at the men. Kevin pulled his rifle up to his hip and pulled the trigger as two of the attackers launched themselves at him.

The M16's rounds tore across the middle of this assailants and blood sprayed into the air. It was then that saw that they were not men.

The things that were pouring from the alleys to the right of the truck were short and muscular, their heads were big, disproportionate to their bodies and elongated. Large eyes stared out from either side of their heads and their mouths were large and opened wide revealing vicious rows of needle like teeth.

The Roscregan men screamed as the things overwhelmed them, forcing some of them against the truck and to the ground. Kevin quickly regained his wits and brought the stock of the M16 down onto the skull of one of the things that had borne Tim to the floor. It shuddered and was pushed to the side by Tim who had a look of sheet terror on his face.

Curly was still on his feet and had pulled a pistol from his pocket, he fired wildly into the creatures that were coming on to them, he didn't dare to shoot those already around him in case he caught his friends.

Switching the M16 to semi-automatic Kevin began to the spray the creatures with bursts. The effect on them was devastating, limbs were wrenched from bodies and jets of blood danced in the air.

From his knees, Tim drew out a pistol but instead of firing began to beat at the creatures that were already engaged with the lads with its stock. A couple more of the lads recovered from the initial assault as their attackers were beaten into unconsciousness and stood, ready to join in creating a wall of bullets that dropped row after row of the monsters.

Kevin could see that there were more of the things coming out from the alleys, and realised that this part of the town must be directly alongside the coast. It was the harbour and these things were coming from the sea. They had to be.

'Lads get into the store there.' He shouted 'Move, move.'

Kevin's rifle suddenly stopped firing, the clip had emptied fast. His old training kicked in and he quickly replaced it and switched to single shot mode. A quick count indicated that there were at least ten men standing including himself. There was no chance that they would be able to drag the wounded away, at least he hoped they were only wounded. They would be overwhelmed. Right now, he needed cover and enough firepower to keep the swarm of creatures at bay. He shouted again 'Move, move, Curly get to the fucking store'.

The Roscregan men moved as one, each man having to reload on the way but covered by the others as they did so. The creatures continued to move against them but they did appear to hold back a little, obviously cowed by the amount of retaliation available to their prey.

Curly booted the door to the supermarket open and ran inside, his eyes took a moment to adjust to the harsh white light. Once inside he crouched behind the nearest set of shelving and took aim at the door. As the men spilled inside he shouted for them to get behind his position and as the first of the creatures burst in through the door he opened fire with fast but precise shots.

Three of the creatures fell dead instantly as Curly's deadly aim opened up their chests. Another sprang in, leaping over the falling bodies but Curly raised his sights a little and put a round into the things leg, it dropped to the floor squealing and lashing in agony, a long pink tongue lashed out from its mouth. A bullet from Tim's pistol blew its eye out and it lay still. No more creatures followed.

No one said a word for a moment but all had their weapons pointed at the doorway. Each was spattered with blood and their eyes were wide with shock and fear.

'Fuck me.' Kevin said.

'What the fuck Kev?' Tim said. Kevin saw that he had a large gash across his cheek but he didn't think that Tim had noticed it.

'I don't fuckin know mate.' He shook his head as he stared at the pile of bloodied monsters. 'But we are out of our fucking league here of that much I'm sure.'

Each of the men replied with a solemn 'Aye.'

'They are gonna regroup and come piling through that door Kev.' Curly said. 'We won't be able to stop them all'.

'Aye, that's that truth.' Kevin replied and took in his surroundings.

'Tim, see if there's a back-door mate, or any way oot for that matter.'

'Aye Kev.' Tim said and turned to examine the rest of the store.

'Check ya rounds lads, do it one man at a time in case they come through.' Kevin could hear squeals and harsh, guttural calls from outside the shuttered windows. His mind raced as he tried to make sense of what had happened and what lay by the door. He tried to shake the thought that there might be lads out there that had survived and were now being set upon by the creatures.

From the back of the store Tim screamed. It started shrill and loud but then became a low, gargled mumble. Kevin braced his rifle and quickly but calmly moved down the aisles looking for his friend. Two others followed, one taking the second aisle. Curly held the others back to watch the door with him.

As he approached the end of the aisle he saw a slowly expanding pool of deep red liquid on the floor. He stepped around and saw Tim on his back. The side of his neck bore a gap so deep that Kevin could see his exposed windpipe spliced open. Stood over him was a man in a khaki warehouse jacket, Kevin thought it was the sort that Arkwright had worn in 'Open all Hours.' He blinked at the thought.

The man was short and stocky, balding, the few hairs he had were set atop an oversized bulging head. His eyes were large and protruding and his lips almost none existent. In his hand he carried a machete that dripped with Tim's blood.

He looked at Kevin with cold indifference as the Roscregan man fixed his sights on him. Kevin fired a shot through the middle of its skull. The Arkwright thing dropped to the floor.

Kevin looked down at Tim. Behind him he heard a whispered 'Mother of God...Timmy.' His friend's eyelids flickered and then closed. His gurgling breaths stopped. Kevin looked around the area, not least of all so that he wouldn't have to look at his dead friend.

There was a counter here, perhaps where the Arkwright man had been when they came in. He must have ducked down behind the counter and as Tim had come around and then swung at him with the machete. He stepped away from Tim and checked an open doorway behind the counter. There was a door on the right of wall of what was a large stock room.

He walked in and examined the room while the others stood guard. The stock seemed to consist almost entirely of tinned goods and baby food. There was a lot of the baby food and a good deal of powdered milk. He checked a few other boxes that sat in a corner. Here were medical supplies, bandages, plasters and antiseptic. There was also a crate of Whiskey.

He lifted out one of the bottles, it was Glenfiddich, fifty years old if it was a day. He removed the lid and took a long, deep swig of it. It was as smooth as silk against his throat and lit a fire in his gut. There was a stack of large drums in a corner. Kevin walked over to them, still taking swigs from the bottle.

On the side of each drum was a label. A fire symbol in black with the words 'DANGER' printed across the top.

Kevin nodded. This would do.

Chapter Twenty Seven

When he heard the first screams Peake almost clapped his hands. He emerged from behind the crate that had been his retreat for the last fifteen minutes and rushed around to Macgregor who had just pulled his men further back.

'The cavalry is here.' He said gleefully. 'As soon as this is over I want you to make sure that their fucking village ceases to exist.'

Macgregor said nothing but watched and listened as the assault on the Roscregan men began. There were more shouts and screams but the sound of gunfire was sustained and this concerned him. If they had rallied from the initial attack the firepower they had could cause problems.

Peake shuffled his feat, clearly excited but also, like Macgregor, nervous at the amount of gunfire. The Father would not take lightly great losses of his children to the humans and it would be *his* skin that was on the line.

Macgregor lifted his rifle and used the scope to observe the activity ahead. The shots had become more sporadic and he could see movement towards the supermarket on the left.

'They've run.' He said. 'They've gone into the Lawton place.' He waved to the men who were armed to come forward. 'Come with me.' He told them.

'Wait.' Peake shouted anxiously what about me? You can't take all the men with guns, what if one of them gets away?

Macgregor looked down at Peake with such malice that for once the Doctor stopped whining. The big man fished into his pocket and pulled out a pistol which he placed into Peake's hand. 'If someone comes, shoot him.' He said evenly. He then started off down the street with his group in tow.

'Giant prick.' Peake muttered. He was now left with some of the older men, some already in an advanced stage of returning. He made a mental note to start looking for a replacement for Macgregor as well as the late Billy Duggan. 'Two psychopaths with one stone.' He said quietly.

When Macgregor reached the truck he walked slowly past it. The Deep Ones could identify those returning instinctively but those who were still fully human only bore the mark of Dagon as a sigil on their skin. It would give off an aura but in the heat of battle it might go unnoticed.

He was shocked to see the number of Deep One dead, their blood was everywhere and had blackened the snow across the road and onto the pavements.

His caution was rewarded as the Deep Ones that milled about the bodies of the fallen Roscregan men ignored him. He could see that there were at least twenty of them gathered about the entrance to the supermarket but they were no longer prepared to risk any more of their number to the withering power of the Roscregan assault rifles. Instead they pulled and banged at the shutters and a few climbed up to the roof.

Macgregor wasn't sure what to do next. Waiting them out was an option but it wasn't one that he thought the Father would like. The creatures didn't like to be ashore for more than an hour or so. Most likely the Roscregan men would try to burst out and escape the village in their truck.

With this in mind he instructed one of his lackeys to move the truck away, back down towards the lodge but this came to nothing when the man returned to explain that the keys were not in it. Macgregor could hot wire it but that would mean his attention was away from the villagers.

He was just about to tell the lackey to slash the tyres, to ensure that it wasn't used for an escape when the front door of the supermarket was flung open from the inside.

The Deep Ones stepped back and Macgregor expected a burst of gunfire but none came. A few of the Deep Ones took cautious steps forward as did Macgregor and then, silently, a fiery object flew from within the supermarket and through the air in a graceful arc. When it landed a wall of flame erupted around the creatures it had fallen next to.

Their screams filled the air. Suddenly three more of the firebombs were launched and they impacted in similar fashion, exploding on contact and coating the Deep Ones with liquid fire.

As confusion and panic embraced the swarm, men appeared at the doorway and fired shots into the fleeing creatures. They then turned towards the truck. As Macgregor had anticipated it was a break out and the Leyland was their goal.

'Fire!' He shouted and the Falls men began blasting away at the villagers. This closer range gave their previously ineffective shotguns far more power even in the hands of men unskilled in their use. Rounds peppered the Roscregan men. As a salvo whizzed past Kevin's head he turned his M16 towards the source and switched the weapon back to fully automatic. He allowed the gun to traverse the area and two shots struck home, one taking a Falls man in the face the other tearing the shoulder of one completely from his body.

Although his attack had been productive it also emptied the clip and he had no replacement. He let the rifle drop from his hands and pulled out his pistol. There was an 'ough' noise from the side of him and he turned to see Mick Heaps on the floor, a rifle shot had struck him in the chest.

'Shit.' Kev snarled, and began to move forward, his pistol ready to fire at anyone or anything that appeared in front of him. Brian Tunny was holding four more of the improvised firebombs in his arms. His brother Brian plucked one out, lit the end of the cloth that had been stuffed into its neck and hurled back into the Supermarket. Curly also grabbed one and lit it. He threw the bottle through the window of the house immediately in front of them. Brian took another and repeated the action on the house next to it.

With the hail of bullets from the Roscregan men reduced Macgregor and his group were now able to focus their own fire and a rifle shot found its mark and another villager fell to the ground. More shotgun rounds ripped at Kevin and this time grazed his head. The little lead beads gouged at his skin and it felt like his face was on fire as his cheek was peppered.

Undaunted he continued to move to the cab of the truck firing as he went. The firebombs were devastatingly effective on the old, dry wood of the houses and flames were seen licking at the windows. Macgregor had backpedalled and found cover from the side of an alley that led to the harbour but could see the fires. He realised that the Roscregan men intended burning the town to the ground.

He chewed his lip, Deep Ones scurried past him, while the guns were threat for them the sight of fire sent them into frenzy and they scrambled for the sea, leaping over each other in panic.

Macgregor popped his head around the corner of the building that covered him and could see Joss lighting another bottle. He took careful aim and fired as the man prepared to throw the bottle. Too late, Curly saw Macgregor and tried to push Joss out of the way but the shot caught him in the side of the chest, the bullet tumbled through Joss's body and exited through his neck. He fell to the floor. The bullet had killed him instantly.

Brian screamed in horror and anger, he had too had seen Macgregor take aim but had no chance to get to either of them. He scooped up the bottle, its taper still burned. He tossed it towards Macgregor, the big man dodged back into the alley and the missile exploded against the corner of the building sending a shower of flames down onto the retreating Deep ones.

Kevin reached the cab and jumped in, his pistol had emptied as he had pressed forward and he changed the clip as he lay down across the cab seats for cover. That done, he fished out Tim's keys from his pocket, opened the passenger side door and fired up the engine.

He shouted to the others, only then realising that more of them had been killed by the Falls men.

'Get in, get in!' He screamed. Mike Simpson the village carpenter and Curly, sprinted for the cab and leapt in, squashing up against Kevin to allow the others to get inside. Curly turned to Brian who was throwing the remaining the bottles at buildings on the other side of the road and bawled at him, 'Brain! Come on man.'

'Go.' Brain shouted 'I'm not finished here.' His face was wet with tears and when the last bottle was thrown he unslung the AK47 from his shoulder and began to fire into the defensive positions of the Falls men.

He gave a 'Whoop' as a head, with large eyes staring at him appeared above a pallet of metallic containers. It exploded as a round entered its skull, tearing it apart.

'What do we do Kev?' Curly shouted. 'They got Joss.'

'We stick to the plan.' Kev said. He put the truck into gear and punched the accelerator. With any luck the town would burn to the floor while he and the others escaped. He had to get them out of here and to the army. They would raise the whole place and vaporise whatever the evil fucking things were that had attacked them.

The truck picked up speed as he headed down the road. He expected the road to turn and head back up to the town at the end, away from the harbour and back to where they had first entered in pursuit of the jeep. He hadn't expected to see the big man step out from an alley ahead of them and fire into the cab.

Having no other choice available Kev slammed on the brakes and tried to turn the vehicle but he hadn't the skill at the wheel of Tim. Instead of a steady swerve the truck shook violently and as the back end flipped around its weight forced the whole vehicle to go over on to its side and then its roof.

Kevin, Curly and Mike were thrown about the cab like coins in a washing machine. The truck came to a rest twenty feet from where Macgregor stood with his rifle. The big man advanced, keeping the weapon trained on the cab door. It swung open, a man dropped out of it onto the floor with a thud. Macgregor didn't hesitate, he fired two shots into the man's chest. He waited for another to emerge, backing up a little so that he could see if the door on the other side opened.

'Come on you fuckers.,' he shouted towards the cab, 'It's time to die so why not make it quick.' He glanced around to the other door again, which remained closed. 'If you are alive when I get you I promise that you'll spend the next few weeks being skinned alive, so why don't you just...'

Four shots rang out like knocks on a door. Macgregor's arms flew up in the air and the impact of the shots turned him, the rifle flew from his grasp as he spun and he dropped to the floor.

Kevin stood with his pistol still pointing at the big man's body. The policeman hadn't realised that the windscreen had popped out of the truck and Kevin had been thrown through the now open frame as the truck had rolled. Poor Mike had been dead already when the door had sprung open. His lifeless body had to the floor, he hadn't climbed out. One of the rounds Macgregor had fired at the cab had taken him out.

Kevin walked up to Macgregor and to his surprise the giant was still breathing. His eyes were open and saw Kevin as he stood over him. Macgregor gave a rumbling laugh and then wheezed a little.

'You know what little man, you and your...' Macgregor began. Kevin put a bullet into his head. Macgregor trembled a little as if he was cold.

'Cunt.' Kevin said.

He expected to be shot at any moment but didn't bother trying to take cover, he was filled a rage that nailed him to the floor. A sound came from the cab. When he looked towards it he saw Curly gingerly dropping down next to Mike's body.

Kevin looked around. He couldn't see anyone, no townsfolk, no creatures. Had they run? He wasn't sure. Down the road the fire was seriously taking hold of the buildings they had bombed which pleased him, but he couldn't see any sign of Brian.

A movement caught his eye further down, in the direction that they had been headed. A large brown door belonging to a three-storey building swung open and from it a figure in a white gown or cassock emerged.

Kevin raised his pistol at the figure, at this distance and in such poor light it was unlikely he would hit but it wouldn't be for lack of trying. Before his finger could tighten on the trigger Kevin realised that the pale, blinking figure was Joe Clarke.

A second person came out from behind Joe. A woman. Clearly a woman as she wasn't wearing a stitch of clothing and Kevin almost felt compelled to look away out of decency.

He dropped his gun arm to his side, and wondered if he was tempting fate too far to think the day had now gotten as fucked beyond belief as it could possibly get.

Chapter Twenty Eight

As Joe opened the door the first thing that came to his attention was the raging fire at the end of the road. Buildings on both sides were covered in an angry orange flame and plumes of smoke rolled into the dark sky. He saw the upturned truck, two men were standing by it and one of them appeared to be pointing at him.

'*Is that Kev?*' He thought. As if reading his mind the man stopped pointing. Melanie stepped up behind him and pressed her body against his, her hands on his shoulder. 'They should leave.' She said quietly into his ear.

'No shit.' Joe replied. He began to walk forward to meet with his friend when he heard Melanie gasp a little. A dull pain sang a song through his ears. His knees went weak and he dropped down onto them. As he reached his hand to the back of his head and tried to clear his now blurred vision he saw that Kevin was pointing at him once again.

'Don't you fucking move Government man.'

Peake's voice. Joe understood now that he had been struck across the back of his head. Despite the instruction, Joe couldn't help but turn and look up at his attacker, a solid kick from Peake's foot was what he got for his trouble. He fell heavily to the floor.

Peake was stood behind Melanie, a hand around her throat and a pistol to her head. It could just have easily been Billy Duggan stood there the scene was so familiar.

'You there,' Peake shouted. 'Roscregan. Put your weapon down or I'll pop her brains just like you did to poor Macgregor.' Kevin didn't move.

'Come on now, you couldn't hit a barn door from that distance and by the time you go for a second try, after the first probably hits her anyway, I'll have but a bullet of my own in each of them.'

At first Kevin remained still but when Peake pulled back the hammer on his pistol he dropped his arm to his side once again.

'Good. Very good.' Peake said and looked down at Joe who was slowly getting to his knees. 'Well, what a fucking disaster you have brought to my little town.' He said. 'You can't even begin to imagine the shit I'm going to get for this.' He increased his grip on Melanie's throat and shook her neck a little, 'and you, you devious little cunt, I'll bet you are source of all this mayhem.'

He looked back to Joe. 'Well I hope she fucked you well enough that it was worth you having to eat your own eyes young man.' Peake chuckled. 'Oh the delights that await you.'

'*Now*,' Peake directed his attention back to Kevin and Curly. 'You two can fuck off back to your little rats nest. I'll have some friends take care of you at a more appropriate time.'

'I'm going nowhere you arsehole.' Kevin shouted back to him. 'I'm going to watch this place burn to the ground and then I'm going to burn you on top o' those fuckin things.'

He cocked his head back indicating the pile of Deep One corpses he had helped to create.

'In that case Roscregan I don't suppose there is any point in me wasting time keeping your friend alive is there?'

Peake took the gun from Melanie's head and pointed it directly at Joes face. He said quietly, 'You know, just between us three I'm actually quite hard right now,' and squeezed the trigger.

Chapter Twenty Nine

Had the Jetty and boathouse not exploded into thousands of pieces at that moment, the shot would have smashed through Joe's face as intended, but the fantastic destruction and subsequent cascade of detritus from the ancient structures was enough to completely throw Peake's aim. The bullet slammed into the floor some distance behind Joe and without looking to see what had caused the distraction he jumped up and charged at Peake.

A vast spray of sea water, fishing weights, and large splinters of timber crashed all along the road, wrecking the remaining harbour buildings and some of the nearby homes. Kevin and Curly threw themselves under the space made by the flatbed of the upturned truck.

Joe grabbed the hand in which Peake held his pistol and bit into it as hard as he could. The Doctor screamed in agony and dropped to the gun to the floor. Melanie pulled herself free as Peake's grip on her neck slackened and quickly stepped away from him. Unbalanced, Joe and Peake fell backwards against the wall of the lodge.

'Joe come to me.' Melanie said firmly.

But Joe wasn't listening, he regained his posture and with a forceful push managed to straddle Peake, his knees locking the Doctors arms down. He began to punch at Peake as hard and as fast as he could. Peake's thin face crumpled as each blow hammered into it. His nose had broken from the first swing and with each subsequent punch blood splashed out and spattered against Joe.

'Joe!' Melanie screamed at him, 'Come to me now.'

Joe stopped, although mostly because his already shocked body was simply too tired to continue beating at Peake. He leaned back from the bloodied Doctor and stood and as he was about to turn to Melanie he recalled that something had exploded on the harbour. He turned to look what had happened and saw the impossible.

The creature towered above the remains of the harbour buildings, a lithe, muscular thing, its scaled skin glistened in the moonlight. Its form was humanoid. It stood on two huge legs that were slightly crouched, its arms were out, as though it were about to leap and grab at something. The head was a terrifying vision, eyes the size of a car turned slowly. Its mouth held two rows of teeth like sabres and great webbed plumes draped down across its shoulders from the head.

The behemoth stared down at them impassively, the great saucers reflecting the fires that continued to spread across the town. Mother Hydra brought a huge webbed hand swinging across her front and the remaining harbour buildings were swept away in a single terrific crash.

'Mother!' Melanie called, and a smile that appeared beatific to Joe beamed from her face. The great hand, which had just disintegrated the harbour buildings, reached down and Joe stood stock still in abject fear. The fingers of Mother Hydra's hand came within a foot of Joe and delicately plucked up the groaning Peake from the floor.

Mother Hydra let Peake fall a few feet into the palm of her other hand and her great eyes swivelled back to Melanie.

'Yes, Mother,' Melanie cried out, 'Yes that's him.'

Joe could hear Peake moaning, remonstrating with the creature, invoking the name of Father Dagon, 'Lord and Master of us all.' he whimpered.

Mother Hydra closed her fingers into a fist and Joe watched, horrified, as Peake's guts oozed out of his mouth while the thing squeezed the life out of him. She tossed the destroyed body into the sea behind her and as he watched its descent Joe was sure he could see creatures, other kinds of creatures, leaping up to snap at the bloody corpse as it fell to them.

Melanie laughed and uttered words in an alien tongue. As she did this the creature lowered its body a little and stretched out its hand onto the floor, the palm up. Joe saw the scaled skin slick with Peake's blood.

Melanie turned to Joe. 'You can leave here now Joe, leave and forget this place. There is a room inside the lodge that is filled with gold and gems, enough to make you rich a thousand times over.'

Joe couldn't speak. His terror was so great that he was still rooted to the spot and thoughts of anything other than listening to Melanie were unable to form in his mind.

'Mother wants nothing more than the sea for our home, but Dagon wants it all because *He* wants it all. You will be safe if you keep away from the seas, the Great Mother will protect me Joe.'

She stepped forward and placed her arms around his neck. She kissed his lips but Joe couldn't respond. He could see her neck and noticed discreet dark lines across her skin that seemed to pulse a little.

'One day you will see your daughter Joe, and she will be beautiful, a child of both worlds.'

Her arms released him and she caressed his cheek with her fingers. 'Goodbye Joe,' she said, and walked onto the waiting palm of Mother Hydra.

The creature lifted Melanie up and a strange sonorous voice travelled through the night air. Melanie sat, crossed legged, still watching Joe. The melodic song ended and Mother Hydra turned and began to walk back into the depths of the sea.

Mother Hydra held Melanie before her as she waded out into the harbour and stopped once the swell was at her chest. Melanie stood and with an agile leap, dived from the monster's claw. Mother Hydra's vast bulk disappeared into the black sea after her. In short bubble of dark water both were gone.

Joe collapsed to the floor as though a spell had broken. His breathing was course and heavy and shock threatened to drive him all the way to unconsciousness, but he fought it off with thoughts of the others who needed him, Kevin and the Roscregan men who had come to rescue him. Unsteadily he got back to his feet, almost tripping on the long robe.

He walked away from the lodge and could see Kevin emerging from under the truck, the other man followed him but more slowly, terrified of what might still be out there. They met by the body of Macgregor.

'What *was* that Joe?' Kevin said

'I don't know Kev. I don't know what any of this is.' Joe replied. 'I should have listened to you.'

'Aye.' Kev replied. They stood silently for a moment. The only sound was that of burning timbers crashing down along the road and the swelling sea that crashed against the ruined harbour.

Finally, Joe spoke. 'What do we do Kev?' There are others here...this place... its rotten to the core, do we burn it?'

'Do you have a better idea?' Kevin replied.

'No.' Joe answered shaking his head.

'Then let's burn it all.' Kevin said. 'And when we are done here maybe we should find out where else these things have infested and put a fire to them as well.'

Joe nodded. London had never seemed further away to him and he no longer cared.

The End

About the Author

Eddie Skelson is the author of the Crowley series, a novel, Winter Falls and short story collection The Whitby Horror and Other Tales. He has also written three books of the series The Township Chronicles and is producing a 1920's supernatural thriller title, Abraham Church.

Born and raised in the Midland town of Stoke on Trent Eddie is rapidly gaining recognition for his dark humour and memorable characters. He has also produced numerous comedic scripts and characters via the Facebook platform.

He earned a Master's Degree in Creative Writing from Keele University and is an avid fan of board games which he has no room for.

You can discover more information on Eddie Skelson via his Facebook page, Website (when he can be arsed to update it) and Amazon.

www.facebook.com/ eddie.skelson.writer

Did you enjoy this story?

Gaining recognition for any kind of art is a tough job. One of the ways you can help to promote independent authors is to leave a rating on Amazon and/or a review on Goodreads. Why not take a moment to deliver your rating? You don't have to leave any comments but if you do you might be helping future readers find their way to this authors work.

Thank you for taking a chance on this little piece of writing and in advance for your rating or review

Eddie Skelson